Birds of a Different Feather

J. SCHLENKER

Binka Publishing, LLC

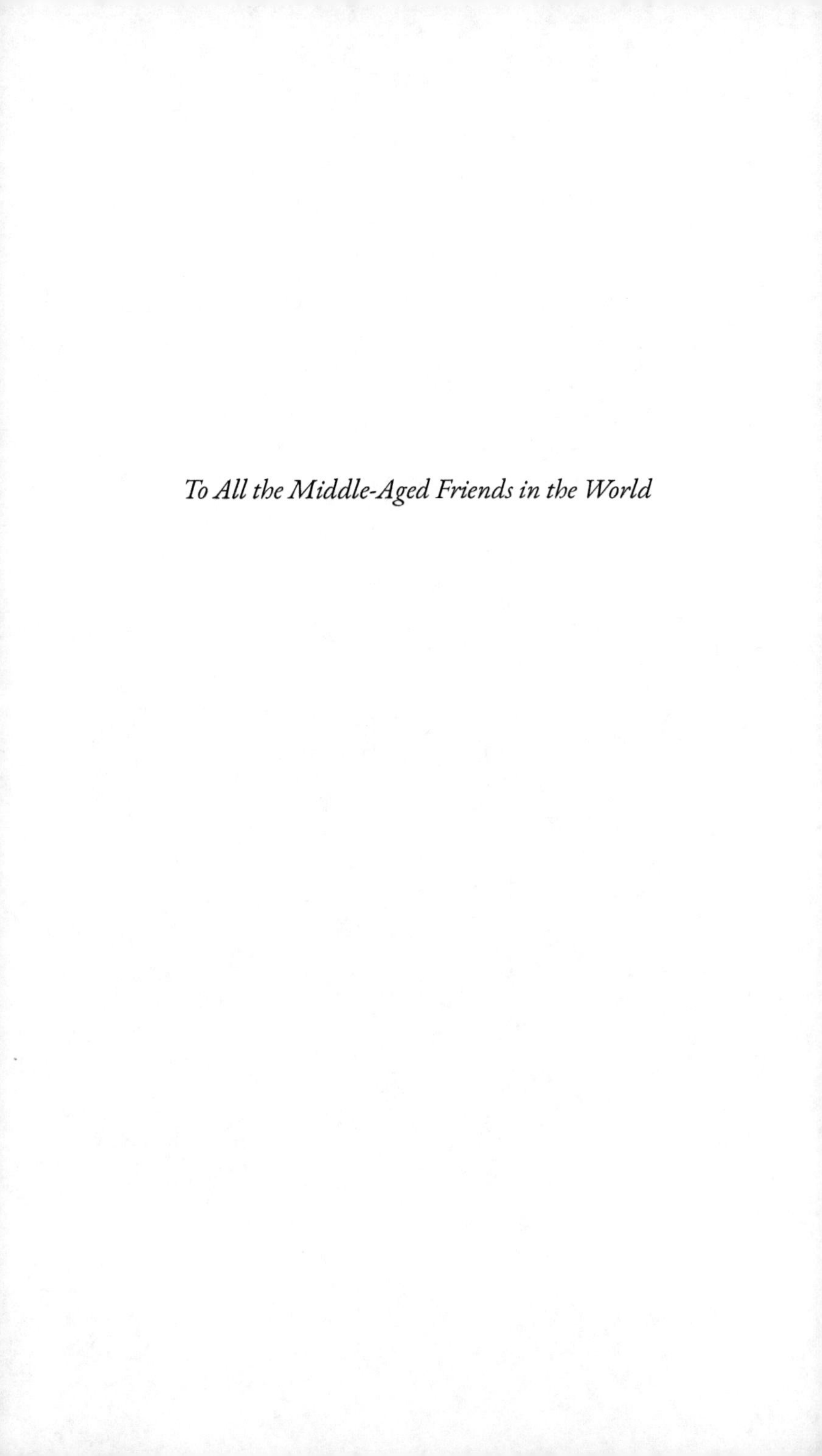

To All the Middle-Aged Friends in the World

"Sweet is the memory of distant friends! Like the mellow rays of the departing sun, it falls tenderly, yet sadly, on the heart."

— WASHINGTON IRVING

Contents

Prologue

Early October 2018

Ethel stood knee-deep amid packing boxes in the apartment she and her husband, Raja, had shared most of their married life. The second-floor apartment served as home, first to them, then to Christine, their daughter.

The past four months had opened a floodgate of tears. Ethel hardly needed more. Dreading both the task and the inevitable accompanying tears she knew sorting through thirty years of memories would bring, Ethel diverted her eyes from the packing boxes to the park across the street. In particular, she gazed at the pond over which a light fog hung.

Fritz, who held yoga classes near the water, referred to the mist as mystical and suggested his students become as light as it was, levitating above earthly worries. "Imagine you're a pinfeather floating in the breeze," Fritz often said. Ethel would miss Fritz's classes.

During the summer, frogs resting on lily pads covered the

water. On many a night of the more pleasant summers, she and Raja cracked the bedroom window, falling asleep to their croaking.

"Ah, searching for a mate," Raja would say with a smile. Then, he would kiss her and whisper in her ear, "I've found mine."

Summer and, hopefully, its woes, were over. Autumn brought a sprinkling of gold, crimson, and orange peeking from the evergreens, arranged in such a way as to radiate the Zen-like vibrations that only a master gardener, in this case, a Japanese Zen Buddhist, might design.

Even though she was only on the second floor—the apartment building only had two floors—it gave her the impression of being above it all, similar to what a bird might experience, one of those birds incapable of making it too far off the ground. If only she were an eagle, a regal bird, not one of those clumsy, ungraceful birds she saw herself as. The only bird that came to mind was an ostrich, which didn't fly.

Ethel moved her eyes from the pond and studied the sky. A series of battles between the golden ball called Sun and an army of silver-colored clouds mesmerized her. She had never given much heed to Seattle's perplexing skies, but today, everything took on a special significance because today would have been her dear friend Ola's birthday.

Ethel's eyes darted from the window to the boxes strewn about the odd furniture arrangement—Raja's doing and over to the haphazard display of books on the wall-to-wall bookcase —her doing. The books held the stories of thousands of lives with secrets, heartaches, and traumas—some real, some fictional.

Ethel moved her eyes back to the window and continued her observation of the sky. The bright yellow ball proved victorious for one infinitesimal moment, its brilliance highlighting an array of colors like a prism. Ethel looked around her to see its origin and discovered it was from the periwinkle-blue sari still draped over the chair's headrest—the chair she had shoved into the far corner of the room because of the man she *thought* had stolen from her. He hadn't, but she never apologized to him, one thing she must set right before moving.

Beneath the sari, she spied the edge of the book. It was Ola's last gift to her. It had gotten misplaced during the events that began in June—events that unleashed secrets, heartaches, and traumas similar to those within the printed pages of the books in her bookcase.

She slid the book from beneath the sari and held it up to the light, admiring the beautiful picture of a peacock adorning the cover. She smiled, thinking a peacock suited her much better than an ostrich. The title read *One Proud Peacock*. If only she could have curbed her pride, she might have avoided some of her past heartaches. She let out a heavy sigh. *No use dwelling on the past.* She was embarking on a new adventure. That was how she must look at it.

"My dear friend Ola," Ethel murmured as she lifted a handful of books from the top of the bookshelf and placed them in a box. With every handful, she remembered the ones purchased from Ola. Half the books on the shelves came from Ola's Wise Old Books.

She squeezed one last book into the box before closing and taping it shut. With a felt-tip marker, she wrote "One Proud Peacock" across the top.

CHAPTER 1

Early June 2018

Ethel jumped at the sound of the last bell. It was Friday, the last day of school for the students, and her nerves were at a breaking point, along with those of every other teacher at Densworth Academy.

Owen, the last student to leave her classroom, turned and waved goodbye to her at the exact time Mr. Densworth, the principal, passed by her door. She couldn't help but let out a distasteful breath. She only hoped Owen hadn't noticed. The child was more sensitive than most. As hard as she tried, Ethel couldn't stay calm when it came to that man. Their relationship had always been strained, and it wasn't her imagination that Mr. Densworth snarled and turned his head away when he walked by her classroom.

Ethel labored over the urge to go to his office after school but decided to put it off until Monday, the last day of school for teachers. With no lingering students to distract them, it was less likely that the suggestions, including evidence to back them up, which she had painstakingly prepared in a spiral-bound notebook, would go unheeded. Plus, she didn't need the man's arrogant attitude ruining her weekend.

She was sure he would see her point, even though he would rant and rave before conceding. It was always the same —like some animal ritual to prove dominance.

Principal Densworth, known for his bad attitude and grumpy disposition, made this time of year harder than it had to be. Both the students and teachers deserved the long-awaited three-month break. Ethel supposed that even Denny, the name both the students and teachers called him behind his back, needed time off.

After tidying up her desk, Ethel locked her room and drove home. No sooner had she gotten out of her car in front of her apartment building than Rhonda, the downstairs neighbor, appeared.

"See you got a package today, and it looked like it might have been from your daughter. How is—"

Ethel cut her off, merely nodded, and hurried upstairs. "Talk later, Rhonda. It's been a long day. Last day of school for the students, and I've got a lot of final grading to do."

Why on earth did she say that? She had already turned in her grades. Students received their final report cards yesterday, something Rhonda, a mother of four children, probably knew. Was it four or five? Ethel couldn't remember. A pang of guilt over her lie spread through Ethel's body.

Regarding Rhonda, Ethel's conversation was one long list of excuses. She was in no mood for Rhonda today or on most days. Rhonda made it a point to know everyone's business in the apartment complex. She had turned nosiness intermixed with compliments into an art form. Rhonda's particular brand of flattery resulted in perfect strangers spilling their guts. Police interrogators could learn a lot from her.

Of course, Rhonda was right. An oblong box wrapped in brown paper with Ethel's address and the return address of her daughter, Christine Sharma, written in bold letters, lay in front of her door. Surrounding both the return and sender addresses were Jackson Pollock facsimiles of red-stamp marks, so typical of a package coming from India. An ivory string tied in a bow provided the finishing touch, something her daughter had picked up from an old black-and-white movie.

"It's so romantic to send a parcel in this manner. Don't you think, Mother?" Christine had once said to her.

Christine alternated between calling her Mother and Mom, depending on her mood. There were days when Ethel thought her daughter belonged to a more civilized time, the turn of the nineteenth century, when life fluctuated between prim and proper and daring and idealized romance.

Maybe it was her daughter's propensity toward being out of step with time that resulted in having no significant other at twenty-six years of age. Her father once stated, "Our daughter is rather plain, don't you think?"

Ethel had replied with a huff, "Raja, how could you say such a thing?" Inwardly, she knew it was true.

Raja had a directness. Sadly, in the looks department, Christine had taken on the worst characteristics of her parents. She inherited her parents' best qualities regarding organizational skills and general practicality. Raja often said, "Christine has a sensible head on her shoulders." Ethel agreed. Ethel, however, had grown less sensible with each passing year. If Raja were here, he would surely comment on the fact, but he wasn't here, having left her to return to his native India three years ago. Upon reflection, Ethel would say that was about when her rationality went by the wayside.

Ethel thought way too much about what Raja might think. Her two best friends, Luce and Ola, had told her so plenty of times. With school winding down for the year and so much to do, she hadn't given her ex-husband as much thought. She was never sure what to call him. They were separated, not divorced, and neither was seeing anyone else, to her knowledge. At least she wasn't. Slight nausea hit her at the thought that Raja might be. "No," she said out loud, shaking her head.

Ethel picked up the package, carefully untied the string, and unwrapped the paper, dropping it on the floor. The box beneath the brown-wrapping paper displayed the company logo where Christine was employed.

Although Christine had superb intellectual prowess, she never aspired to success, except possibly in matters of spirituality. She worked as a run-of-the-mill clerk at a shipping company, dividing her time between India and Seattle, especially in India, where, when not at work, she sat cross-legged at the ashram she frequented.

Hi Mom,

When I saw the periwinkle sari, I knew it was you. Given Ola's fascination with Egypt, or Khemet, as she prefers to call it, it is obvious the red one is for her. I still remember when she helped me with the report I had to do on Egypt in high school. It was one of my few A+'s. Of course, the remaining white and brown one with flecks of Granny Apple Green, Luce's favorite color, is for her.

Oh, and I have some exciting news—the kind of news I can only share in person. So, don't beg me to tell you because I won't. I plan on coming home for Thanksgiving and will tell you then. You will see for yourself.

Love and Namaste,

Christine

A relatively brief note for Christine, written somewhat haphazardly. Her letters—Christine preferred letters to emails most of the time—were always written with meticulous detail and penmanship, were usually wordy, and were filled with run-of-the-mill happenings at the ashram or her work.

So, what could this exciting news be? Knowing Christine, it could be as simple as her meeting the one true swami or finding the perfect ashram. Christine darted from swami to swami and from ashram to ashram. A thirst for the meaning of life seemed to be Christine's calling. But excitement? Ethel couldn't remember her daughter exhibiting the sensation. Christine had lived her twenty-six years in a state of uniqueness, hovering somewhere above worldly affairs while giving the appearance of pragmatic mediocrity. Ethel hated to admit her daughter was not exceptionally smart, not strikingly good-looking, and had no particular interest in anything. She flitted between various pursuits, ranging from the mundane to strict spiritual practices. The one constant with Christine was her dependability— as solid as a rock, the child every parent wants—the kind who takes care of you in your old age.

Suddenly, the thought Ethel had pushed away so many times resurfaced. Could her daughter have finally met someone—the love of her life, something physical, more down-to-earth than platonic or spiritual? Christine did say Ethel would see for herself. Was her daughter bringing a boyfriend home with her? Or possibly a fiancé? No. It was probably too much to hope for, and speculating was useless. November seemed a long time to wait, but she would have to. She knew her daughter well enough that no amount of coaxing would get her to reveal her secret before then.

Ethel laid the note aside to examine the contents of the box. She pulled out a tin container of tea wrapped in tissue paper. Ethel knew it was tea before even unwrapping it. The familiar fragrance of Darjeeling, her favorite, permeated the box. Every time Christine sent a package, it felt like Christmas morning. She must have a cup of tea in hand before opening the rest of the contents.

Ethel carried the tin of tea to the kitchen and poured fresh cold water into the kettle because correctly made tea always starts with cold water. She placed the kettle on the stovetop and turned on the electric burner. Ethel yearned for a gas stove, the kind she cooked on while living in India when she and Raja were first married. The open flame always made the water boil more perfectly. Or was her life more perfect back then?

Ethel placed her teacup on the side table and pulled out the first sari. She stroked her hand across the silk fabric she knew belonged to her because it was almost the shade of blue she wore on her wedding day, the one Raja's cousin, Gita, said most suited her. It was also the color of the sky she remembered gazing upon in youth with her grandmother. How she wished she could talk to her now. Her grandmother always had sage advice regarding the simplest to the gravest matters.

"Your mother was angry that day. She didn't mean what she said. We all say things we don't mean at one time or another. I know she loves you very much, and she looks down from the bluest of skies and smiles at seeing what a nice young lady you are growing up to be."

Her grandmother's words came back to her like it was yesterday. Only it wasn't yesterday. Ethel was six years old when she said it.

Ethel's parents had died in an automobile accident on their trip home from the piano recital, the one Ethel pleaded with her mother not to attend.

"Mother, I don't want to play in front of thousands of people."

"Ethel, there will hardly be thousands of people there."

"Hundreds then," Ethel retorted. Even though Ethel was only in first grade, she was good at arithmetic.

"Not even hundreds. Maybe one hundred tops."

Ethel stood with her arms crossed and her lips in a pout.

"Listen, Ethel. Do this for your parents, won't you? I bought you the new dress especially for the performance."

"But I wanted a red dress, and you got me a pink one."

"What if I call Jessica's mom, and if it's all right with her, you can go home with her after the recital? I'll give you both the money to buy ice cream afterward. You would like that, wouldn't you?" Jessica was Ethel's best friend. They were in first grade together and took piano lessons from Mrs. Eldon.

In thinking back, Ethel couldn't remember when she didn't have a best friend in her school years, even in college. They were never that long-lived, usually changing with each succeeding year. Luce and Ola had been her longest and most faithful friends.

Ethel had casually mentioned to Christine a month earlier that she was thinking of saris for Luce and Ola's birthdays. "Of course, their birthdays aren't until the fall, but I plan on shopping for them soon."

Ethel acknowledged that she procrastinated, especially when carrying out her ideas. Christine, even from an early age —perhaps as early as the womb—internalized this weakness in her mother and, like the immune system battling a virus, instinctively sought to rectify and counterbalance the deficiency.

Ethel knew when she remarked that she planned to shop for saris locally for Ola, Luce, and herself that Christine would process the statement as a not-so-veiled plea to take matters into her own hands. Christine would insist that the saris come from India, not Seattle. In this sense, mother and daughter worked symbiotically. Ethel gravitated toward the bigger picture but was ill-suited for the essential toil of seeing her ideas through. How often had Raja said, "Always such big ideas, Ethel? If only you would carry them out."

Raja also said Ethel relied on Christine too much.

"You're wrong, Raja. Christine loves tasks. She thrives on them. She came out feet first, ready to run full steam ahead."

He countered, "Then how do you explain that she was two weeks late?"

Raja didn't know that although Ethel wasn't a breech baby, she was also late.

"Ethel, for shame, if you had only been earlier. You kept admiring yourself in the mirror in your recital dress, and we were late. You threw everything off. You were even late in your cadence at the end of the piece. You could have made your mama so proud. Always late to the show. Even for your birth," her mother said, shaking her head.

"I hate the piano. I never wanted to take piano lessons. My grandmother wouldn't make me take them, and I'm going to live with her."

"Oh, you are, are you? How do you propose to get there? She lives in New York, and we live in Chicago. Do you know how far that is?"

Her mother bent down and hugged her. "Ethel, I'm sorry. Mama should not have said that about you being late. I've had a terrible morning. Please be a good little daughter, will you? Be helpful." Her mother hugged her again. "Go on. Jessica and her parents are waiting. I will pick you up later."

The time her mother chastised her about the piano recital was the last time she ever saw either of her parents alive.

At age six, Ethel *did* go to live with her grandmother.

Ethel would undoubtedly have died that day, but she was with Jessica, having ice cream. Her grandmother said God spared her for a reason.

Ethel had reflected on that day so many times. Her parents had always doted on her, but on that day, her mother was not her usual self. She remembered her parents fighting, a rare occurrence.

"All couples fight," her grandmother told her. "Ethel, it wasn't your fault."

"I wasn't helpful to my mom, and I should have been. From here on out, I will go out of my way to be helpful."

The next sari she pulled out was Luce's. Yes, it had Luce written all over it. However, talking Luce into wearing it would be a different matter.

Ethel gasped when she pulled out the sari meant for Ola. It was beyond anything she could imagine. It was so appropriate for her friend. Ethel had to call her at once. She would only tell her that Christine had found the most stunning sari for her. Never mind that Ola's birthday wasn't until the fall. She would not give the details of the sari. Ethel would save that part for Ola's birthday.

Ethel knew Ola would want to hang it on the wall rather than wear it, which gave Ethel a sense of gratification, considering only Ola's most relished items went on her office wall. She might even display it in the bookstore, over the section of books on India, for everyone to see. How could she resist waiting three months to give both Luce and Ola their gifts? Yes, Ethel had to call Ola right away. She would only hint at her gift, not mentioning the hand-painted hieroglyphs.

"Something hand-painted on red silk, especially for you, Ola. I won't say anymore. I can't wait for your reaction when you see it."

All seemed normal enough when she talked to Ola on the phone. There was no sign in her voice that anything was wrong, only a twinge of satisfaction, probably imagined on Ethel's part, when she told her how unique her sari was. "Different, not like the ones for Luce and me."

Ethel had never known Ola to become overly stimulated by anything other than some insights gleaned from an unusual book find. Still, she hoped this gift might evoke an inkling of pleasure. Anytime Ethel could rouse a reaction from Ola, it was like adding a feather to her cap.

There was no feather for her cap this time. Ola seemed distracted. Ethel would see her in a few days and ask her about it.

"Remember, Monday is my last day of school. I will see you for lunch on Tuesday," Ethel said before ending the call.

CHAPTER 2

Early June 2018

Ethel awoke at 2:30 a.m. on Tuesday with a romance novel still on the bed beside her. It had been so long since she had read something light-hearted and trivial. She wanted something simple to make her fall into a deep sleep, something to divert her from the thoughts of the previous day's events. The musty-smelling book with yellowing pages, having been on her shelf for ages, didn't work —not in the sleep department—but the contents of its pages were the reason for her dream, the dream that took her to another time, another place, and made her temporarily forget Mr. Densworth and the fact that she was no longer a teacher.

In her dream, she and Raja were both young again and carefree. She tried to savor what she remembered, but it faded as soon as she turned over in bed.

She reached for her phone on the nightstand and checked her school email. Possibly, Mr. Densworth had already regretted his decision to let her walk out the way she did. She scrolled down. Nothing.

The man was beyond unreasonable. Radical was what he

had called her. Couldn't he see her ideas were revolutionary and progressive? Principal Densworth insisted on running the school like they were still in the Stone Age. She certainly wouldn't miss the disputes they had. She and the principal, a distant relation of the school's founder, went head-to-head more times than Ethel cared to count.

"What now, Mrs. Sharma?" he roared whenever she entered his office.

Yesterday was no different. Contempt had become his usual reaction upon seeing her, as was his secretary's stifled, polite manner, gulping down what Ethel imagined to be a heavy sigh. She would then excuse herself for a coffee break.

On the last day of school, Ethel thought he might be open to changes—ones she volunteered to oversee herself. She held up the notebook containing articles noting the success of various programs underway in other schools. He didn't bother to take it when she reached it toward him.

In a patronizing tone, one of his more civilized tones, he said, "Mrs. Sharma, we already have enough programs in this school. Do you see this pile of paperwork?" He pointed to the corner of his desk, where a hefty stack of chaotically scattered papers resided behind several jars of candies. The man had an insatiable sweet tooth and the dental work that went with it. His teeth were so white that they stopped short of being translucent. Ethel cupped her hand over her mouth to prevent him from seeing her smiling at her visualization of them glowing in the dark. "Do you think I want to add to that pile?"

"Well, perhaps I could go over a few of the things I have compiled in the notebook, and you can review them and let me know what you think. For instance, we could incorporate meditation as a deterrent in place of detention for unaccept-able behavior and more cafeteria selections to accommodate those children who are vegan or vegetarian."

Mr. Densworth growled as fiercely as a lion might and said, "If this school has a vegetarian child, and there are none to my knowledge, he or she can remove the burger and eat the bun, lettuce, and pickle."

Mr. Densworth's secretary, Roberta, spent much of her time sidestepping him to avoid his moods. When she wasn't doing that, she was reminding him about something he had forgotten, one of which was to wear his glasses, which, when he did, kept slipping down his enormously wide nose, having no indentations with which to grip properly. His nose looked like one you might find on a lion. Yes, she thought. The man reminded her of a lion, the way he roared at the kids. They all scurried from his path like a herd of zebras whenever he approached. And that thick mane he was so proud of, always running his fingers through the strands, was probably dyed that unusual tawny brown. Ethel might find him handsome if it were not for his disposition.

Ethel had met his wife, a sweet, timid woman who was much younger. They say opposites attract.

Ethel knew her ideas were sound. Not to be deterred, she continued, "Mr. Densworth, if you would just take the time to read—"

He cut her off. "Unlike you, Mrs. Sharma, I do not have time to read. I would love to read a novel, something I haven't had time for in ages. However, I will be stuck within these four walls reviewing reports and budgets while you are on summer break. I hope you'll enjoy reading outside in beautiful weather." He stroked his hand through his hair, removed his glasses, placed them on his desk, and looked at her sternly. "The answer is no, and that's final."

"Mr. Densworth, I don't see how I can continue to work under such rigid dictatorship and close-mindedness."

"Are you saying you quit, Mrs. Sharma?"

She stuttered, "Why, yes, I guess that is what I am saying."

A slight smile came to his face.

Ethel fought the urge to throw the notebook she had worked so hard on at him. For a moment all breath had been sucked out of the air for her. Her breath returned; his smile remained. She turned and burst through his door to the outer office, where Roberta had returned to her desk. The secretary sat frozen with a look that said she had heard all, at least the quitting part. Or had she been fired? Neither Ethel nor Mr. Densworth had kept their voices down. Probably everyone in that part of the building had heard the outburst.

"How you work for that man, I'll never know," Ethel said, attempting to restore her dignity, before walking out into the hallway, which, thank goodness, was empty.

Ethel's first instinct was to hold her head down in shame as she passed the open-doored classrooms, but she took a deep breath, let it out, held her head proudly, and walked down the hall.

She ducked into the janitor's room, grabbed an empty box, carried it to her classroom, gathered all her personal belongings, and took them to her car. All the teachers' vehicles were still in the parking lot. Most of them planned on meeting at a restaurant to celebrate the beginning of summer vacation. She could hardly see herself joining them, given that she would be the topic of conversation. She fought back tears upon getting behind the wheel. As soon as she was out of sight of Densworth Academy, she pulled into the far end of a mall parking lot, placed her head on the steering wheel, and screamed.

She placed the book on her nightstand, fluffed up her pillow, and let out a heavy sigh, determined to have a good night's sleep during the few remaining nighttime hours. The man was not worth losing sleep over. Tomorrow was a new day, and she would figure out the rest of her life then.

CHAPTER 3

Early June 2018

The ding of Ethel's alarm came too soon. If only she could capture the moment between sleep and wakefulness, the space between thoughts when there were no cares in the world. During that time, the personality she knew herself as didn't exist. The moment was infinitesimal, however, and too soon, all the previous day's events flooded back in.

Today was the first day of summer vacation, even though the vacation was permanent this time. She had always made it a point to treat herself on the first day of break, and she saw no reason for this day to be any different.

The treat was seldom anything planned, usually something spur-of-the-moment. Later in the afternoon, she would go to the bookstore to visit Ola. She had also always made it a point to go by the bookshop to see her friend on the first day of summer vacation, a ritual they had practiced for nearly a decade. Usually, Luce would join her, but her boys, Martin, Lou, and Dewey, were signed up for a slew of summer activities, and the first week after school was the only time the entire family could get away.

"I hope you understand," Luce said to Ethel with down-turned lips. The look of despair at not being able to join her and Ola was mixed. While Luce enjoyed their visits, Ethel knew how excited her friend was to have her whole family together without distractions.

"Santiago sprung this little getaway on us as a surprise."

Ethel would hardly call the Bahamas a little getaway. Luce had a way of downplaying that they could afford such things, but mostly, she minimized how romantic and devoted her husband, Santiago, was after all these years, when Ethel's husband, Raja, was no longer in the picture. She did the same with Ola. Except in Ola's case, there was never a man in the picture that Ethel or Luce knew about, unless you counted Ola's strange relationship with Cornelius. "Such an odd duck," Raja had often commented.

Ethel appreciated Luce's consideration in not flaunting her perfect life in front of the two of them. It had not always been so. After a series of disappointments in the romance department, Luce had landed in a dream marriage. The only thing Luce ever complained about was not getting enough time with Santiago and the boys.

"I hope you understand."

A teacher, above all others, understood all those extra-curricular activities expected of students.

"It will be just fine, dear. You have a fantastic time."

She would go to the bookstore with or without Luce. Why should this day be any different? Well, it will definitely be different. She would have Ola one-on-one. Although Ethel wasn't one to confide, she thought she might burst if she didn't tell someone she was no longer a teacher at Densworth Academy. Who better to confide in than Ola? Besides, she would eventually find out anyway, as would Luce.

But first, her morning yoga class in the park across from her apartment—the reason she set her alarm. Then, her treat.

Ethel rose from Shavasana, placed her hands in the gesture of Namaste, nodded to Fritz and the other yoga students, rolled up her yoga mat, placed it under her arm, gathered her bag from the grass, and began to walk.

While stopping to look at the map app on her phone, by coincidence, although she didn't believe in coincidences, she found herself standing in front of a beauty salon. She had been thinking of doing something about her lackluster hair for a while. The sign said, WALK-INS WELCOME. Perhaps some off-color remark by Fritz, her yoga instructor, prompted her to enter the shop.

"Coincidences. Call them a method for getting your attention," he said, referring to the potty mouth he attributed to past-life incarnations. Fritz had a flair for throwing in sideline witticisms amongst his typical pearls of Vedic wisdom.

"You gotta run more than your mouth to escape the treadmill of mediocrity." Mild compared to some of his offhanded remarks.

Something snapped upon hearing those words, not her back, even though she was in Kapotasana, commonly known as pigeon pose, when Fritz, contrary to his usually soothing voice, emitted the words brusquely. A mixture of profound and salty sayings spouted from Fritz's om-shaped lips like a croak, reminding Ethel of a frog. Yes, a frog. She had never thought of Fritz in that manner, but the man, a marvel for his age, fiftyish if Ethel had to guess, was as lithe as a toad in the way he could effortlessly bend his body in and out of the most challenging yoga positions. It had taken Ethel a full six months to master the pose.

Ethel could give a good yoga talk, encouraging Luce and Ola to take it up, which they never did. But talk was all it was. Ethel rued the day they might actually show up and witness her losing her already precarious balance, setting in motion the entire class of aspiring yogis falling off their brilliantly colored mats like dominoes. It had never happened, but she imagined one day it might.

She had passed Baboons' Beauty Shop a zillion times. Zillion. Ethel had embraced the word zillions, a habit she had derived from Owen, one of her students. If Ethel could describe Owen in one word, it would be orange. She would miss Owen, his unruly mop of red hair and carrot-like, freckled complexion. The worn brown jacket he wore reminded her of dreadlocks. Owen was one of the nicer kids in her class who didn't mind hanging out with an autistic boy named Michael. Owen had a genuine talent for drawing. Pictures were one way he and Michael communicated.

Baboons' Beauty Shop was a quaint little establishment. The owner had a fondness for baboons—no, more like a fetish. Posters and zoo snapshots of the strange-looking creatures adorned every square inch of space not given to hairstyle shots. Who knew there was such a thing, but Ethel supposed there were as many strange hobbies as there were people. The owner must have collected them the way Owen collected baseball caps. The child wore a different one every day. Ethel repeatedly had to remind him to remove his cap while in class.

Driven by the desire to shed at least a portion of her mediocre life, Ethel pushed through the glass door with the signage, FIND YOUR WILD STREAK. Ethel assumed they meant hair.

"Something exotic," she told the hairdresser, a young girl probably Christine's age.

The hairdresser handed Ethel a thick piece of cardboard, something akin to a hardware paint chart, only with sections of imitation miniature ponytails in brilliant colors. After studying it for a while, Ethel handed it back to Barb. "I'm afraid I'm out of my element regarding these things. You choose."

Barb held a few fake hair strands against Ethel's cheek (Ethel suspected they were synthetic blends of something to resemble hair) and said, "Matcha Tea. I think this color will suit you best."

Ethel looked in the mirror one last time at her dishwater-blonde thinning tresses before sitting in the swivel chair. She could always dye it back before school started. Before school started? *What was she thinking?* None of that mattered now. School *would* start, but not for her.

She thought for a moment. She might as well go for the whole ball of wax. *Whatever did that phrase mean?* Maybe it had something to do with the time before electricity, when people used candles.

"Maybe a cut, too," she said to Barb, who smiled in delight at the possibilities while massaging her fingers through Ethel's hair.

The same young girl, Barb, who turned out to be the owner, washed, combed, blow-dried, and brushed something that looked brownish onto her thin strands, all while plying Ethel with every personal question within reasonable boundaries, a few teetering on the line.

Two hours later, when Ethel was in mid-sentence, Barb broke through. "Perfect." The word registered more like our time is up—something Freud might say. Somehow, Barb had extracted from her the details of her heated confrontation with Mr. Densworth, and how she had stormed out, quitting, along with other details of her life, some of which she had never confided to anyone. It was as if the hairdresser pulled out her secrets through her hair follicles. Did all hairdressers have some secret formula for doing this? She only hoped hair stylists practiced a creed of confidentiality the way psychiatrists did.

Barb held the mirror to the back of her head while Ethel faced the large mirror. Barb awaited eagerly for Ethel's reaction.

Ethel could only imagine walking into the classroom with this new look. Being on the other side of town from Densworth Academy, she supposed she was unlikely to encounter any of her students. She had to remind herself—former students.

"It's radical, isn't it?" she said to Barb, thinking she did indeed fit Mr. Densworth's description of her.

"My motto is we must express our inner being on the outside. I believe this is you," Barb said.

Possibly, that is why hairdressers ask so many questions—to get at the core of their client's inner being.

Ethel studied this new person looking back at her in the mirror. She pursed her thin, beak-like lips, which had grown narrower with each passing year. Maybe a Botox injection was next on the list. She raised the corners of her mouth into a smile in increments, turning her head to the right and the left.

"Yes, I rather like it."

Ethel stepped onto the sidewalk, feeling like a new woman. Matcha Tea strands cascaded down one side of her face. Barb said her new look was all the rage, even for the more mature woman. Plus, it gave her face some plumpness. Ethel agreed she had a thin face. The weight seemed to travel to her middle and stop there. However, Barb could have left off the part about the mature woman.

Wearing her hair to one side of her face, with strands dipping over her right eye, was new. She often wondered how the girls in her class could stand bangs covering half of their eyes. How could they see? Walking down the street, she couldn't help but push the strands aside the way someone might swat a fly.

Ethel's first thought was to show Ola and Luce the new her. With Luce on her trip, Ola would have to do for now.

Ola's eyes would widen at first, but then she would shrug it off. Even though Ola could be single-minded and deadly serious regarding her studies, she was pretty much anything goes when it came to everything else. She would likely say, "Well, enjoy the new you."

On the other hand, Ethel knew Luce would give her new hairstyle a full critique.

CHAPTER 4

Early June 2018

Eager to get Ola's thoughts on her hair, Ethel headed straight to the bookstore after leaving Baboons' Beauty Shop.

Cornelius greeted her, his chin resting on a stack of books he was carrying. "Good morning, Ethel."

"Closer to afternoon, now," Ethel replied.

Like an acrobat, he repositioned the books to one hand, and with his free hand, he picked up a book that appeared totally out of place on the edge of the book display and handed it to Ethel.

"Cornelius, I always appreciate your recommendations, but when will I find the time?"

She studied the whimsical design of a peacock on the cover. "Impressive cover," she said while handing it back to him.

Cornelius placed it back on the corner of the display unit and waved his free hand through the thick air of old-book smell in a gesture Ethel took to mean never mind. The stack of books occupying his other hand, because of their perfect bindings, Ethel took to be new acquisitions. The aroma of both old and new pages hung in the air like a thick fog. It was the satisfying aroma Ethel sucked in with delight each time she passed through the bookstore's door.

Cornelius's hand gesture reminded her of a bird ruffling its feathers, one that was agitated. Cornelius brought to mind an old owl, like something out of a cartoon—thin, short, and stodgy—sporting a respectable mop of silver-streaked hair with a perfectly groomed mustache to match. Although he didn't wear glasses, she could envision him wearing a monocle.

Cornelius carried an air of respectability about him, just the right touch of cologne, all prim and proper, like a Fuller Brush salesman, a relic of the past. Ethel had always admired his perfect posture despite the aches and pains she knew he had, not that he ever complained. She only knew about them through Ola. This was Cornelius's appearance on most days, but on rare occasions, he could look withered and older than his years. This was one of those rare days. He was only sixty-five, six years older than Ola. At one time, sixty-five would have seemed ancient, but not so much anymore, considering Ethel was about to turn the corner down Sixtieth Avenue herself.

"Don't have time to read?" he shrieked. Cornelius even sounded like an owl. Ethel had interpreted his hand waving through the air wrongly. Cornelius was most passionate about books. Ola could not have found a better person to assist her with the bookstore. Ethel thought of them more like partners, since Cornelius, as far as Ethel could tell, made most of the decisions concerning the running of the establishment. Despite brick-and-mortar bookstores teetering on the brink of obscurity, especially the small independent ones, Ola's Wise Old Books seemed to flourish. By physical standards, the shop was hardly small, winding around corners like a maze, depositing readers to perfectly delightful cubbyholes where they could exercise solitude with the printed page. Ethel contributed this to a loyal customer base who lusted after the rare and hard-to-find books of an esoteric nature, which the bookstore specialized in.

Ethel remembered a conversation she once heard Ola having with a customer. "Oh, we have best-selling novels like the rest. I tend only to read the blurbs and synopses of the fiction we carry. I can't possibly read all these books, but I must keep up. Customers often like to discuss what they're reading or ask for recommendations. And then, there are the two book clubs that meet here monthly. Not that I have too much involvement, but I like to keep on good terms. After all, they are buying their books from us, well, except for Mrs. Thurman. Someone bought her one of those electronic reading devices. You would think she might at least have the good manners to hide it in her purse when she waltzes in here, but no, she flaunts it. She even had the nerve one day to show me her new leather cover for it. I smiled and acted like it didn't bother me. I'm more inclined toward the serious student who comes here."

Fortunately, Ola gave this spiel to one of her most ardent customers, a grotesquely thin, bearded man who wore wire-rimmed spectacles and tied his scraggly hair back into a ponytail. Ethel surmised his academic endeavors prevented such frivolities as eating or visiting a hair salon. He was carefully studying a volume whose title had long ago faded.

Over the years, Ola and Cornelius had become the head deaconess and deacon of a bookish cult. The fact that the bookstore was within walking distance of the university helped.

Realizing his nervous excitement, Cornelius composed himself, subduing his unruly hand by smoothing down his tweed jacket—the brown one with the burnt-orange elbow patches, which Ethel saw him wear so often.

"Maybe then you have time to write? Finish that book you keep talking about?" he said, stepping back slightly as if waiting for a progress report. But there was no progress to report. Ethel had not opened the writing program on her laptop for months. The words that had flowed from what she surmised were coming from her higher chakra after one enlightened meditation dried up halfway into chapter two.

"Cornelius, I will take the book, but I came in to see Ola," Ethel said, changing the subject. "You know, we always get together for lunch on my first day of summer break." She tilted her head from side to side, hoping Cornelius might say something about her new hairdo. It was in vain.

Ola, the owner of Ola's Wise Old Books, usually hid away in her office, entrenched in some first edition or rare text she had happened upon. It was Ethel who always came to the bookstore to see Ola. To her dismay, Ethel had never once been invited to Ola's home. Ethel had hinted at it frequently, but Ola always changed the subject whenever she did. So, they sat in Ola's crowded office space, which only appeared small because of the many books and various papers, maneuvering a tea service and tray of tiny cakes or whatever pastry Cornelius brought in since he sometimes joined them for the first half of teatime when there were no customers. He said the remainder of the hour was for woman talk, walking away red-faced, slightly embarrassed.

They kept the water hot with a small electric teapot that Ethel feared would catch something on fire. Ethel wondered if the reason Ola never invited her to her home could have been because of a hoarding disorder. Ola moved and re-stacked papers and books to clear out space for the teapot on the shelf behind her desk, a ritual she followed daily. Each time she did it, Ethel worried everything might come toppling down like an avalanche, the books and other items in her office being so precariously arranged.

Ola's office bore no resemblance to the immaculate arrangement of books in the bookstore itself. Ethel attributed such flawless product display to Cornelius, whom she had seen more than once gather discarded books, meticulously inspecting them before returning them to their proper place. Ethel had never once seen Ola performing these tasks.

Ola had never married, and neither had Cornelius, to her knowledge. Both were big on privacy when it came to such matters. Ethel understood that the two had run the bookstore together for decades. Why they had never tied the knot in all that time, Ethel didn't know. They appeared meant for each other in every way, even down to their preferences in food.

Breaking for afternoon tea was a must, even though neither had any English heritage, Ethel knew about. And what would tea be without petite sandwiches and scrumptious pastries? Neither could live without French macarons, and it showed on Ola. But then, Ethel was no one to judge. She had grown a little on the pudgy side herself. Cornelius stayed as thin as a rail. Ethel wondered if owls could be skinny.

"She called in sick," Cornelius said bluntly.

"Sick? What's wrong?"

"She didn't say. I'm in a horrible quandary today with Ola out. I must get these latest books cataloged." Not giving Ethel time for follow-up questions, Cornelius spun around on his sneakered heel and hurried away. Well, as briskly as his arthritic legs could carry him. He had abandoned his highly polished Florsheims, substituting them with sneakers possessing extra cushioning.

Ethel picked the book from the corner of the table, held it up, and called out in Cornelius's wake, "You forgot. I need to pay for the book."

He turned. "It's a gift. Ola set it aside for you, meant to give it to you herself, but, well...." He turned and shuffled off toward the back of the shop before finishing the sentence.

"Okay," Ethel said, although she doubted he heard her. Not like Cornelius at all, Ethel thought. Stressed about Ola, no doubt. She hoped it wasn't serious, but everything in Cornelius's perplexing demeanor said it *was*. Besides being serious, it was suspicious.

<hr>

"I must call her as soon as I get home," Ethel mumbled as she left the bookstore.

She arrived at her car. Distracted by Cornelius's odd behavior concerning Ola's illness, she fumbled through her purse, looking for a key she no longer needed because the door unlocked automatically when she got near enough. An old memory resurfaced about when she first met Cornelius. Oh, he seemed affable enough, but there was something in his mannerism that suggested he was hiding something. As time passed, Ethel dismissed the feeling. The man was a perfect gentleman. She might not have given it another thought, but his conduct today, the way he was shoving the book at her, almost berating her over not starting that novel, and then abruptly brushing her off, was most peculiar. It brought to mind what Raja had said after dinner one night.

It was the first and only time Cornelius and Ola had come

together to their apartment for dinner. After they left, Raja said, "I see people from all cultures every day, and there are a lot of odd relationships out there, but this one takes the cake." Raja took a particular delight in using clichés.

"How so?" Ethel asked.

"He's hiding something."

"What on earth could he be hiding?"

"I don't know, but both are a little strange. It's like their existence revolves around the bookstore. And why have they never married? Maybe they're both hiding something." He laughed.

"What's so funny?" Ethel asked.

"It's probably all nonsense, what I get for reading Agatha Christie novels before falling asleep. I'm sure if there were anything nefarious going on, you, of all people, with that laser-pointed scrutiny of yours, would have discovered it by now."

Yes, he was right. After all these years, she would have known if something were amiss regarding Cornelius. Except for remaining a bachelor, he was devoted to Ola. However, he was noticeably worried and stressed. Ola had to be sicker than he was letting on.

CHAPTER 5

Early June 2018

"Ethel came by to see you." He paused, expecting Ola to respond. She didn't. "I did as you asked. I didn't tell her. You said you wanted to be the one."

Still nothing from Ola's end except her steady flow of breath.

"I said you were sick, but I felt like I was lying to her."

One long breath came before Ola said, "Don't worry about it, Cornelius. She will understand."

Ola was feeling on top of the world when she awoke two days earlier. She attributed it to the alignment of the stars. Although she didn't understand astrology, she needed no one to convince her of its significance.

She looked in the mirror, zooming in on the spot along her right jawline. "Yes, time to get you removed. And then a facial, no, a whole spa treatment. I might even go to Ethel's yoga class. She's always begging me to come. Time for a new me," she said to her reflection in the mirror. Hearing her voice speak the words aloud sealed her confirmation.

Ola thought it was nothing more than a stubborn wart, although she had never had a wart in her life. However, considering it was spreading and worsening daily, she felt compelled to take action.

Ola avoided doctors. Whitecoat syndrome was what both Luce and Ethel called it. Possibly so, but neither of them knew what it resulted from. On some nights, Ola still woke up in a cold sweat, reliving the news she had received thirty years ago from those in white coats.

"You have to get over this fear and see what a good dermatologist says about that spot," Luce scolded her.

With Ethel, it was always some Ayurvedic regimen. At the same time, Ethel was adamant about regular checkups. Out of desperation, she tried Ethel's recommendations but saw no results.

"Please don't tell Ethel they didn't work," Luce said.

"I think you know me better than that, Luce," Ola replied.

Both Luce and Ola knew it would only provoke an onslaught of further suggestions, which Ethel would likely supervise.

"See a doctor," Luce pleaded.

"Yes, it was time," Ola mumbled after agreeing to meet the possible Mr. Right via email. Calling him Mr. Right was jumping way ahead of herself. A blind date from a dating website was risky, but she was suddenly ready to take risks. Maybe it was the fact that she would turn sixty in October. If not now, when?

She closed the computer on her home office desk. A date, her first in, well, it had been so long she couldn't even remember back that far—at least not a going-out-to-dinner date followed by a movie. There had been days she had felt like moving on, but guilt convinced her it would be disrespectful. So, she dismissed the thoughts.

She had never put Cornelius in that category, the actual date category. There were plenty of lunches together and late dinners when he had stopped by her house, some of which led to sex. It had happened on several occasions, but had ceased with the purchase of the bookstore. She would have been happy to continue the arrangement. But Cornelius apologized for his behavior, saying it was wrong. A lapse in judgment, he called it, and that it wouldn't happen again. Although she hardly took a break from the bookstore, she left for a week, telling him she was visiting a sick aunt. She suspected he knew there was no aunt. She needed the time alone to recoup and gather her thoughts. Mostly, she needed a week to cry. She contemplated not returning to the bookstore and going back to working in a library, but when her tears finally dried, she realized she loved the bookstore and that she loved having Cornelius as a friend more than a lover. He had been there for her in the roughest of times.

Ola wasted way too much time trying to figure Cornelius out. It was useless. There was something about him that defied explanation. She knew he had been married, although he never spoke of it. She couldn't imagine there were any other women in his life. There would have been clues. She had been to his apartment plenty of times, and he to her house. The thought of him being gay had occurred to her, but she quickly dismissed it. He gave off no vibes of that nature. No, there was something deeper, something even their close friendship couldn't penetrate. She accepted it and moved on. Or so she had thought until one day, when Ethel suggested online dating.

"I might try online dating when my divorce is final," Ethel had said rather casually.

"Oh? You're filing for divorce?"

"Well, no, I haven't started the process, but sometimes, this limbo I'm in gets so tiring. A teacher at our school met her husband online, and she's no spring chicken—in her late forties. We ought to give it a whirl. What do you say, Ola? Look how happy Luce is."

"Luce married young, and she didn't meet Santiago online. We're in our fifties." She paused and sighed. "I don't know. I'll give it some thought."

That answer seemed to satiate Ethel. Her friend had never even brought up divorce before. Ola had always thought Ethel was perfectly content with her arrangement with Raja—separated, estranged, or whatever one might call it. If Ethel was thinking of moving on, surely *she* could.

"We could do it together," Ethel said.

"Do what together?" Ola asked.

"Search online for dates."

"I thought we were off that subject for now."

"It might be fun. There are a lot of happily married couples who have found each other online."

"Who, other than the teacher you mentioned?" Ola inquired.

"I don't know of anyone else specifically, but I've read about them."

While Ola could see herself and her friend drinking wine and having a pleasant laugh over perusing the choices and reading the bios of those who resorted to this, she waved Ethel off. "I'm too old for such nonsense."

"Too old! Hogwash," Ethel said. "Neither of us has turned sixty yet." What Ethel said next hit Ola like a brick. "Quit wasting your life waiting on Cornelius."

Ethel was right. She had put her life on hold for far too long, embarrassing herself with an amorous hint here or there, something casually thrown into the conversation, hoping to pursue something more than friendship with Cornelius, restarting what didn't get off the ground that first time, all to no avail. And for what? Cornelius seemed to like the current arrangement of employer and employee. Their relationship was something more than just platonic and best friends, yet not enough. She and Cornelius had been through so much. Stuff that Ethel didn't know.

Sometimes, she thought about telling Ethel about her past, but what would opening old wounds that were finally closing after all these years accomplish? Maybe she and Cornelius had been through too much together for it to work; perhaps that's why he called it a mistake.

Still, Ethel's remark hit Ola hard. She could no longer fathom a pajama-party scenario, drinking white zinfandel with her best friend while they scrolled down various testosterone options. No, she would proceed independently, noting those who appealed to her and making a list of the pros and cons of each. It would be a serious pursuit—businesslike and analytical.

First, she had to Google dating sites. Ola didn't have a clue. She wondered if Ethel had already explored it. Her friend had much more gumption than she. Ola shrugged the notion off. If Ethel had done so, she would have said. Ethel always spoke her mind.

Ethel had been urging her to see a doctor for months. "If you think makeup is hiding it, it's not," Ethel had said. Ethel had a bluntness that Ola both cringed at and respected.

Ola turned to the right and the left and straightened her dress in front of the full-length mirror. She had finally decided on her red dress. Luce had always said it was perfect for her. She didn't know about that. Black might have made her look thinner, but red had always been her color, and the three-quarter-length sleeves helped hide her flabby arms. Perhaps too bold—maybe. This whole rendezvous was daring.

She did another quick turnaround in front of the mirror and smoothed out some wrinkles with her hands. *Linen, what was she thinking?* She should call it off. She glanced at her phone to check the time. She began typing an email with hands so sweaty she feared shorting out the keyboard. Why was she so nervous? It was probably too late. No, don't back out, she told herself. She hit delete. He might already be at the restaurant by now. She doubted he would see an email. She would go and enjoy a good meal if nothing else.

Considering she had shared three emails with Roger, it wasn't necessarily a blind date in the truest sense of the word. She had seen his picture, which was a bit blurry. Despite his age, he looked young in the photo.

Ola sighed heavily, grabbed her purse, and drove to the restaurant. She told herself if she couldn't find a place to park, it would be a sign, and she would leave.

The parking lot was only half full. She slid her car in easily, close to the door. She entered but couldn't remember if she was to meet him out front. The lighting was low. Possibly, he was in the restroom or already had a table. Or maybe he wouldn't show. She carefully scanned the tables at the mid-priced Italian family-style restaurant they had both agreed upon. She only saw one lone man sitting at a booth in the back. He was in his twenties. She debated between leaving or getting a table for one and treating herself to a nice meal when she spied a man waving at her from the opposite corner. Could it be that he sent his father?

It was when her date, Roger, this much older man than the one portrayed in the picture on the dating site, shrieked with a disgusted, bunched-up face halfway through the parmesan eggplant, "Your face is bleeding?" that Ola put down her fork and excused herself to the ladies' room.

They both passed on dessert and the movie.

A day went by, and Roger hadn't bothered to call. Ola had to admit he nonplused her, and even though he made polite conversation throughout the dinner, they were an unlikely pair. Like an elongated toothpick, he towered above her five-foot beach-ball frame. He had narrow eyes with bushy eyebrows. Compared to her thinning brows and eyes resembling those found in a Margaret Keane painting, they must have been a sight, something the other couples in the restaurant Ola imagined whispering about.

Ola talked about rare and ancient manuscripts while he stared blankly, after which he said, "I don't read many books. Oh, maybe a crime story once in a blue moon."

They say opposites attract, but he *did* list books among his likes. Had someone prompted him on his bio about what appealed to mature women? Did he not even see that she ran a bookstore? But then, while she cringed at some of the things he listed as his interests on his bio—action movies, poker, and NASCAR—she still hit the response button to his ad. He seemed the safest of the list of candidates. At least he omitted candlelit dinners followed by lengthy massages, which most men listed as their favorite things to do. He must have found her as dull as himself, the impetus for responding to her.

The following day, she took her turn at a walk-in clinic, afraid that if she waited for a doctor's appointment, she might talk herself out of it.

If Ola had known it was more than a wart, she would have asked Ethel to go with her for a shoulder to cry on, as she was driving back in a flood of tears. Too bad the windshield wipers were not inside the car. The prognosis didn't even hit her until she got into her car. In a hot car, Ola gripped the steering wheel for an indeterminate amount of time. Only the sweat dripping down her nose from sitting in the hot vehicle prompted her to release her grip.

How long had she sat in that sweltering hot car? The parking lot, devoid of shade trees, was as ruthless and metaphorically cold as the clinic's interior, with its artificial plants and ubiquitous artwork on the walls, paintings that looked like they came from one of those starving artists' warehouses. Ola had once read that the images were manufactured on an assembly line—someone skilled at painting water painted lakes; another good at painting trees painted those; a person adept at painting figures painted people, and so on. Whether this was true, she didn't know.

The woman doctor asked her if she was okay after making her recommendations, the ones she must have recited by heart, just as a policeman recites Miranda Rights. Her concern even seemed staged, a poor rendering of Shakespeare for one lowly member of an audience. When the doctor relayed the news, Ola felt her eyes widen even bigger than they already were.

"The first step is a biopsy, but if you were to open a medical textbook, you would see that your particular carcinoma is the classic example. Now, there are several options."

While the doctor continued, Ola faded out. Something about three different courses of action: radiation, something else she didn't understand, and surgery. Ola heard the words plastic surgery but didn't have the foresight to question why this was even a possibility. If only she had brought Ethel. She would have been asking tough questions. But then, Ethel would have also been making the decisions as if Ola weren't even in the room.

The doctor rendered her closing act in the same dry style as her opening before transitioning into her curtain call.

Ola remembered the day she met Ethel. This tall, authoritative woman entered the bookstore in search of a gift for her wedding anniversary.

"Something of Hindu origin, in Sanskrit. Do you have anything like that?" she asked.

Ola knew of nothing in Sanskrit offhand, but Cornelius said they might have something in the back and excused himself, leaving Ola and Ethel standing there. Since there were no other customers to tend to, Ola felt obligated to, at the very least, make small talk, something she failed at miserably, while Cornelius dug through boxes in the back. Knowing how thorough Cornelius was, Ola predicted a long wait.

"For your husband, you said?"

"Yes, he's from India. He teaches computer technology at the University of Washington." She said it with an air of pride. Ola couldn't help but notice how her head lifted a full inch with the proclamation.

Even though Ola deduced the woman wasn't a professor herself, thinking she would have mentioned that both she and her husband taught at the university, Ola asked, for lack of anything better to say, if she also taught. It was apparent she had just come from some white-collar job, dressed in a skirt and blouse.

"I teach middle school at Densworth Academy." Ola feared that she might ask if she might have grandchildren there, but she didn't. Instead, she talked about shaping the minds of the young and what a noble calling teaching was.

It was midway into what Ola thought would be a lengthy spiel when Cornelius finally reappeared, holding a book up. "Would a copy of the *Mahabharata* be a suitable gift?" he asked.

After that, Ethel became a regular customer. It was one day when Ethel, with her flamboyant brand of salesmanship, sold a young couple, the wife of whom was expecting any day, a whole set of first-edition Beatrix Potter books, money the couple probably needed for diapers and formula, that Cornelius said, "You need a woman friend, and Mrs. Sharma seems to be of sound character. You should invite her for lunch. Something nice."

A week later, Ethel entered Ola's inner sanctum for tea and a vegan charcuterie board, as Ethel had stated she was a vegetarian upon receiving the invitation. They became fast friends. After only a month, Ethel said, "You must meet my friend, Luce."

Between bites, she added, "We could become the female version of The Three Musketeers. One for all, and all for one."

Ola could not help but notice the grin on Cornelius's face as he walked past Ola's office door, which caused Ola to smile. Ethel seemed to have a perpetual smile during their lunch.

It began raining as Ola drove from the clinic. Rain had not been in the forecast, but neither was cancer. Plastic surgery? The doctor should have known by her lack of makeup and fashion sense that she wasn't a vain woman. What *registered* with her was the doctor saying the cancer appeared to run deep and was likely in her bloodstream. After sitting in her car in shock for that indeterminate time, she drove straight home. She hardly wanted to go back to the bookstore and face Cornelius. He knew her too well and would know something was wrong. She needed time to think.

Upon entering her house, which she only knew at night and on Sundays, she threw her purse on the couch and went to her computer to Google what the doctor had said. After reading various sites, she sat at her desk, took a deep breath, ended it with a heavy sigh, leaned back in her chair, and shouted to the walls, "I'm a goner."

The bottom line was that she had waited too long. The next thing Ola Googled was Egypt. Typing Egypt into the search bar happened automatically, subconsciously, on her part. She had always dreamed of seeing the pyramids, the numerous tombs, statues, and ancient hieroglyphs in person, not in a museum or on the pages of a book. After finding various tour groups, she selected the one she thought best suited her. A husband-and-wife team led it. Both had studied sacred sites worldwide. Dr. Leonard Walker held a Ph.D. in Egyptology, and his wife had a Ph.D. in religious studies.

Nine glorious days of experiencing the wonder of what she considered the world's most mystical land. She could see the magnificence of the pyramids firsthand and enter the Great Pyramid's inner chambers. She had read of people having transcendent experiences. A chill traveled up her spine as she thought about having her picture made standing between the paws of the Sphinx, something to put up on her office wall.

The tour boasted a five-star hotel, a cruise down the Nile, and a balloon ride over Luxor. What appealed to her the most about this tour was that it would be led by a couple of Egyptology scholars whose mission was to unravel ancient wisdom. Additionally, it was limited to twenty-two people, including the Walkers, a manageable and intimate number. She might even make friends on this tour.

Making friends? For how long? What if there was no hope for her? She could die during the trip. She shook her head in an effort to ward off the negativity, doing her best to concentrate on the website.

There were no chat boxes for questions; only an email address was provided. The tour was a week away. Her passport, which was only used once for a book symposium in Canada, was up to date. What did she have to lose? She got an almost immediate reply to her email. It was from Dr. Walker.

The tour had been solidly booked months ago, but there had been a cancellation this morning—definitely a sign. Ra was with her. She smiled, thinking that in a short time, she would walk in the footsteps of ancient holy ones while visiting the ageless temples.

Ola paid the total amount and hit the final booking button without hesitation.

Two days later, she received a call from the clinic. "We have your biopsy back. We will need to schedule you for surgery right away."

"I will call you when I return from Egypt," Ola said bluntly.

CHAPTER 6

Mid-June 2018

Ola hadn't visited the bookstore for a week. Ethel continuously left messages on her cell. In response, Ola sent one brief text. "Don't worry about me, Ethel. I'm taking a much-needed rest. I will call you later in the week."

When Ola finally rang back, she asked, "Ethel, can you drive me to the airport in the morning?"

"To the airport?"

"Yes, I'm taking a trip."

After a pause, Ethel said, "This came up suddenly. A book symposium or something for business?"

"No, I'm finally taking a trip I've long dreamed of."

"To where?"

"I'll explain tomorrow. I leave early. I hope that's not a problem. It's the first flight out. Can I leave my car at your apartment?"

"Yes, I'm sure that won't be a problem. But—"

"I'll be there at five sharp. I can't miss my plane. I must get there on time. Should I give you a wake-up call?"

"No, I can get up, but Ola—"

"See you in the morning," she said, all bright and cheery, before abruptly ending the call.

It had only been a couple of hours earlier that Ethel, with tears in her eyes, saw Ola off at the ticket gate. It was the first time Ethel had cried in... Well, she didn't remember the last time. She didn't even cry when Raja had left, even though both Ola and Luce said she was repressing her feelings.

How could Ola do such a thing, announce such a heart-wrenching prognosis while she was driving, with no more emotion than saying, "Turn here?" It occurred to her that Raja announced he was returning to India in much the same way. A month later, Christine matter-of-factly pronounced that her father had found her a job there. It seemed as if everyone in her life sprang life-altering pronouncements on her in the most casual manner.

With Ola, Ethel knew something was up, but expected nothing like this. Ola had been avoiding Ethel's calls all week. And that text, telling her not to worry. How could she not worry? She had gone to the bookstore twice to check on her, and both times, Cornelius had said she was recuperating at home. *And all is well? Hardly.*

"Be happy for me, Ethel. This is the adventure of a lifetime," Ola said after checking her bag. "I hope I packed the right clothes and accessories. I followed the instructions the best I could."

"I'm sure you'll be fine, Ola. Just beware of all the hagglers trying to sell you souvenirs."

"Yes, that was in the email. The people running the tour

have done this plenty of times. I'm sure all twenty of us are in capable hands."

"Yes, I'm sure you're in excellent hands." Ethel managed a half-hearted smile. It wasn't until her friend began the walk toward the TSA line that Ethel's smile turned genuine. Ola was right, and Ethel was happy her friend was taking this leap, or at least was trying to be.

"Ola," she called out.

Ola looked back. Ethel blew her a kiss. Ola smiled and waved. Ethel stood there until Ola got swallowed up in the crowd of fellow travelers, some bored, some weary, some disgruntled, and a few noticeably excited, like her friend.

Ethel had spent the drive to the airport urging Ola not to put off the surgery and radiation. She was still postulating when Ola's voice broke through, hitting her like a ton of bricks. "Ethel, you're being selfish."

How could she say such a thing? What if she lost Ola—her good friend, maybe her best friend, now that Luce was preoccupied with raising teenage boys?

"Of course, I'm being selfish. I don't want to lose you," Ethel retorted. What Ethel hid behind the melancholy of Ola's possible fate was selfishness. It hurt Ethel that Ola hadn't even considered her for the trip.

It was as if Ola had developed some new clairvoyance with the cancer prognosis. She put her arm around Ethel. "You know I would have liked nothing better than for you to accompany me, but there was no time and only one slot left. I had little choice. You know Egypt has been a lifelong dream of mine."

Yes, Ethel knew. Had Ola considered Cornelius for the trip and not her? A pang of guilt surfaced at her jealousy. Possibly, she had asked him, but he said no. She said there was only one slot left—someone canceled at the last minute. Ethel was being paranoid. Yes, she was happy for Ola.

Ethel drove directly back to her apartment, but even on such a dreary day, she wanted to be out. What did it matter if it was raining? It constantly rained in Seattle. Maybe the rain might clear her head. She parked the car in the apartment lot. Rhonda was out tending to her garden. Rain or shine, you could almost be certain of Rhonda's presence there. She would have to walk past her if she went up the back stairwell. Rhonda meant well, but Ethel wasn't in the mood today. She was sure she would insist on giving her something from her garden. Avoiding the stairwell, Ethel removed the umbrella she always carried in the backseat and set off on foot in the opposite direction, with no particular place in mind.

What an awful day to travel. She brushed the thought aside that Ola's plane might be grounded. Ola might see it as a sign to stay, go through with the operation and radiation, then go on the trip. They could go together. She had a bit of mad money put aside. No, she told herself. *Quit the pity party, Ethel*. How many times had Raja accused her of pity parties? Besides, the rain was not much more than a sprinkle.

Ethel walked, lost in thought. She looked around to get her bearings, but the buildings were unfamiliar. The drizzle suddenly turned into a downpour. It wouldn't last. It never did, but no sense in catching a chill or cold. Nor did she want green dye running down her face, something she feared ever since her impromptu new hairstyle, even though Barb told her it wouldn't happen.

Ethel laughed. Ola's reaction to her hair was priceless. "Seriously, Ethel? What in the world brought this on?"

"Do you like it?" Ethel asked, tossing her strands around.

"Can you see out of your left eye?" Ola almost always pulled her hair back.

"I'll admit, hair falling over my eye takes some getting used to, especially green hair. Sometimes, I feel as though I've run into a bush."

Ola snorted. "I think it might be the true you. Yes, I believe I like it."

Ethel found herself in front of a quaint little shop, the outside reminiscent of something stuck in the 1950s, nestled—no, more like wedged—between two gray-metallic newer structures with clean, crisp, futuristic window displays. It was like a beacon calling out to her. This storefront was out of place and otherworldly, perhaps a portal to a parallel universe. If so, it was what she needed: a refuge from all that was happening in her life. She ran over, stood beneath the awning, and shook the excess rain from her umbrella before ducking in.

"Nasty out there," she heard a voice say.

"Yes, yes, it is," she said, looking up. The voice belonged to a squirrelly-looking man somewhere in his late forties.

"Are you looking for anything in particular?" the man asked.

"No, I'm afraid I must confess I only came in to get out of the rain. And I was in awe of your storefront."

"Happens a lot—the rain and the storefront," he said.

"Definitely in Seattle, the rain, that is," Ethel added.

He smiled. "Make yourself at home until you want to brave the outside again."

With her back resting against the door, Ethel looked in three directions. The shop was a compilation of everything imaginable. The smell was old, and the atmosphere was magical. She had entered an entirely delightful world merely by opening a heavy oak door with THE EMPORIUM, etched in gold across the glass, halfway up. The name fit, and the interior was as fascinating as the exterior.

She had nowhere to be—no appointments. She set her umbrella by the door and gingerly meandered through the crowded aisles, winding like a maze into hidden junctures not unlike the Tardis. There was an odd assortment of objects, none of which appeared new. It was a shop Ola would enjoy. On the other hand, Luce would likely excuse herself to one of the more modern shops next door.

Ethel examined various trinkets. There were old keys—an entire box of them. Who would buy such a thing? She picked up a bravery medal attached to a faded ribbon. She wondered who it had once belonged to and what brave act it commemorated. Second-hand clothing materialized in the strangest places among the miscellaneous merchandise, suggesting that this outfit might pair well with this item. She held a tie-dyed dress up against her torso.

"It complements your hair." The voice came from a woman who stood only a foot from her. She hadn't noticed her before. "You should get it," she added.

"Oh, I don't know." Ethel looked down at the dress and then back up to see the woman walk around a corner and disappear. Maybe a ghost, she thought. A ghost saleslady would undoubtedly be at home in this shop. Ethel looked at the tag. The price was out of the fifties as well, even though the dress looked like someone had worn it during the sixties, possibly even at Woodstock. She removed the dress from the hanger and draped it over her arm before veering off in a different direction from the woman.

There was no rhyme or reason for anything's location in the store. Peeking from a far corner, she spied a statue of the Sphinx, bringing Ola back into her thoughts. The shop had been a slight reprieve from sadness. Ola had hardly left her thoughts since Cornelius's odd behavior in the bookstore. Then there was Ola's aloofness—not going to work or returning her calls—and finally, the news. She picked the Sphinx statue up for closer examination, noticing the outline of dust surrounding its now vacant spot.

"Mrs. Sharma," a male voice called. Upon hearing her name, Ehtel placed the miniature Sphinx back on the counter and turned to see who might know her. A man roughly in his early twenties smiled timidly at her. Ehtel guessed him to be a former student.

"I'm sure you don't remember me," he said. He was at least six feet tall, with dark brown hair and big brown eyes. Earbuds dangled from his ears. He reached up to turn off the music.

"Give me a moment." She studied his face. "One of my former students? Correct?"

"Yes." He smiled.

"I'm afraid you're hard to place with the stubble on your face. My middle school students didn't have beards. Also, I'm used to towering above my students. You've obviously had a growth spurt since I taught you."

"Sam Scranton," he said.

"Sam? Sam, the writer?"

"Why, yes," he said, displaying an even broader smile. "Just graduated from U Dub. Majored in Creative Writing with a minor in business."

"I am so glad to hear it. I remember your stories. Let me see. Didn't you write one about a squirrel who went on a grand adventure?"

"Mrs. Sharma, I'm amazed you would remember that."

"Well, I didn't..." she corrected herself. "I don't have that many A+ students." There was hardly any need to put her teaching career in the past tense. She knew Mr. Densworth would call any day and beg her to return. She hadn't even told Ola or Luce about the incident. After considering it, she concluded it would all be sorted out before the fall semester. The idea of going back and saying it was all a misunderstanding had crossed her mind several times, but each time, she cringed. It would make Mr. Densworth so happy to have her groveling before him, begging for mercy like some prey he was about to devour. No, she would wait for his call. It was sure to come.

Sam laughed.

"You've grown into a handsome young man." Did she see a hint of a blush? She remembered him being shy, a bit of a nerd.

"Thank you." He did a small half-roll of his eyes as if he were embarrassed. Few young men these days displayed such self-consciousness.

"So, are you shopping? Perhaps looking for story ideas? So many rare finds in this shop. I bet each item could tell a story."

"As a matter of fact, I have gotten some ideas from some of the stuff here, but I work here. My pop owns the place."

"Oh," Ethel said. She paused. "It is a rather unusual shop."

"I've worked here, helping Pop out, ever since I could reach the counter. Been saving my money."

"For college?" Ethel asked.

"At first, but I ended up getting a full scholarship."

Ethel stepped back a bit. "That's fantastic, but I remember you as a conscientious student."

His cheeks lit up again, and he looked down at the floor. Suddenly, a memory resurfaced—of how bragging about his stories in front of the other students made him react the same way.

He looked back up. "I'll only be working for Pop the rest of this week. I'm taking some time off. Headed to France for a month."

"Oh, I see. I've been to France twice, once in Paris, the other time on the French Riviera. It will be the experience of a lifetime for you. Early on, my husband and I traveled quite a bit."

No need to tell Sam she was estranged from her husband. She looked down at her ring. She had never taken it off. She wondered if Raja still wore his wedding band.

"No doubt you'll be in Paris?" she asked.

"Yes, but I'll be backpacking across the country, staying in hostels. I've saved money, but not that much."

"You must visit Shakespeare and Company."

"It's at the top of my list."

"Oh, to be young again."

"Maybe when you retire, you and your husband can travel again."

"Maybe," she said. "Well, I must pay for this dress and be off," Ethel said, moving the dress meant for a much younger woman slightly under her arm. "A gift," she said.

"Really? I thought it was for you. It matches your hair."

Ethel felt her face turning red as she reached her hand to her head. She had forgotten about her hair.

"Hmm, I might consider keeping it for myself. We'll see. Well, it was so nice to see what a fine young man you turned out to be, Sam."

"Thank you, Mrs. Sharma. It is so good to see you again."

The rain was slackening as Ethel left the shop. She looked at the sky to see a hint of sun erasing the gray. With her umbrella closed, there was a new lightness to her step. Yes, to be young again and travel. She had so many fond memories of their trips to France.

CHAPTER 7

Early to Mid-June 2018

"No, Santiago, you don't understand. She's my best friend, and I literally told her she couldn't go around rescuing everyone."

"What's so bad about that?" he asked, not bothering to turn around in bed.

"It's the way I said it. And when I said it. She was upset about Ola, and I was mean. I thought she was going to cry. She said, 'I only want to help.'"

"Luce, I'm sure you weren't mean. You don't have a mean bone in your body. Besides, you're upset about Ola, too," he said in a drowsy voice. Luce loved that voice. She loved almost everything about Santiago, even after twenty years of marriage.

"I know. I'm probably overreacting, but I kicked her when she was down—when she was the most vulnerable."

He turned around in bed. "Ethel, vulnerable?" he grunted with open eyes and a surprised look.

"It's more than Ola having cancer. Ethel is no longer working at Densworth Academy."

"What do you mean?" he asked, sitting up in bed.

"I called the school. The secretary said that Mrs. Sharma no longer works here."

"That's strange."

"Yes. I even had her repeat what she said to make sure there was no mistake."

"You didn't tell Ethel you called the school looking for her?"

"No, I felt like she should be the one to tell me. She told me about Ola having cancer, and I acted as if I had heard it for the first time. Ethel had already worked out a regimen for Ola. That's when I said what I did."

He reached over and hugged his wife, looking into her eyes. "Aw, don't worry, honey. She'll understand. You and Ethel have been friends for a long time. You've known Ethel longer than you've known me."

Luce shook her head. "And if she knew Ola told me about the cancer first.... Well, you can only imagine."

"Ethel's one proud bird, for sure," he said.

Luce laughed.

"What's so funny?"

"Ethel, a bird? I guess she *is* like a mother hen."

"A mother hen? Maybe, in a way. It seems like Christine was more the mother," Santiago said.

"Christine was born an adult."

Santiago let out a loud cackle.

"What?" Luce asked.

"I just had a thought."

"And that was?"

"Ethel reminds me more of a peacock."

"A peacock?"

"You said she was a mother hen, but she reminds me more of a peacock than a hen."

"A peacock. That's interesting. I think you mean a peahen, though. The peacock is the male."

"Honey, you'll work it out. Can we go to sleep? I have an early day tomorrow."

"I'm sorry," she said.

He reached over and kissed his wife. "No reason to be sorry. It's refreshing not to be talking about some trouble the kids caused today."

"Yes, you're right," she said.

"Good night."

"Good night," Luce replied. Santiago was already breaking into a snore.

It was three days into Ola's vacation. Luce lay in bed and wondered if she was happy about finally seeing the pyramids. She had talked about them for so long. Well, as happy as she could be, considering she would have to have an operation and begin radiation when she returned. Maybe entering the pyramids would cure her. Ola often talked about such things. While Ethel put her faith in Ayurveda, Ola sang the praises of the mysterious power of the pyramids and this other place she had recently discovered, Göbekli Tepe. If it were true, it would be a double bang for your buck, Luce thought—the vacation of a lifetime plus being cured of cancer.

When Ola called Luce after her return from the Bahamas and suggested they meet for coffee, Luce was surprised. It wasn't like Ola to leave the bookstore in the middle of the afternoon. "Okay, I'll call Ethel," she had said.

"No, please don't call Ethel. It's you I want to talk to."

"What about?" Luce asked.

"I'll tell you when I see you."

"Okay." The word stumbled out of Luce's mouth in three syllables rather than two.

So ominous, Luce thought. It was always either Ethel and Ola, she and Ethel, or the three of them together; rarely was it just Ola and Luce, unless she went to the bookstore without Ethel. It was usually when the boys needed a gift for a birthday party. She always felt obligated to buy three gifts, one each from Martin, Lou, and Dewey. The boys complained their friends would think their family was cheap or, worse, poor if she didn't. She didn't want to argue with them. The boys protested when they had to take books as gifts, but it was a take-it-or-leave-it deal. Ola always gave her a discount.

"Can you give me a hint, Ola?"

"We'll talk when we see each other. The coffee shop near the bookstore? And don't tell Ethel you're meeting me."

"Yes, that's fine. Can you give me an hour?"

"Yes."

Luce hopped into the shower. What in the world could this be about? Ethel, no doubt.

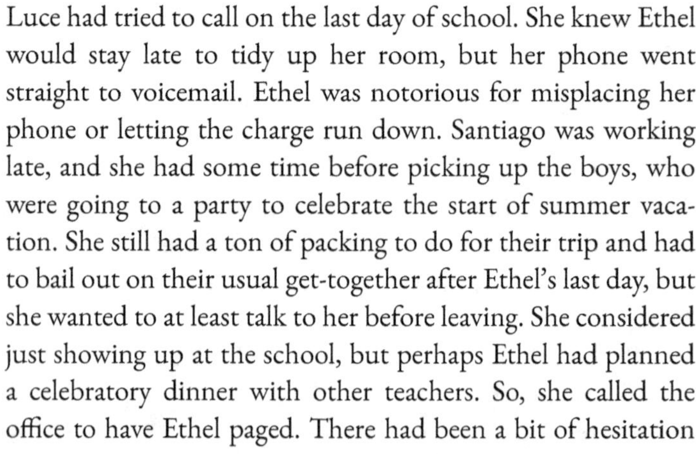

Luce had tried to call on the last day of school. She knew Ethel would stay late to tidy up her room, but her phone went straight to voicemail. Ethel was notorious for misplacing her phone or letting the charge run down. Santiago was working late, and she had some time before picking up the boys, who were going to a party to celebrate the start of summer vacation. She still had a ton of packing to do for their trip and had to bail out on their usual get-together after Ethel's last day, but she wanted to at least talk to her before leaving. She considered just showing up at the school, but perhaps Ethel had planned a celebratory dinner with other teachers. So, she called the office to have Ethel paged. There had been a bit of hesitation before the secretary said, "I'm afraid Mrs. Sharma no longer works here."

"There must be some mistake."

"No mistake," the secretary had replied.

"I will not let this ruin my vacation," Luce said, still flustered over the news, while throwing the last item into her suitcase. "Nor will I even mention it to Santiago until we return."

Luce saw Ethel only once since returning from the Bahamas. Ethel acted as if everything were perfectly normal. Luce knew if she brought up her phone call, Ethel would be beside herself with embarrassment. So, she pretended nothing was amiss. She knew whatever had happened with Ethel must be the reason Ola wanted to meet with her.

She toweled dry and put on black leggings and a light sweater. Seattle was still chilly in June. She put on some face powder and lipstick, quickly turned in the full-length mirror, and said aloud to her image, "I have to exercise."

Grabbing her car keys, she headed out the door.

She was already seated with a Frappuccino when Ola walked in, reprimanding herself for the indulgence after seeing her butt in the mirror when she stepped out of the shower. She had recently been rethinking the full-length mirror opposite the walk-in shower, which had been Santiago's idea.

"It will be nice," he said.

"Nice? More like naughty is what you have in mind."

He had given her that sly look of his. He had a way of fixating his notorious bedroom eyes on her entire body, making her think she was the only woman in the world. So, what if her butt had spread out a little? It was the price of having three babies at once—babies they had worked incredibly hard to achieve.

"I think I might have one, too," Ola said, coming up to Luce's table.

Luce raised an eyebrow. She had only ever seen Ola have a hot cup of tea, sometimes with cake or a pastry, but never a Frappuccino.

"What is it?" she asked.

"It's a blended iced mocha with extra whip."

"Be right back," she said.

Luce was halfway finished with her drink by the time Ola got through the line. It seemed everyone needed a pick-me-up at two o'clock in the afternoon.

"So, what's this news you have for me? It's about Ethel, right? It's why you said not to call her. You know why she is no longer employed at the school?"

"What?"

"That's not what this is about? I called the school on the last day to have her paged. You know how she always misplaces her phone or forgets to charge it. Well, the secretary told me she no longer works there."

Ola looked surprised. "Do you think she might have gotten fired? I can't believe Ethel would quit teaching."

"Possibly... probably—the reason she hasn't told us. Why did you want me to meet you if this isn't about Ethel?"

"I have cancer." She said it matter-of-factly, like a news reporter delivering the evening news.

Luce could feel her face sagging. She pushed her drink aside. "Ola?"

"I know, rather blunt, but how else can you give someone news like this?"

"What kind of cancer?"

"It started with this place on my face. Now they say it's in my bloodstream."

"Oh, Ola. What treatment are they recommending?"

"Operation, followed by radiation."

"When?"

"After I get back from Egypt."

"Egypt? You're going to Egypt?" Luce couldn't help but smile. "This is why you are telling me and not Ethel."

"Yes, we both know she would tell me not to go. Plus, she would have to oversee every trip to the doctor."

"Like a mother hen," Luce said.

"Yes, something like that. Please drink your drink and be happy for me. I'm finally going to Egypt."

"Ola, are you not planning on telling Ethel? About the cancer, I mean."

"I plan on asking her to drive me to the airport. I was thinking about telling her on the way."

Luce laughed. "Oh, Ola, I'm sorry. This is no time for laughing. Sorry, I couldn't help myself."

Ola burst out laughing, too. "You're right. It's funny."

"She'll be furious," Luce said.

"I suppose so."

Luce didn't see Ola anymore before she left. She had only called to wish her well and tell her to have a safe journey. She hoped that was the case, and she was having the time of her life.

And as far as why Ethel was no longer teaching, she supposed Ethel would tell both her and Ola in her own good time.

She would call Ethel tomorrow after she returned from taking Ola to the airport to see if they could meet for lunch or something. It would be on her, of course. If Ethel had lost her job, she might be watching her expenditures. Maybe Ethel found another teaching position at a different school. It was no secret how Ethel felt about the principal.

Luce sank her head into the pillow, turned onto her side, and put her arm around Santiago, telling herself that both Ethel and Ola would be fine.

CHAPTER 8

Mid-June 2018

Upon returning to her apartment, Ethel made herself a cup of tea, the Darjeeling that Christine had sent her, and pulled out old picture albums from the bookcase. She hadn't looked at them in ages. She moved her hand over a layer of dust before opening the first one. How skinny she and Santiago both were! Most of the pictures were of her. Raja had always been the family photographer. He complained that her photographs were out of focus. He was right. She couldn't help but smile, holding up the blurred pictures she had taken of him during their first year of marriage.

"Hold the camera steady," he said while pretending to be Julia Child. He was making a pot of chai, of all things. How on earth could she hold the camera with precision while laughing at his antics?

"Julia Child is a French chef. I seriously doubt she cooks Indian dishes," she had chided.

Ethel looked around the room. There were so many memories. Not counting their time in India, this was her first and only apartment, the home where Christine grew up. All things eventually ended. After losing her job, she would need to find a cheaper place. It would be a fresh start. It seemed as if everything in her life was changing.

She flipped through the album, stopping to take a long, hard look at certain pictures. Their marriage had been exciting in the beginning. They both had careers—she, a middle school teacher, and Raja, a professor at the university. He was never really happy in the United States, even though it had been his decision to move to Seattle. It threw her for a loop when he announced they would make their home in Seattle.

"But I thought we would live in New York," she said.

"I got a job in Seattle."

Initially, they discussed having a house in the country, one they would fill with children. Instead, they settled for this apartment near the university and took their chances regarding conceiving.

Both decided a house, particularly one with a large lawn, was too much work, which neither was suited for. Nor, with careers, were either ideal parent material. Luckily, because of fate or past karma, Christine was born a model child. Sometimes, Ethel thought Christine was raising them, not the other way around.

Raja agreed, saying, "She must have been our mother in another life. She is merely continuing the role."

Raja agreed with Ethel a lot. He joked it kept the peace. He habitually attributed most things to a past life whenever they disagreed. Disagreements were infrequent, and they never escalated into full-fledged arguments, during which they raised their voices. If Ethel even hinted at the beginnings of a shouting match, Raja would say, "Please, Ethel, we are two educated people. Let's keep this civil."

Ethel flipped the page and saw a picture of a couple she

didn't at first recognize. Then it all came flooding back. It was the couple in the downstairs apartment. Yes. Over-the-top Stephanie and Travis. Marital disputes ending with make-up sex was an art form with them. The loudness of their voices initially maintained a steady pace, moving in sync with the beat of a metronome, their tones increasing in progressive intensity with each point and counterpoint, culminating in a perfect crescendo. Then, dead silence. Ethel imagined them falling back into the rumpled sheets and becoming dead to the world. Why could she and Raja not find something to disagree about so vehemently that it would end in sexual passion?

The couple eventually moved out. Although they were both younger than her and Raja, they had become pregnant about the same time she and Raja had.

"Yes, it's time for a bigger place. Travis and I want two children, maybe three," Stephanie said while rubbing her swollen belly.

It amazed Ethel how she could talk about her husband so tenderly after such tense disputes.

"How about you and the professor?" She always referred to Raja as the professor, probably because she didn't remember his name or had trouble pronouncing it.

Stephanie once commented, "Foreign names are so hard to pronounce, don't you think?"

Ethel replied, "I suppose American names are as hard for someone unfamiliar with them. We are not thinking that far ahead. Just want to get through this one."

Ethel's morning sickness lasted most of the day. She knew she looked pale, even for a Seattle resident, and standing beside Raja made her appear like a ghost.

Pregnancy was designed for women like Stephanie. Ethel imagined her in a past life as one of those women walking beside a wagon train with her brood of thirteen children as strong as the oxen pulling the wagons—always faithful to her man, no matter what.

"I'm sure you'll want another one as soon as you're done breastfeeding this one," she said, all bubbly.

Ethel kept quiet about breastfeeding. Midway through the pregnancy, she decided to use bottles.

"A girl, you said?" Stephanie asked.

"Yes, and I remember you said you were expecting a boy."

"Jordan. Already have the name picked out. Do *you* have a name yet?"

"We've decided on Christine, after my grandmother," Ethel said. Picking a name was the only thing that was easy about this pregnancy. At seven months, Ethel hadn't even had the energy to finish decorating the nursery. She barely had the zeal to drag herself through the school day. Luckily, her pregnancy occurred while Mrs. Evans was the principal. God forbid she would have to endure morning sickness *and* Principal Densworth. Mrs. Evans, a mother of two, was sympathetic.

"I wish you and the professor the best. We can send each other pictures of our babies."

"Sure thing," Ethel responded, even though she knew it was only polite conversation between two next-door neighbors whose only commonality was being pregnant at the same time.

Travis and Stephanie moved out, and Rhonda Jones moved in. Ironic, considering Travis and Stephanie were moving out, thinking the apartment was too small for one child, and Rhonda had two teenagers still at home. The woman talked incessantly. There were two other children already out on their own, or maybe that wasn't right. Rhonda babbled on as fast as a horse in the Kentucky Derby—the words whizzed by her. Ethel wasn't sure how old Rhonda was, but by appearances, she must have had her first pregnancy at the onset of puberty, and the whereabouts of Mr. Jones was anyone's guess. His absence was the only thing Rhonda didn't talk about.

Ethel looked around the living room. Not every memory was so wonderful. Walking through the living room was a cross between tiptoeing through landmines and a recent police investigation. With everything on her mind, she hadn't had the energy to maneuver the obstacle course designated as her living room. The odd arrangement of furniture was Raja's idea.

"Why would you keep the furniture this way for a husband who hasn't been here in three years?" Luce once asked.

Luce was Ethel's first, most enduring, I'll-be-there-for-you-through-thick-and-thin friend. Luce was also the most direct.

As much of a friend as Luce, Ola was a little less direct. One might say she was more discriminating with her words. "Hardly Feng Shui, but if it makes you happy."

It didn't make her happy. It made *Raja* happy. The couch ran diagonally across the room, totally off-center and incompatible with the area rug. Then, there was the chair that Ethel pushed intentionally into the far corner.

"With the sofa like this, I can see out the picture window if I choose, or I can peruse the titles of the books in the bookcase along the wall, or watch television. I don't have to strain my neck in any direction," Raja had said as if he were applying some mathematical computation the way he might with his students. Ironically, Raja was rarely home to enjoy any of it.

Anyone who entered her inner sanctum looked puzzled, even the delivery people who peeked through the doorway. Ethel laughed it off and responded, "Marital compromise."

"Married! He's not even here. The only reason you would leave the furniture in this awkward arrangement is that you secretly long for Raja to come home," Luce said.

Even though Ethel ardently denied it, she knew in her inner core that Luce was right.

Ethel had every intention of rearranging everything with the purchase of the chair, but the scene that transpired after its delivery gave her an uneasy feeling. Its banishment to the farthest corner of the room became permanent. She bought it shortly after Raja's departure. It was both an impulse purchase and a sort of consolation prize. There were days she couldn't bear to look at it.

"Nothing more than a misunderstanding," she told Luce. "I'm sure it happens frequently in his line of work."

"His line of work? He owns a furniture store. He delivered it himself because his regular deliveryman was off sick. That poor man. The way he was breathing so heavily coming up the flight of stairs, I thought he might have a stroke. He wasn't young, you know. Ethel, you practically accused him outright of stealing your grandmother's prayer beads."

"I did no such thing, Luce." But she knew she had, and she still hadn't apologized. Tomorrow, she would make it a point to go there and do so. If not tomorrow, soon.

It had been over three years since Raja announced he was leaving for India.

"I don't understand. Is there something wrong with one of your parents?"

"No, they're fine."

"I can't go, Raja," she blurted before thinking. Guilt quickly took over. It had been six years since they last visited his parents. Ethel promptly followed with, "I'm sorry, Raja. When do we leave?"

Raja had an uneasy look when she asked, but replied, "Immediately."

"For how long? We'll be back before school starts. Right? I must take care of some household things."

"Ethel." He stuttered when he said her name. She realized by the look in his eyes that he meant he was going without her.

"If you must, I suppose. I can manage here without you for a while."

One reason they never argued was that as the years progressed, they spent less and less time together. There were no scheduled blocks of time to fight. Raja was a workaholic but organized, scheduling chunks of time for almost everything. Raja spent much of his life on campus, sometimes even sleeping in his office, only coming home to shower before returning to work. Ethel never once thought there was another woman, not even one of his students. Her husband wasn't built that way.

Raja wasn't that handsome, at least not as time wore on. The one thing he had going for him, besides his intelligence, which attracted Ethel to him, was his thick black hair. It had thinned over the last several years of their marriage, and she imagined he might even be bald now.

In her mind's eye, she could still see him standing there with his suitcases, ready to leave. His brown eyes had lost their luster over the years. How had she not noticed? The physical attraction that was so prevalent early on had vanished years before, around the time Christine entered college. Instead of giving them more time for themselves, their daughter's absence gave them more time for their careers.

What did he see when he looked at her? Not what he used

to see. His eyes were red, not from crying but from eyestrain. Teaching computer technology meant always viewing a screen or poring over manuals.

When she told him she wouldn't go, even though he hadn't even asked, it was the one time she expected an argument, but none came. If anything, there was a look of relief on his face.

"But what will you do?"

"Teach. Like I do now."

"Do you have a position?"

"Not yet, but I will soon. My family has connections at the university in my hometown."

Raja was the only teacher in his family. The rest were priests or doctors. His family belonged to the Brahmin caste. Even though the caste system was banned by law, it still underpinned Indian culture in the way it existed in America. Maybe even more blatantly in America.

The abruptness of his departure hurt the most. Couldn't he at least have talked it over with her? She knew he wasn't happy in the States, and she should have said something to him. Perhaps that was what he was waiting for. He might have asked, "Ethel, do you want to return to India? Live there?"

It could have been a fresh start for them. Taking time off from their careers might have improved their marriage. Who was she kidding? She would have tried to persuade Raja to stay in Seattle or move to New York. India appealed to her exotic senses when she was young, but not at this stage of her life. Raja knew she wouldn't have uprooted her life.

She sighed. Now, she had lost her job and had plenty of free time. Ola was off to Egypt. Luce and Santiago had returned from their vacation in the Bahamas only days ago. Christine was making her home in India, or so it seemed. Sam was going off to France, not that she actually knew Sam, but it seemed as if everyone was leaving or had left her. The urge to be somewhere else was pulling at her as well.

She could afford to travel. Not so much on a teacher's salary, but Raja had not left her high and dry. Like clockwork, he sent monthly stipends, not substantial amounts, but plenty to help with the household expenses. Ethel labeled it guilt money.

CHAPTER 9

Mid-June 2018

Ola neglected to tell Ethel she wiped out her savings for this trip. Ethel might have asked how she could afford such an extravagance. There was nothing subtle about her friend. It could be the worst and best of Ethel's traits. You always knew what was on her mind, even when she tried to conceal it. But the questions didn't go in that direction. As soon as Ola mentioned cancer, Ethel's questions regarding this trip stopped dead. The word seemed to floor Ethel as much as it did *her* when the doctor told her the news. Ethel was indeed a genuine friend. She had brought her out of her slump more than she would ever know.

When Ola first met Ethel in the bookstore, there was something about her. Cornelius saw it, too. She had a way of taking charge of situations. A benevolent usurper of power, she swept in like a bloodhound, not to destroy but to protect.

Things with Ethel could get a little out of control, especially if the person in Ethel's path of making a difference in the world tried to block her. Ola suspected that was the case with Mr. Densworth. Ethel had bent her ear enough about the man. Luce's too. Ola surmised Ethel and her principal had more in common than Ethel knew. She suspected Mr. Densworth of being as prideful and stubborn as Ethel. At any rate, Ola sometimes considered Ethel the inner voice spoken aloud on behalf of many troubled souls.

If there had been time, she might have taken the other money—the insurance money Cornelius had encouraged her to use—and invited Ethel to accompany her. But considering the prognosis and haste of the trip, it wasn't possible, plus, she could only imagine the suffocation she would feel under Ethel's watchful eye. The entire trip, Ethel would hover over her, asking if she was all right and telling her to rest.

She should have told Ethel that she would have been her first choice, not Cornelius. It would be nice to take a break from the man she saw six days a week, and sometimes on Sundays, especially if it was related to the books. Cornelius and the bookstore had saved her, but she had been growing weary of both as of late, even before learning she had cancer. The deep yearning to have something more had been bubbling to the surface for some time. Besides, Cornelius never expressed an interest in travel. He was content enough to study the world within the confines of pages, even if it was only through bookkeeping and ledgers on some days.

"Are you going to let the money rot away in a bank account?" Cornelius had asked. It sounded like something Frank would say. She had never thought of it before, but Cornelius reminded her of her brother. Why had she never seen it?

"What difference does it make which money I use?" But it did make a difference to her. Transferring from savings to checking was easier than waiting for an insurance check. "I was afraid it would not come in time," she told him. But that wasn't the real reason. Even though Ola elected to do her only bucket list item properly, which meant splurging on first class, she could not bring herself to spend that money. It seemed wrong. She wouldn't even have had it if it weren't for Frank. She remembered arguing with him that taking out an insurance policy on such things seemed wrong.

"We have to be prepared for everything, Ola," he told her.

When it happened, Ola thought her brother must have had foresight into what was to come, but quickly dismissed the idea when his wife left him. He didn't see *that* coming at all.

Her poor brother. Working in finance and insurance, he provided too well for everyone but himself, especially his wife, who had sized him up as a sucker all along and left him for another man. It wasn't long after that that cancer took him. Did it run in the family? She could hear Frank scolding her for not seeing a doctor sooner, just as she had scolded him for not moving on with his life after his wife left him. Frank didn't even live long enough to see that she would have reason to use the life insurance. Ola sighed. Her bloodline seemed to be cursed.

She might have gotten one hour of sleep the night before. Too much to think about. The seat next to her was unoccupied. She knew little about first class but couldn't imagine the seat remaining vacant. She stretched her legs and yawned, wanting to close her eyes, but there was too much commotion with the plane loading still underway. She reminded herself there would be plenty of time for sleep.

It had been Mrs. Sisko this and Mrs. Sisko that from the flight attendants as soon as she took her seat—another reason she didn't want to drift off to sleep yet.

"Would you like something to drink?" the young man,

sporting the latest designer glasses and gelled hair, asked while bending over her seat. He reminded her of the Tintin character, although his name tag read "Craig." Yes, he looked like a Craig.

She hesitated.

"Coffee, tea? An alcoholic beverage? They all come with first class."

Did he sense this was her first time in first class? Probably, first-timers gave off a vibe detectable by seasoned flight attendants. Maybe it was the guilt registering across her face as the flux of bodies moved past her toward the abyss of cramped spaces known as economy.

Maybe wiping out her entire savings account for this adventure hadn't been such a brilliant idea, but it would probably be her last trip. She was feeling good now, probably from the excitement of this journey, but she knew that unless a miracle occurred, her health would go downhill fast. She had given no thought to treatment costs. Cornelius had assured her that her insurance was up to date—*good old Cornelius*. If the timeline were different, she might think Cornelius was Frank's reincarnation, maybe the reason the relationship couldn't be anything other than platonic. Now, she sounded like Ethel.

Like Frank, if there was one thing Cornelius was meticulous about, it was detail. Precision was evident in everything he did, including the operation of the bookstore. Ola had a much broader perspective, finding it hard to concentrate on tedious details. It was second nature to Cornelius, probably coming from his previous life as a detective. She put the insurance matters out of her mind—one of those nuisances of life to be shelved for now—even though she knew there would be a co-pay she would have to deal with on her return. She had brought it up to Cornelius before leaving.

"We'll worry about that when the time comes," he had said. "You just enjoy your trip for now."

Suddenly, the thought of funeral expenses entered her mind. She still had the insurance money. Even at this point in her life, touching it seemed blasphemous. She had already planned for Cornelius and Ethel to be the sole beneficiaries listed in her will. Who else was there to leave what little she had to? Luce didn't need it. She should at least discuss her plans with Luce upon her return. Luce would understand, and she was good at keeping secrets.

"Alcohol? This early?" she asked. Then it hit her. "Craig, a mimosa, perhaps? Maybe two. I will let you know if I can handle another one after the first." A mimosa, she told herself, was perfectly fine to have this early.

The flight attendant smiled the way a young man might smile at his grandmother, and said, "One of my favorite drinks to make, Mrs. Sisko."

Ola had never been a drinker, besides the occasional glass of wine shared with Ethel and Luce and a few times with Cornelius. She had Googled so much regarding cancer after the prognosis. She read that alcohol was linked to both causing and spreading cancer, and she certainly knew about its effects on the liver. She also read that laughter is an excellent therapy for cancer patients. While she didn't expect this trip to be comical, she associated laughter with an elevated mood, which, thus far, this adventure had put her in. Hopefully, the trip's elation would nullify the drinking she planned to do, considering the number of drinks included in the trip package.

A young man in a gray business suit boarded, placed his

briefcase and carry-on in the bin overhead, and slipped unobtrusively into the seat next to her. The plane was nearing take-off, but he seemed undeterred. The flight attendants were already checking the overhead bins and ensuring that people were in their upright positions with seatbelts on. This entire process, which was new to Ola, was old hat for him. He glanced her way and nodded. She returned the gesture.

When Craig returned with her drink, he asked, "Mr. Parker, would you like anything before we take off?"

Mr. Parker, already settled in with his headphones (he provided his own) as if traveling in first class was his second home, waved him off. Ola understood from his deliberate manner that there would be no conversation between them for this leg of the journey. He was probably headed to New York, the next stop, on business. Ola put on the headphones provided by the airline and perused the movie selection on the display station. It had been so long since she had seen a movie.

On the second and last leg of the trip, a dark-complected man with graying hair asked in a pronounced accent if he could put her bag in the overhead bin before taking the seat beside her. Unlike her first seatmate, he was the talkative type. He had been to New York to see his brother, who was a doctor. After he warned her about what to expect and look out for, Ola told him she was joining a tour group.

"Oh, well, then. You should be well taken care of."

"So many instructions. I have my packet here and studied it during my three-hour layover in New York, but I'm sure reality will differ from what's on paper and in the books."

"Don't worry. You'll be fine. Just be prepared. It will not look like it's pictured in movies. They always romanticize it, not that it's not romantic, but there's lots of commercialism," he said, shaking his head with disdain. "Hey, but without the tourist industry, where would Egypt be?" he added. "People will try to sell you stuff constantly. The dollar goes a long way in Egypt. If you're buying something, never accept the first price offered. Haggle. Egyptians respect haggling."

Excitement and anticipation wore Ola down, as they did most passengers on the journey's second leg. A few hours into the flight, only a few muffled voices came from beyond the barrier between economy and first class. Her seatmate had dozed off long ago. Having nothing more to see than the clouds and blue ocean below her, the heaviness of her eyelids won out.

Upon arriving at the Cairo Airport, the nice man grabbed her bag from the overhead compartment and wished her a safe journey before veering off in another direction at the airport.

The first task was obtaining a visa, for which she had to have cash and her passport ready. After using the restroom, she felt more at ease handling the long line she saw before her. Her instruction packet said a man would greet her during this process, but she didn't know where to go. The line of people, barely moving, appeared to be heading for what looked like a bank. Ola stood perplexed when a heavyset man holding a Walker Tour Group sign approached her.

"I'm a part of the Walker Group," she said, waving, fearing he might go past her.

He asked for her flight number. When she told him, he looked at a piece of paper. "Mrs. Sisko?"

"Yes, that's me."

He showed her the list of group participants and had her sign her name alongside her typewritten name on the roster. He smiled and said, "I need your visa and passport cash."

He took both, telling her to wait where she was while he walked past the long parade of weary travelers. She worried she had trusted too quickly for a moment, but before she knew it, he returned with her passport and said, "All taken care of. If you follow me, we'll take care of immigration."

The man who could have been an angel took her past the long, meandering line to where no one else was, and she was through immigration in a snap. Next, he grabbed her checked bag and led her to where she boarded a bus that took her straight to the hotel.

Straight, except for one exception.

A black sedan sat in the middle of the road, blocking traffic. A man was bent over in the last stages of replacing a flat tire. A woman in a burqa sat beside the automobile on a fold-up chair with a matching fold-up table, lifting the covering over her mouth in a way that kept her mouth out of view, leisurely sipping a cup of tea. A servant stood alongside her like a secret service man might guard a president, ensuring traffic didn't get too close. After possibly ten minutes, their bus proceeded around the entourage. Ola turned her head as they passed to see the servant helping the woman back into the car and placing the table and chair in the trunk. She shook her head, thinking how different the customs were here.

The bus passed men on camels, donkeys, and every sort of tourist-carrying conveyance, open-air and air-conditioned, before arriving at their hotel entrance.

She gave the receptionist her name and told him she was with the Walker Tour Group. A bell boy swiftly grabbed her bags and ushered her to her room. He knocked. A woman's voice said, "Come in."

He swiped the card key to enter her room, deposited her biggest bag on the vacant luggage stand, and took his leave after Ola placed a tip in his open hand.

A slender, well-kept woman, approximately Ola's age, was

placing the contents of her luggage in a drawer. She looked up, smiled, and extended her hand.

"You must be Ola. I'm Peg, your roommate."

Ola smiled. "So glad to meet you, Peg."

Ola looked around. "This room is so nice, much bigger than I expected."

"You can always expect first-class with the Walkers. I understand this is your first trip to Egypt. I want to show you something."

Ola followed Peg to the balcony. The sun was setting over the most marvelous sight. Across the Nile River was an unobstructed view of the pyramids in the distance. The vision of them, the way the last vestiges of the sun made them appear as a mirage, took Ola's breath away.

"This is my third time on the tour, but the sight of them never gets old. I'm sure you'd like to freshen up. Get ready for the meet and greet."

"Yes, I feel like sand is embedded in my skin."

"I know what you mean. I've already showered. The bathroom is all yours."

Ola viewed the pyramids at sunrise from their hotel balcony. She could only see their top, but the mirage-like appearance they gave off last night had molded into something solid, firmly anchored to the earth. They were as grand as expected, but modern civilization creeping in from all sides was competing with time and weather in eroding that grandness. Having read as much as she could on Egypt, she knew in the back of her mind that this was the case, but preferred, like most, her heart's view of the ancient monuments.

She elected to view all the ancient sites the way books and movies romanticized them, gleaming in the sparkle of sunlight or as mystic beacons reaching to the stars under a subdued moon with sweeping sand as far as the eye could see.

She also pictured them as silent, soundless, tranquil manifestations rising from the desert. Nothing could be further from the truth. Filth of all sorts, litter, a plethora of sounds from bus engines and vehicles and their accompanying horns, the braying of donkeys and camels, unpleasant smells, and voices in so many languages of various intensities merging into one never-ending roar abounded. She stood amid it all, merging the sights and sounds into the sound of Om—what she felt must be the Great Pyramid's intention all along.

Dust—so much dust. She had no clue regarding many things she found to be the actual reality of Egypt.

She heard the tour guide's voice, "This way."

She was so happy to be a part of this group. She could never have maneuvered all the madness on her own. She and her travel companions stepped onto the air-conditioned bus. Dr. Walker and his wife stepped on last. The doors closed, shutting out a good portion of the exterior noise.

She had immediately connected with her roommate, Peg, a widow from Portland, Oregon, who was traveling alone. Peg, like her, was an avid explorer of all things mystical. But then, that was true of everyone in the group. Many, including Peg, had been on other tours with the Walkers.

"You will learn so much," she said to Ola.

They wore name tags attached to a lanyard. Their names were typed in bold letters, along with their country, on a card encased in a stiff, zip-locked coating to preserve them for the trip and keep out the dust. Ola found it helpful to remember everyone's name, even though introductions were made the night before.

The bus passed through the roads and neighborhoods surrounding the pyramids on three sides. What Ola didn't realize was Giza's enormous size—its population in the millions.

Cabarets and other forms of risqué Cairo nightlife bordered Al Haram Street, the last road leading to the pyramids.

"Not what you expected, hey?" asked Burt, who was in the seat behind her and Peg. Burt, a middle-aged Canadian with a nicely trimmed beard, was traveling with his wife. At least two-thirds of the trip's participants comprised wealthy retirees or those like Ola, who were spending their last penny on their life's dream.

She was glad to meet new people. The only people in her life were Cornelius, Ethel, Luce, and various long-time customers she knew by their book preferences and occasionally by their names.

"No, not at all."

"We'll visit the Great Sphinx tomorrow. A Pizza Hut sits a quarter-mile away. From there, you have a superb view." He laughed.

"The tourist sites don't want you to know this stuff is here. All the images you see in books are shot from a specific angle. The pyramids appear remote because they are situated on a limestone plateau and stand at a higher elevation than their surroundings. If you study the pictures closely, you can see city lights in the background if the photographer didn't bother to Photoshop them."

Ola noticed the rather expensive-looking camera with a telephoto lens on Burt's lap.

She had met everyone on the bus at the meet-and-greet the night before, hearing their various stories. It was all so much to take in after such a long trip. She was only beginning to put the faces with the name tags. The brochure stated that lifelong friendships would be formed on this trip.

"We are all like-minded individuals on a spiritual journey," a woman named Liz said after introducing herself at the initial get-together at the hotel on the first night.

"You won't be the same person," said a man who stepped into their circle of five. He bore the name tag Ray, with "Ra" in parentheses. He held a glass of white wine, as did Ola. It wasn't long before he strode off toward Dr. Walker, who was talking to his team of guides.

"Ray has been doing these tours since they started," Louis said. Louis was traveling with a woman. Ola had learned earlier from Peg that they preferred spiritual partnership over the constraint of marriage. Ola watched as he grasped her hand during the conversation, gave her a subtle smile, and thought whatever they wanted to call it was working.

Ola didn't know if pouring out her heart to Peg on that first night was prompted by the ethereal nature of her fellow sojourners, the otherworldly pull she was feeling from being in such proximity to the sacred sites, or the amount of alcohol she had consumed since embarking on the trip. Maybe all of the above. She only knew it was a welcome release as Peg held her. She wondered why she had not been so bold as to do so with Ethel, her best friend, but knew she must do so upon her return.

CHAPTER 10

Mid-June 2018

L uce called early. "Ethel, I've been concerned about you. I worry I might have said something I shouldn't have."

"It's all water under the bridge," Ethel told her friend.

"Yes, you're right. We must both do what we can to help Ola now. Do you want to meet for lunch tomorrow? My treat."

"You don't have to."

"No, I insist."

Moments before Luce's call, Ethel had come from the kitchen, where she had put water on to boil. She had stood rigid, staring out the picture window at a pigeon on the windowsill. It made her think of Luce. It was white with some brown markings. Besides varying shades of green, Luce primarily wore neutral colors, such as white and brown. Or perhaps because pigeons had an uncanny sense of direction, which Luce also had. Ethel could get lost in a shopping mall. Or was it the discussion she and Luce once had about pigeons?

"Such annoying creatures," Luce had said.

"I think they're beautiful. I don't get what the big deal is with pigeons. They are almost the same as doves, only a little bigger. Everyone loves doves," Ethel countered.

"Well, they aren't doves. And if your car got bombarded by their poop the way Santiago's does in his office parking lot, you wouldn't think so highly of them. It looks like confetti after a parade, except it can't be easily cleaned."

Luce was overprotective of Santiago, and he of her. Ethel envied their marriage. Santiago had worked his way up in a growing real estate agency, now owning many buildings himself. According to Luce, he was the top salesman, something Ethel did not doubt. She also knew females were his main customers. Santiago had this way of walking into a room. His mannerism said, 'All is well, ladies.'

He had a thick mop of black hair, the bluest of eyes, and dimples that should have had 'no diving' written across the rugged jawline that encased them. His Cuban accent and the way he sometimes stumbled with certain words that caused him to break out into a grin merely sealed the deal.

Before meeting Santiago, Luce had gone through less-than-desirable relationships. Ethel went through the consolation phases of Luce's break-ups more times than she cared to count. They all followed the same pattern. At first, it would devastate Luce. She would hardly have the energy to drag herself to work, despite loving her job.

Before marrying Santiago, Luce worked in a department store surrounded by clothes, shoes, and house furnishings—her second love right after the wrong men. Sadly, she couldn't afford what was in the high-priced store where she worked. Luce, however, was optimistic, saying one day she would no longer be working there but would be one of their preferred customers. Her determined friend vowed she would gingerly stroll through after leaving the salon, caressing the leather of the couch with her freshly done nails before giving the saleslady, whose eyelashes batted eagerly for a commission, the address of where to have it delivered. The address would be located in one of Seattle's finest neighborhoods. Luce, an avid Oprah fan, used a vision board.

Then Luce would eye someone new and fall in love faster than a thoroughbred at the Kentucky Derby. Luce had no trouble attracting men. Men flocked to Luce the way a shiny new toy captivated a child, at least initially. The problem was that the men drawn to her also had the maturity of toddlers, quickly moving on to the next toy.

In the beginning, Ethel judged Santiago to be no better than the string of men before him. He came off as a smooth-operating womanizer who would break Luce's heart, but he proved her wrong. And Luce, who never wavered from her affirmation of being one of the prime clients of the department store she worked in, which catered to the wealthy, realized her dream of instructing the sales staff to have her latest purchase delivered to the biggest house in one of the most sought-after neighborhoods in all of Seattle.

Ethel knew that when Luce said she and Santiago were planning a family, despite her friend having everything working against her, she was determined to make it happen.

⁕

Ethel watched as the bird flew off toward the park. Maybe she was flying off to her hatchlings. Her apartment had such a delightful view of the park. She would miss it so. She had been crunching numbers, and there was no way around moving to something cheaper.

Ethel looked over at the saris draped across the chair. They were still where she had left them two weeks ago. "Oh, Ola," she groaned as she looked at the hand-painted Egyptian symbols on the red silk.

Ethel had met Luce nearly a decade before meeting Ola. It had always been her and Luce, the best of friends. Then Ola, dear, sweet Ola, came into the picture. Two best friends turned into three best friends.

Luce had once remarked, "We are birds of a feather, a different feather in that we are unique, but still with commonalities, the underlying glue that binds us together. Maybe we were best friends in another life." Luce always referenced reincarnation, feeling it was the basis for most things in Ethel's life, to which Ola always nodded approval.

The whistle of the teakettle gave Ethel a start. Deep in contemplation, she had forgotten she had put the water on to boil. She made her way into the kitchen, a short trek from the living room, which was the adjoining room. She placed the loose tea in the pot, covered it with the filter and lid, and tidied up the countertop, giving the tea time to steep. After a few moments, she poured it into her favorite mug, a gift from her students. It said WORLD'S BEST TEACHER. A group of her students made it during art class. She smiled, thinking how Mr. Smith, the art teacher, had blamed her because the students had gotten the glaze too close to the mug's base, causing an awful mess in the kiln. For an art teacher, that man had a horrible disposition. Probably jealous to discover the students had not made the mug for him. Perhaps she was judging him too harshly. Compared to Mr. Densworth, his disposition was downright jolly.

She returned to the living room, holding the mug of hot brew, a surplus of thoughts racing through her mind.

The pigeons. What was the city going to do with them?

She must get ready for her daughter's arrival for Thanksgiving. She would more than likely be in a different place by then. They had talked over Skype once since Christine sent the package. Neither of them brought up the exciting news. Nor did Ethel tell Christine she had lost her job. She still had hopes Mr. Densworth would call.

The conversation she and her daughter had seemed to always border on the mundane. The maze of red tape and office politics at the shipping company where Christine worked was enough to give one a migraine. Still, her daughter, who took after her father in being meticulous with details, handled it all like someone floating above the chaos. Like a wren, without a care, Christine chirped melodiously the goings-on beneath her.

Regarding office politics, it was the same wherever you worked. It was undoubtedly true at the middle school. Ethel regretted not discussing Bradley with Mrs. Elsmore. Handling him required a unique finesse, and dealing with his mother was frightful. Should she call and warn her? All rambling thoughts, none of which had anything to do with what was actually troubling her, all the things that had brought her to this point in time.

Ethel guessed the conversation over lunch tomorrow would center on Ola and Luce's trip. She wasn't ready to bring up the fiasco with Mr. Densworth, or the fact that she was no longer a teacher. The thought had occurred to her to call Raja. He was still her husband, technically. It's not like they hadn't spoken to each other in the last three years. There had been emails between them. Rather humdrum and boring. They would talk about Christine and the weather in Seattle or Mysore. Ethel would tell him if she ran across a professor Raja might know, although she made it a point to avoid anyone who might ask about Raja. She was always afraid they would ask why she was here and he was in India. Something that, after three years, she still had no satisfactory explanation for. But as to calling him out of the blue, what would he think? Possibly, she was dying. She needed to talk to someone. Although she knew she could confide in Luce, her pride stopped her, and Ola had bigger problems. She would sleep on it and perhaps draft an email to Raja.

On Facebook, Ethel was friends with Raja's cousin, Gita, if you could call that true friendship. They exchanged only the occasional likes and niceties between them. Out of not wanting to appear desperate, Ethel couldn't bring herself to ask anything personal regarding Raja.

Initially, she told Luce and Ola that Raja had returned to India because his parents were getting old. After six months, both finally stopped asking about their health. She was sure they had both checked the university's website and saw he was no longer listed as staff.

Luce finally asked when Raja would be home.

"It's complicated, Luce."

"Complicated? I'm sure it's complicated. All relationships are, but Ethel, I'm your oldest and closest friend. I know there's something more going on here beyond the complicated. If you need to talk, I'm here. Don't let your pride get in the way."

Pride was one reason she hesitated about getting a divorce. That and the hope that the situation was temporary. But how could she keep insisting it was temporary? Three years in Yuga cycles amounted to a fly's life, even less, but not when it came to humans and matters of the heart. It was permanent, at least in this lifetime. It's not something she confided to Luce or Ola, although she was sure they suspected, especially when Luce suggested she should move on with her life. She wanted them to see her as an independent woman making it on her own and as a compassionate woman who didn't want to hurt Raja.

Ola and Luce had asked her more than once why she continued to stay married to a man she hadn't seen in three years.

"Why bother with a legal mess until it is necessary? Life is difficult enough as it is," she told them. In a matter of a few weeks, it had grown even more so. "Besides, Raja doesn't want a divorce, and I think it might devastate him if I were to file."

And as for being independent, neither knew that Raja regularly sent money. It was directly deposited into their joint checking account. She hadn't bothered to set up her own. The amount always varied, nothing extravagant, but it was enough for a bit of savings, plus all the extras such as yoga classes and shopping at one-of-a-kind boutiques instead of discount stores, not that she made a habit of buying lots of clothes. No, she was rather down-to-earth when it came to apparel. She had to laugh, thinking about the tie-dyed dress. Without thinking, she ran her fingers through the jade strands to one side of her face. They were a part of her now.

So, with what money she had put aside from Raja and even with a small pension check since she wasn't yet sixty-five and this would be early retirement, she *could* afford to travel a little—nothing extravagant, just one good trip.

What if she went to India? Surprised Raja. She could always say she was visiting Christine. She could hear Raja now. So practical. "But Christine takes regular trips home. She's coming for Thanksgiving." Or she might run into a different situation altogether.

Did Raja even know Christine would be home for Thanksgiving?

There were numerous tasks to complete in preparation for travel. She would have to let go of the apartment, which she would have to do, regardless. What if she decided to stay in India for an extended time? She would have to either store the furniture or sell it.

Of course, she couldn't travel right away. Not with Ola sick. When she was well. Perhaps in the fall, when school starts again. Yes, that would be her excuse for quitting her job. She would announce to Ola and Luce that she was joining Raja in India.

The apartment was in her name. Security, Raja called it. Raja had always been a staunch advocate for women's rights. Or maybe it signified something different—some forecast of things to come. *Don't be silly, Ethel,* she told herself. In fact, upon reflection, this whole sentimental journey down memory lane and Ola's prognosis were causing her to lose all sensibility. What was she thinking? Mr. Densworth would soon call, begging her to come back. It wouldn't come to retirement. She had dedicated over thirty years of her life to the school.

She thought back to her first day of teaching. She was so nervous. Mrs. Evans, the former principal, was the opposite of Mr. Densworth.

"You remind me of myself when I first started," she had said. "Remember to show them who the boss is. This age group can take over if you give them the slightest opportunity."

Mrs. Evans was always there for her. She was there for all of her teachers. But after six years, she retired, and in came Mr. Densworth, a young man full of noble ideals in the beginning. Ethel watched as those lofty principles got squashed by bureaucracy and school politics. Maybe she judged the man too harshly.

Ola would return from Egypt and announce that the miracle she hoped for from the pyramids had indeed happened. Then, Ethel would take a two-week trip to France over the summer, returning with her own miraculous experiences. She, Luce, and Ola would discuss their most recent getaways during their weekly get-together.

Ethel poured herself a fresh cup of tea and imagined all the places she wanted to see again: d'Orsay, Shakespeare and Company, and The Louvre, even though she found The Louvre a tad on the stuffy side. It was the same with Versailles. She enjoyed the grounds of the stately palace the most, where the not-so-ostentatious cottage in which Marie Antoinette lived during the last part of her life was located. She would have to revisit Giverny, the beautiful gardens, the lily pond, and Monet's sunny, bright kitchen. It would be splendid this time of year. She might even run into Sam at Shakespeare and Company. She smiled, remembering the sidewalk cafes, where she would sip a glass of wine while watching life pass by. And the fabulous boulangeries.

Her stomach growled. The thought of French food was making her hungry. She looked at her phone and saw it was nearly one. She must grab a bite to eat. She remembered a crepe shop not too far from the apartment, near the university. A nice walk. She set down her half-finished cup of tea, slipped on a comfortable, loose-fitting pair of pants and top, put on a dab of makeup, grabbed her purse, and headed out the door.

When she arrived, she saw no trace of France—no outdoor tables with patrons unbound by time constraints, sipping wine, or servers irreverent toward their customers. Well, they were, but not in the French manner. Instead, a line of busy yuppies, professor types, and college students stood in a self-serve queue placing orders, eyeing their phones during the interludes. Her mind played tricks on her—an intermingling of memories and wishful thinking. She walked away, almost running, as a sudden rush of long-repressed emotion rose uncontrollably to the surface.

She reached her apartment complex, climbed the stairs, and fumbled with the key like a drunk fooling with the lock. When she finally opened the door, she threw her purse on the table beside the chair covered with the saris.

The sight of the chair triggered another suppressed memory—of driving back to the furniture store a week later and accusing that nice man of theft. Perhaps not outright accused, but she had implied it.

He was such a lovely man, too. The whole time he was carrying the chair up the flight of stairs, he talked about his wife and their four children. He mentioned not being able to decide on a name for their youngest, referring to him as Baby for weeks. They finally agreed on Don.

She had been so distraught over her grandmother's missing rosary beads. Who else could have taken them? They had been on the table right next to where he had placed the chair, and no one else had been there.

One day, when Luce and the boys visited, she saw Martin playing with them. Ethel shrieked, and Martin jumped. "Where did you find those, Martin?" she asked.

Martin pointed to the chair's crack.

"Your grandmother's prayer beads?" Luce asked.

"Yes," Ethel said rather dryly.

"The ones you ranted and raved about for months, saying they were stolen, blaming that poor furniture store owner? The one who was kind enough to deliver your chair on a weekend, himself, because he had given his regular delivery man the day off?"

"All right, Luce. I get your point," she had said.

Tears streamed down Ethel's face. She wiped both cheeks and plunked her body down on the floor, not wanting to deal with removing the saris from the chair. She couldn't stop crying. Even though it was June, she reached for the afghan draped across the couch. She needed the weight over her body, a substitution perhaps for Raja.

She thought of his last caress. He had set his suitcases on the floor and squeezed her tightly. He had even kissed her. It was a passionate kiss. Nothing like that had occurred between them for the longest time. There was a brief pause. For a moment, she thought he had changed his mind, and their marriage might start anew—be the way it was in the beginning. But he reached down for his luggage. She stared as he headed out the door—his backside no longer slender, his hair no longer black but gray and thinning, and his gait heavier and less confident than she remembered.

She called out, "I could drive you to the airport."

"No worries. I'll take a taxi," he said, not looking back.

It was all so casual. She hadn't cried until now, always either too numb or in denial.

Luce had encouraged her to cry, scream, yell, anything. "Ethel, I know he didn't return to India because of his parents. And even if it were the case, he would have returned home by now. It's not normal how you act, as if his absence is nothing. It would upset most women if a husband walked out of their life, even if it *were* consensual."

She thought of Ola, losing her job, and the man who owned the furniture store she had accused of stealing her prayer beads. She wondered if Stephanie and Travis were still together. According to divorce statistics, there was only a fifty percent chance. She wanted to do more than cry. Finally, she *did* want to scream but feared a neighbor might call 911. So, she cried uncontrollably into the afghan and woke up hours later with mascara running from her swollen eyes down her cheeks.

CHAPTER 11

Mid-June 2018

Ethel awoke to a loud racket outside. She looked at the clock beside the bed to see that she had overslept before running to the window to see a moving truck parked out front. Two men were unloading a lift chair and carrying it inside the apartment downstairs, the one next to Rhonda's. Of course, Rhonda was outside supervising.

How old *was* Thaddeus? According to Rhonda, he was approaching his hundredth birthday. A nurse checked on him daily, and his daughter came at least three times a week. Poor Thaddeus. Ethel couldn't imagine living that long. The man moved like a tortoise, with a body all humped over to match, but he seemed to manage on his own. Ethel had only seen him move with any dexterity when his daughter attempted to force him into an assisted-living home. It caused an awful stir. He became so agitated about moving from the apartment where he and his wife had spent fifty years of their marriage that they had to bring him back after two days.

His daughter threw her hands into the air and said to Rhonda and all the other neighbors standing around, "It's what he wants. At least he will die happy."

That was ten years ago, and Thaddeus seemed to outlast them all. According to Rhonda, his daughter had all kinds of health issues and was on a slew of medications, while her father only took a prescription for high blood pressure.

Ethel looked at the clock. It was nearly ten, and Luce would be by to pick her up before eleven. She needed rest, a reprieve from the reality happening in her world, although she sometimes wondered if the waking world was, in fact, the dream world.

She maneuvered to the kitchen for a cup of coffee, needing something more substantial than tea. After hurriedly sipping it down, she searched her closet for her loose-fitting black pants. Then she remembered they were still in the clothes hamper. In disgust, she said out loud, "What else?"

Thinking she would have time, she put them in the washing machine and set it on speed wash. Nothing. Only red flashing numbers and letters lit across the panel. She picked up her phone, Googled her brand of machine, and typed in the code.

"What do you mean, hardware failure?" she screeched back at her phone. "What else could go wrong?" A smile came to her face. "Nothing," she said out loud.

Her grandmother said things always happened in threes. She had lost her job and learned that Ola had cancer, and now she either needed a washing machine repaired or a new one. Maybe Luce could recommend someone. Santiago knew people, as he had to handle matters related to his rentals.

She showered quickly. After towel-drying, she looked into the bathroom mirror. Were those wrinkles there before? It was as if the features of her face, like perfect little soldiers obeying time, had organized themselves into the outer edge of middle age. She stepped back, taking in her entire body. Did she grow into this body, or had her youth melted away over the years, the way a wax figure's features might melt too close to a flame? She thought of her mother, who never knew this feeling, having died young, and her grandmother, who only ever looked old to her. She felt the wisdom her grandmother's ancient body had been shrouded in had somehow eluded her. Would she soon have to have a lift chair like Thaddeus? Rhonda would check on her daily, bringing special soups and herbs from her garden.

Ethel vigorously rubbed lotion on her legs, arms, and face and applied a touch of makeup, thinking twice about applying powder. The girl at the makeup counter told her that women her age should avoid powder. Women her age? Really?

Ethel remembered Luce hadn't seen her jade hair. Her reaction would be priceless. She opened her closet door again, preparing to filter through an array of clothes before finally deciding on something, but one item stood out. The tie-dyed dress. Why not? It was loose and comfortable.

"Letting your wild streak finally come through?" Luce exclaimed when Ethel opened Luce's car door. As she got in, Ethel looked back at the apartment building to see Rhonda staring through a slightly pulled-back curtain. "A mid-life crisis? Is this what this is?" Luce asked while Ethel fastened her seatbelt.

"Possibly," Ethel replied.

Luce was one to talk after that rampage she went on when her boys entered puberty. It flabbergasted Ethel to see the word

Freedom tattooed across her friend's backside with three butterflies.

"Freedom from what?" Ethel had asked. "You're a privileged white woman married to a real estate developer living in Laurelhurst."

Luce merely shrugged.

"Also, you hate tattoos," Ethel said. "Why, I remember once you said you didn't understand why someone so young wanted to cover up perfectly flawless skin when we walked past that teenager."

"I'm not young, and my skin is hardly flawless. Besides, I felt like something radical, and a tattoo was what came to mind first," Luce said.

"But you're afraid of needles."

"A small price to pay for freedom, don't you think?" Luce realized what she had said and laughed.

"What did Santiago say about this?"

"He hasn't seen it yet, and what can he say? He has a tattoo."

"He does?"

"Yes, not one you would see, or at least I hope you wouldn't."

"What kind?" Ethel asked.

Luce just gave Ethel a sultry smirk—a gesture having nothing to do with another woman. What a scene Luce caused when she thought Santiago was seeing another woman, one of her friends who worked at the department store with her. Gloria, if Ethel remembered the name correctly. It turned out to be a misunderstanding. Gloria had helped Santiago pick out Luce's engagement ring.

"He could have asked me to help with that," Ethel said when Luce told her it had all been a misunderstanding.

"He wanted it to be a surprise."

"I can keep a secret," Ethel exclaimed.

"Sure you can," Luce said with a roll of her eyes.

Ethel knew this tattoo was a loud and clear message regarding the triplets, who were always a handful, but more so when they turned thirteen. After all the trouble she and Santiago went through to have those three—the fertility clinics, the side effects of the various drugs, the shots, the invasion of privacy, not to mention the cost—and now, Luce was ready to put those kids up for adoption, not that there would have been any takers. Ethel was glad she didn't have Martin, Lou, and Dewey in class. Being their godmother was a hard enough row to hoe.

"So, freedom," Ethel exclaimed.

Luce laughed. "Better sooner than later. Oh, I made reservations at a new restaurant on the waterfront. Hope they don't have a dress code."

"It's Seattle. Hippies are second nature," Ethel replied.

"I know. I was joking," Luce said.

While at the restaurant, the two discussed Luce's family vacation, but mainly focused on Ola. Halfway through lunch, they decided they needed a girls' day out upon Ola's return.

"We'll give her a few days to rest up from her trip," Ethel said.

"Oh, definitely," Luce said. "You should wear that dress. We can all wear our fanciest or most bizarre costumes, like three young girls having a tea party in our parents' backyard."

"I love it," Ethel said. "Oh, how people will stare."

"And be envious," said Luce with a wink.

CHAPTER 12

Late June 2018

Over the years, Ola had grown so accustomed to "Rhapsody on A Theme of Paganini" from *Somewhere in Time*, the song that played each time she entered the bookstore, that it barely registered with her during the thousands of times she crossed the threshold. However, on the two brief times she went into work after returning from Egypt, the melody was fresh, piercing her soul with a new meaning. For a moment, she felt like she could enter a different time or possibly even a different life. The sweltering sun of the desert, the relentless sand, and the high-pitched bleats of the camels, all overshadowed by the vastness of the pyramids in her mind, replaced the cool air and sophisticated atmosphere of Seattle on those two occasions she entered the bookstore. The vision, a portal between worlds, that seemed to happen on the threshold, ended when the door shut behind her.

Today, she was home, the place she had done her best to avoid over the years. She studied the interior of the cottage. So much hope abounded here at one time. She loved how the living area was one large, open space that spanned the front of the house to the back. She loved her beautiful mahogany desk, not only because it was such a handsome piece but because it had belonged to her brother. Angled just right, it was easy enough to enjoy her morning coffee when Amelia was young, watching her from her playpen, or later, when she got older, from the window while she had tea parties with her dolls in the backyard.

Lloyd always kept the lawn immaculate. With the cancer and trip, she had neglected to call her usual yard work service this year. What used to be so pleasant had turned into an over-grown jungle, one where animals might find great delight. She sighed, determined to make the call today. It was already ten o'clock in the morning, and she was still in her pajamas, on her first cup of coffee.

She envisioned Cornelius at the bookstore, sipping coffee and holding a Danish he had picked up on his walk to work. Everything about Cornelius was predictable and regimented. He said the discipline to walk stemmed from his early days at the police academy—the donuts, a habit picked up at the precinct. He always walked, rain or shine, even though his apartment was nearly two miles from the bookstore. He said it allowed him to continue eating pastries. While she had almost become as broad as she was tall over the years, Cornelius had hardly put on any weight. Ola's sedentary lifestyle over the years bit her on the very butt she sat on so much during the trip.

The website had said there would be a lot of walking, but nothing too strenuous. When it came to the part about medical conditions, she checked none. Peg had kept her secret.

She attributed most of her tiredness and the need for brief rests to weight gain and being out of shape.

Cornelius had grown accustomed to her not showing up for work since returning from the trip. He would carry on without her. He would break for lunch at noon and call and check on her. She would tell him she was fine and not to worry. He would reply with, "Come in whenever you're ready." Both knew she wouldn't be coming back.

The bookstore, Cornelius, Ethel, and Luce had replaced her former life—the one with her husband and daughter. Although the bookstore and her friends helped her cope, she realized they had become crutches over the years—no more.

Ola returned from the kitchen with a fresh cup of coffee, set it on the desk, and pushed her laptop aside. She opened the bag with the hotel's logo and pulled out the leather journal, a gift from Peg. The smell of leather permeated her senses.

"You must have this," Peg had said while passing the display window of the hotel gift shop. Her roommate, who had become her new friend on the trip, had seen her eyeing it when they went into the gift shop together the previous day.

"I don't need it. I just liked the design." Before Ola could say anything else, Peg disappeared and, within ten minutes, returned with the bag, handing it to Ola.

"Let me pay you," Ola said, opening her purse.

"No, I wouldn't hear of it. It's my treat. Whenever you write something in it after returning home, you might think a nice thought about me and record it." She laughed.

"Thank you. You're too kind. I will hardly need something to remind me of you, and I can't imagine thinking anything other than nice thoughts about you."

Ola had abandoned journaling years ago, but the beauty of the light-tan, stressed-leather journal with the Eye of Horus, looking as if it were from the time of Khufu, mesmerized her.

She thanked Peg again and said, "I will record every leg of my trip."

"Oh, you'll have no time for writing. Wait until you return home."

Peg was right. Writing in the pages of a journal when there was so much magnificence all around her somehow seemed blasphemous. She tucked the journal away at the bottom of her suitcase, where it remained throughout the rest of the trip.

Each day brought a new adventure. At night, back at the hotel, after washing the desert sand from the crevices of her body, she either spent her time in discussions with the tour group in the hotel bar or lobby or poured out her heart and soul to her new best friend, Peg, before exhaustion set in.

Ola traced her fingers over the embossed emblem on the journal cover. Besides being said to ward off evil, the Eye of Horus symbolized regeneration. She no longer saw her cancer as evil. She had hoped for a miracle, a cure, from the pyramids. She smiled, thinking the transformations hoped for sometimes came differently and much more encompassing than what mere humans could envision.

She opened the journal's pages and began with meeting Peg.

She and Peg were practically inseparable on the trip. They made an odd pair—Peg, tall, the picture of robustness with her slightly tanned skin and healthy glow, while Ola was short, plump, and stodgy. Ola wanted to be like Peg in the next life if reincarnation existed, and she believed it did. Peg moved about so gracefully, so self-assured. When Ola complimented her poise, Peg said she wasn't always like that. It came through years of searching for the proper balance.

Peg told her getting in on this trip at the last moment was divine intervention. It was almost unheard of for someone to cancel one of the Walker trips, and even then, there were waiting lists.

Divine intervention. Something Ethel would say, although sometimes she felt Ethel rattled on about such ideas more than she believed in them.

"My friend talks about such things a lot," Ola told Peg. It was their first night in the hotel together, and Ola had already mentioned Ethel. By the third night, they were sharing their life stories.

In tears, Ola said, "I never thought I would bare my soul to a perfect stranger like this."

Peg hugged her. "Ola, we're not strangers. I'm sure we've known each other in many lives."

Peg opened up about her own life. Everything she related to Ola didn't reflect her perception of the woman who sat cross-legged on the white bed linens. Peg had a bad first marriage, one that lasted entirely too long. She sighed. "I guess I was afraid of change."

She regretted that her children had to go through it with her, witnessing the fighting and bickering. Ola could not imagine Peg fighting with anyone. They divorced when her two children were in their teen years. She regretted how difficult those years had been.

She found her twin soul in Joel when her children were in college. They were together for twenty years.

"We were too indulgent, always eating out, both of us gaining weight, no exercise. We didn't have the energy we had in the beginning, but then who does? Joel's heart attack was quick. He should have had annual checkups. At first, I was on a downward spiral. I guess you could call it a dark night of the soul. Something snapped in me.

"I knew Joel wouldn't want the same for me. I started attending yoga classes and consulting a nutritionist. The yoga instructor was how I learned about these tours. And I make it a point to have annual checkups." She paused. "Oh, Ola, I hope you don't think...."

"No, no worries. I should have gone to the doctor long before I did."

Peg smiled. "These trips give one a new lease on life. I so wish Joel could have experienced the pyramids. We had a good life, but even with good marriages, everything isn't perfect. He was a workaholic. He had a successful business and ensured I was financially cared for after his death. We took vacations, but they were always short ones. He would never dream of taking off for two solid weeks, even though we could afford it. There was always something needing his attention. He was a micromanager."

Micromanager. That term fit Cornelius to a tee, as did her brother, Frank.

"I wish I could say I don't have regrets," Ola said.

"We all have regrets. It's a fact of life. We have to learn to accept."

Ola didn't know what caused her to divulge her life story to Peg so freely—her marriage, her child, how Cornelius helped her on the road to recovery, and then meeting Ethel and Luce.

"And you never told Ethel or Luce any of this?"

"No, I don't know why. Sometimes, I wanted to, but I thought I was finally finding some normalcy in my life. I didn't want to dredge up all the grief and anger again."

"I understand," Peg said.

So many times, people said they understood, but how could they? Possibly, that was one reason for not telling her two best friends. They both had children—healthy children, children who were alive. How could someone understand who hadn't been through what she had? Peg hadn't been through it, but Ola felt her empathy.

Was there something in the sand, some sacredness that shot up through the pyramids into the constellations that opened the floodgates of her soul? Egypt was a strange mixture of adrenaline—the modern versus the old, the hustlers, nightlife, and sacred sights—all magical. The people who lived in the shadows of the pyramids and those who found themselves compelled to visit them were all flawed individuals with a past to come to terms with and learn from—souls on their individual paths to enlightenment.

Ola promised herself she would tell Ethel and Luce about Amelia and Lloyd upon her return, but after returning, she still couldn't bring herself to, not face-to-face. There would be the journals. She once had thought of destroying them, but now knew she couldn't. Ethel would read them and either pass them on to Luce or relate the contents to Luce in person. Or perhaps they would read them together.

Ola opened up her laptop. She emailed Peg, expressing her gratitude for her friendship. Next, she emailed Cornelius. She had already conveyed her wishes to him, but wanted it in writing. She could depend on him to take care of every detail scrupulously. Lastly, she emailed Christine.

CHAPTER 13

Early July 2018

Ethel had called the day after Ola returned from her trip. "We have to have a day out before your surgery. Mine and Luce's treat," Ethel said. "Wear your best dress. The red one. Both Luce and I love that dress. We'll do it up in style."

Feeling drained of physical energy ever since returning from Egypt, Ola sighed and fumbled for the words to beg off, but stopped herself. Life was for living, what little she had left of it.

"On one condition," she said.

"Anything," Ethel replied.

"The two of you must agree not to hover over me and ask me how I'm feeling constantly."

There was a slight pause. "Agreed," Ethel said.

Ola knew she had lost weight, not because she had stepped on the scales; she had thrown those out years ago, but from what she saw staring back at her in the mirror. As far as her emotions and spirit were concerned, she felt lighter than ever.

Her surgery was scheduled for Monday, with radiation treatments to follow shortly after. She would call the doctor's office tomorrow and let them know she had no intention of going through with any of it. She could only imagine Ethel's reaction.

Her perspective had changed since returning home. Her experience inside the pyramid had altered her perception of life. Going into the bookstore wasn't the same. Her office felt musty and dark. Only facsimiles of what she had experienced in Egypt hung on the walls.

While she thought the ecstasy she had experienced in the King's Chamber might have cured her, she had come home to find the cancer had spread. This revelation neither made her sad nor resentful. If anything, a sense of peace pervaded her whole being. She thought about one of the first books Cornelius had brought her, *The Egyptian Book of the Dead*.

She rehearsed how she might tell Ethel and Luce. The thought had occurred to her to announce it during dessert or over a glass of Chardonnay. They had planned this outing with such care and affection during her time in Egypt. The thought of putting a damper on the excursion gave her pause. But they were her best friends, and she owed them the truth.

It was a magnificently rare and beautiful day in Seattle as she slipped on her red dress, the one her body had filled every inch of when on her date with Roger. By the time of her trip to Egypt, it had loosened into a comfortable fit, and now it practically hung on her.

"Some wild adventure today—that's what I want," Ola announced with a big smile as she stepped into Ethel's Prius. Luce waved from the back seat.

"Whatever you want. After we eat at your favorite restaurant," Ethel said as Ola strapped herself into the seat belt.

"Yes, today is *your* day," Luce said. "What's in the bag?"

"I have something for the three of us." She pulled out three tiaras, each adorned with a feather. "Different feathers. Luce, I remember you once saying that even though we were birds of a different feather, unique, we would always be bound together."

"Aw," Luce said, with tears forming in her eyes.

There was a peacock feather for Ethel, a white feather for Luce, reminding Ethel of a dove or pigeon, and a brownish one for Ola, which she thought might have belonged to an owl.

"How cool," Luce exclaimed. "Should we put them on now?"

"Of course," Ola said.

It was lunchtime at the Athenian Restaurant and Bar, one of the city's oldest establishments. Their table had a view of Puget Sound and the snow-capped Olympic Mountains. Ethel had called ahead. Ola could only imagine the sob story Ethel had told the maître d' to get what appeared to be their best table. Upon seeing the three decked in questionable clothing, sporting feather tiaras, he likely suspected them as three escapees from the loony bin by the look on his face.

They ordered wine while they watched ferries slip in and out of the waterfront dock. Only small talk had transpired to Ola's delight as they wickedly commented on the patrons, imagining their lives while laughing, knowing they were the day's spectacle.

The first glass of wine was followed by a second glass with mozzarella sticks when Ola exclaimed, "Something marvelous happened to me inside the King's Chamber."

With eagerness, they listened as Ola related her experience.

"We all sat cross-legged on a dusty stone floor around the empty sarcophagus. Our group had elected to turn off the electricity and sit in complete darkness. The Walkers led us in a chant."

"Who are the Walkers?" Ethel interrupted.

"Oh, the Walkers are such glorious people. They were our tour guides. Both are founts of wisdom when it comes to ancient Khemet.

"The chamber had perfect acoustics, which made our chanting sound as if we were playing the pipe organ.

"Suddenly, I felt myself falling. It was the weirdest sensation. It was like a free fall. Before I knew it, I was floating in the universe. I was without a body. I felt so much love. There are no words for it. I was cradled in God's metaphorical arms. But it wasn't God, or it *was* God, but not in the way people typically imagine God. The term I understood was Source. It was Home. I knew I was Home, my actual home—everyone's real home.

"There was no time, and I perfectly understood this. I don't know how now, but during the experience, no time was natural. I knew I had access to all knowledge and wisdom and could ask any question, but I was in such a state of bliss that I had none, not at first.

"Stars surrounded me. I then realized I was *also* a star; these stars were other souls like myself. I saw the Earth below. Earth, in comparison, seemed a dark and dreary place. I think, telepathically, I must have asked a question. I wanted to know why we were on Earth. Immediately, I was told telepathically that it was a school, a place of learning, something necessary. I only knew I wanted God or Source to take me at that very moment. I had no interest in being on Earth anymore.

"It was then that I started returning to my body the physical shell sitting on that dusty floor in the pyramid. I was so disappointed to be back, even if it was in the place I had always dreamed of being in during this earthly incarnation.

"The bus ride back to the hotel was silent. I think everyone was reflecting upon their own experiences. At the opening reception the day before, and on the way to the pyramids the next day, there was excitement and exhilaration as we all got to know each other, discussing our lives, our expectations for this tour, and what had led us to this particular juncture. Following our visit to the Great Pyramid, peace and contentment had replaced the previous anticipation.

"That night, at dinner, we were no longer separate voices. We were one, despite having varied and unique experiences. Some felt they were levitating. Others saw astounding visuals, deceased loved ones, or had visions. A few fell into a deep sleep."

Ethel and Luce sat in reverence upon hearing Ola's story.

"I'm so glad you didn't listen to me," Ethel said after a moment.

"Didn't listen to you?"

"About you not going on this trip. Waiting. I was selfish. You said I was, and I truly was. I'm so sorry, Ola."

Ola reached across the table and grasped Ethel's hand and then Luce's. "You were only looking out for me. Who knows? If I hadn't become sick, I might never have realized my life's dream. I was meant to be there. The experience gave me a lot to think about during the plane ride back. Everything has changed. Both of you and Cornelius are my best friends in the world. Please understand, and don't argue with me when I tell you this." Ola paused. "I don't plan on having the surgery or the radiation."

"Ola—" Ethel said as Luce put her free hand on Ethel's arm.

"Hear me out, please. You see, the cancer has spread. It's just a matter of time now. Currently, I feel fine. A little tired, but fine. Even with the surgery and radiation, the doctors predict only six months. I will not spend my last days going through all of that."

"Oh, Ola," echoed Ethel and Luce. Both had tears in their eyes.

Ola continued to grasp both of their hands. "No, no, don't feel bad for me. I'm ready. I've had a glimpse into what is coming."

The waiter came. "Are you ladies ready to order?" Ola was the only one smiling.

"Yes, I believe we are," Ola said. "I'm having the cheesecake after the main course, which will be the halibut. How about you girls? Ethel, you can forgo being a vegetarian for one day, can't you? Even Buddha didn't fully ban meat."

They both sat wide-eyed, stunned. "We'll all have the same," Ola said, handing the waiter her menu.

During dessert, Ola said, "Cornelius has taken care of all the details. I will, no doubt, be admitted to hospice when the time comes, and then my funeral—a small affair. The burial will be private. You will understand in due time, so please don't protest."

Ethel and Luce only picked at their meals. However, Ola ate heartily while discussing her funeral, as if she were reciting laundry instructions.

After consuming desserts, Luce asked, "What shall we do now, Ola?"

"This was plenty," Ola said.

"It's your day out. We must do something more than an extended lunch," Ethel said. "Or are you too tired?"

"No, not at all."

"Well then, name it," Luce said. "A movie? A walk around the pier? A museum? The aquarium?"

"I'm perfectly content sitting on a bench, people-watching, and looking at the view."

"The check, please," Ethel told the waiter. Luce swooped it up when it arrived.

"You have to stop doing this," Ethel said.

"It's only money," Luce said.

They all broke out into a boisterous laugh. The people in

the restaurant would have stared, except they had grown accustomed to this odd trio.

The three strolled through Pike Place Market and watched the fishmongers hurl fish at each other and fake fish at unsuspecting tourists. One woman screamed as the fake fish made a surprise landing on her head.

"I know it's coming, but even so, I always jump," Luce said.

They walked through the crowds, admiring the flowers, crafts, fruit, and vegetables, coming upon the original Starbucks.

"We should stop," Luce said.

"Yes, a Frappuccino might be nice," Ola said.

"We'll be in line forever," Ethel said.

"I thought we had all day," Ola replied.

"Ola, I believe you are enjoying life," Ethel said.

"It's about time, isn't it?"

"They give samples while you're in line," Luce said.

They found a bench near the waterfront and sat, Ola between them, drinking their Frappuccinos while watching the boats come and go.

After a meditative pause, Ola said, "I always hoped some catastrophe might take me out. So much simpler."

"You're not out yet." Ethel reached one arm around Ola. Luce followed suit.

Early July 2018

At dusk, Ethel and Luce dropped Ola off at the bookstore, where they had picked her up. She insisted that she go back and check on some things and that Cornelius would take her home. It was strange that neither Ethel nor Luce had been to Ola's home. Ethel mentioned how odd it was that they had never been invited. Luce joked, "Probably has a family we know nothing about," and laughed.

Ethel wanted to bring it up again on the drive to Luce's house, but their energy having been expended on the day's emotions—a jumble of contradictions both wanted to file away if only for an evening. Luce exited the car and, before closing the door, leaned in toward Ethel and said, "We'll talk when we've had time to digest this."

"Yeah," Ethel replied with downcast eyes.

Luce still stood, bending down, with the passenger door open. "Did you call the guy about your washing machine?"

"No, not yet."

"Santiago said he was good."

"I know. I just haven't taken the time."

"Are you still going to the laundromat?"

"Yes."

"You know you can bring your laundry here until you get it fixed?"

"Thanks, Luce, but it's too much trouble."

"It's no trouble."

"With three boys, your washer and dryer go nonstop. Besides, I like to go to the laundromat."

Luce raised an eyebrow.

"It takes my mind off things. I like to people-watch."

"Yeah, I bet there are some odd characters there. Well, have a safe drive back home."

"I'll call you in a few days," Ethel said.

"Okay," Luce said, shutting the car door.

Ethel watched Luce traversing the stone path through her professionally manicured lawn up to the door. She punched in her code and entered.

Ethel arrived back at her apartment, parking near the courtyard, which would have been a perfect parking spot except she would have to walk past Rhonda's garden. Rhonda was almost always tending to it, but today, she wasn't. Ethel breathed a sigh of relief. She was in no mood to listen while Rhonda rattled on about this or that; the almost one-sided conversation usually ended in Rhonda insisting she take something—carrots, cabbage, or parsley, the things Rhonda was big on growing. Not that Ethel wasn't appreciative. During the growing season, Ethel and the rest of the apartment complex could almost entirely bypass the grocery store's produce department.

"From the garden to your mouth gives one the most nutrients. No middleman," Rhonda would always say. The woman was a wealth of horticulture information, and Ethel imagined her green thumbs reaching to her elbows.

Ethel went inside and removed the feathered tiara from her head. "A peacock feather?" she asked out loud. "Why on earth would Ola choose a peacock feather for me?"

She flopped down on the couch, feeling every ache and pain in her body. What did Ola feel? She would never profess to any discomfort. Was she playacting, for their sakes? Was she hiding her suffering? She had resigned herself to giving up. Luce, Cornelius, and she must do something about this.

And what about their weekly meetings? The three of them usually met in Ola's office during the summer. Their peculiar get-togethers, where they discussed every subject from A to Z, would be no more. So many times, they sat in Ola's office, Ethel's apartment, or Luce's spacious house, one perk of having a husband as successful as Santiago, engaging in conversations that ranged from different areas of philosophical thought to the downright bizarre.

The discussions didn't always involve Luce. Luce almost had to forcibly pry herself away with a crowbar from Santiago and the boys. The triplets were a handful. With a husband and three boys, Luce was always on the go, attending to day-to-day chores such as cooking dinner, packing lunches, and carting the boys to various activities—those down-to-earth tasks that both Ola and Ethel privately envied. Luce had a housekeeper, but being a fan of cooking shows, especially Rachael Ray, she handled most things culinary herself. She claimed cooking was like meditation to her. When Luce *found the time away from her family responsibilities, she provided the counterbalance to their seriousness, contributing her unique style of mundane tête-à-têtes*. Luce was indeed the glue that held the trio together.

"Do you know how long it has been since I've been out

dancing?" Luce once said while looking at a picture of whirling dervishes on Ola's office wall.

"Luce, we're talking about elongated skulls and what significance, if any, they had toward reaching ecstatic states," Ethel scolded.

"Yes, I know. I would be ecstatic if only Santiago and I could go out dancing. Last week, I saw the most beautiful pair of leopard heels in a store window." She let out a dreamy sigh with half-closed eyes while entranced by the poster of the dervishes with a Rumi quote on the bottom: "In the house of lovers, the music never stops, the walls are made of songs, and the floor dances."

Luce had a way of tethering them to the ground from their hot air balloons. Even though Ethel mocked her friend for such errant thoughts in solemn discussions, she and Ola usually burst out in laughter. Ethel envied how her friend, without even trying, could elicit such a natural response from Ola. Sometimes, Ethel suspected Luce of purposely throwing in tidbits of triviality, terse parables, to get both out of their heads. At any rate, Luce was the comedy relief they sometimes needed.

She would miss the conversations the three of them had, especially now that she had no job. Nothing but idle time for her whimsical endeavors, she told herself. *Whimsical*, she thought, a gracious way of saying half-heartedly. On many occasions, Ola had accused her of being half-hearted.

"I can't concentrate, Ola. There are so many things to do. I hardly have time for so many causes. I have school too, you know," she snapped back.

"Ethel, I'm just saying, pick one thing and put your heart into it. You spread yourself thin: women activist groups, animal rights, yoga, and what about that novel you keep saying you will write?"

"I'm not like you, Ola. You tuck yourself away in this

bookstore, wiling away your time studying all this occult stuff."

"You make the word occult sound sinister. It's not, you know. Occult merely means hidden."

"What do you hope to find?" Ethel asked.

"Some meaning," Ola answered.

Had Ola found it in the Great Pyramid? Did she think her death was the answer?

CHAPTER 15

Mid-July 2018

In pajamas growing stiffer each day, Ethel stood peering into her closet. The tie-dyed dress, some miscellaneous tops, and one pair of gray sweats remained. Not her favorite pair, the ones that expanded in the hip area with each wear. In one of her more melancholy moments, she had exiled all her professional clothes, which she taught in, to garbage bags and placed them in Christine's old room. She thought of selling them on eBay, but some desperate part of her clung to the hope that Mr. Densworth would call and plead for her to return for the fall semester.

She must go to the laundromat, and it wasn't even Saturday. She lacked the energy and the will to call the repairman Santiago recommended. The old Ethel would have forged ahead, armed for the challenge, overseeing every move of the repair or shopping for a new machine, dickering with some young sales associate for the best deal. The latest Ethel, depressed over Ola's condition, losing her job, and her uncertain marital status, along with the added contemplation of her life purpose and approaching mortality, was up for neither.

A month had passed since she first went to the laundromat, taking only a few items to test the waters. It was only a block from the apartment complex. She crept in covertly, expecting some dark dungeon-like space with Gollum lurking in the darkest corner. Instead, she found a well-lit room with the background noise of water jets and spin cycles, where no fewer than ten people were loading, unloading, and folding clothes in a room so hot that it felt like Bikram yoga. She looked around to see people from her apartment complex. Ethel knew not all apartments in her complex had hookups for washers and dryers.

Finding an empty machine without an "Out-of-Order" sign, she put her one load in, followed by the appropriate number of quarters, and sat in one of the multi-colored plastic chairs, a splash of color to contrast with the white machines and gray concrete floor. Why had she not brought a book to read? She picked up a year-old *People* magazine from a rack and casually sifted through the worn pages.

Weeks passed, and Ethel had still not called a repairman or looked for a new machine. She found she rather liked this new arrangement. While most people considered the laundromat a chore, Ethel found it not only a respite from the world but also a form of entertainment. Going on Saturday mornings, when the laundromat was at its busiest, had become routine. Getting a glimpse into the lives of the laundromat crowd made her life seem less troubled.

After separating the colors from the whites and depositing a multitude of quarters in the only two machines available, absent of out-of-order signs—the same machines that never got fixed—Ethel retired to her usual back corner with earbuds in her ears and a book in her lap. Both were merely props, ruses to hide her eavesdropping. No music traveled through her earbuds, and she had read the book she had brought with her, *Life of Pi,* twice already. She cast her eyes downward on the print, although she wasn't reading, while her fingers drifted between the marked pages with her favorite passages. She regularly looked up from her book. All of her favorites were here today.

Craig, who had just returned from a morning run, was jamming his entire wash into one machine: mostly running shorts, two pairs of jeans, and some polo shirts. Ethel had not known Craig before coming to the laundromat. From his clothes, Ethel thought he was a rather conservative gay man.

Today, he was alone. But on numerous occasions, Ethel had seen him with his boyfriend. Unmarried, Ethel assumed. Neither sported wedding bands. Ethel hoped they hadn't broken up, even though Jerry, who appeared to be in his late fifties, might have been considered too old for Craig. Craig was in his early thirties, if Ethel had to venture a guess. They were complete opposites—Craig always joking, while Jerry broke from his serious pout long enough to laugh at Craig's quips. From the snippets of conversation Ethel caught, she surmised that Craig worked at some animal research facility, possibly related to the zoo, or perhaps the zoo was a secondary topic. With the swishing of the washers and the buzz of dryers, it was challenging to piece bits of the exchanges into legitimate facts.

Jerry was reserved and mature, someone Ethel might be attracted to if he were heterosexual. She guessed him to be a professor at the university, possibly in a scientific field. She kept meaning to Google him but kept forgetting. He and Craig often talked about animals in hushed tones, which made Ethel wonder if some nefarious animal testing might be underway. Luce, who frequently accused Ethel of jumping to conclusions without cause, would attribute it to Ethel's suspicious nature, while, on the other hand, commended her on a vivid imagination. "You should write that book, Ethel," her friend encouraged.

After starting up the washer, Craig looked her way and said hi. His high-pitched voice cut through the thick, moist air in the room like a beacon guiding the way should anyone need to escape the room's heavy confines of steam. Poor man's sauna, Luce called it. "But then, you don't go there for your health," Luce jibed. She wanted to tell her friend that she did indeed go there for her health—her mental and emotional health, which couldn't help but contribute to her physical health, but Ethel didn't feel like arguing the point. Her friend certainly didn't turn a deaf ear when Ethel recited the latest gossip.

The swishing sound of all the machines dropped a few decibels. Ethel looked over to see that both washing machines her laundry was in had quit almost simultaneously. She laid her book on the chair, walked over, removed her wet clothes, and placed them all in the larger industrial dryer—the only one available. She moved back to her chair, glancing at Hiram and Thor, who were in the opposite corner.

When Ethel first heard them use the names, she thought they were some absurd pet names they had given each other. Later, she realized those were their given names, which she discovered when they forgot to remove the name tags from their fiftieth-class reunion. With names like those, they had to end up together—two old bachelors, Ethel had surmised, together since high school. When they had come out was unclear.

Thor reminded Ethel of a regal tiger, while Hiram, the way he cackled when he laughed, conjured up the image of a hyena. Both, nearly seventy, carried their ages well. Thor, always immaculate, every hair in place, had sad hazel eyes bearing a slight tinge of yellow, suggesting a come-hither look. He wore cologne that fought a courageous battle with the dampness of the enclosed space. Not what one expected on a trip to the laundromat. Possibly on his way to an appointment afterward. They not only epitomized opposites attracting but went above and beyond. Elderly, gay, and bi-racial, they could have been the poster children, or rather poster mature adults, for the LGBTQ movement. Hiram sported a more relaxed demeanor, wearing a Seattle Seahawks t-shirt, loose jeans, and sneakers.

Ethel turned a page in her book to maintain her cover, lest they catch her observing them.

Even their bodies were opposite—Thor, large and muscular, and Hiram, small and wiry. There was something about Hiram, a mysterious nature exuding from his black pores. Yes, he was hiding something. In her mind's eye, Ethel could vividly see Luce's eye roll at all of her speculations.

Both were meticulous in the handling of their apparel, buttoning each shirt before folding with precision, carefully creasing the pants in the right spot while placing them on hangers, and the way they handled their collection of multi-colored socks and boxer shorts (of course, they wore boxer shorts) was an art form in itself.

Both nodded politely to Ethel on their way out.

They made it out the door just in time to avoid Rhonda. Everyone in the apartment complex and the surrounding area knew Rhonda Jones. Rhonda always wore her hair tied back, not bothering to cover up her curiously elongated ears, which made Ethel wonder if the woman had a hint of Vulcan ancestry. The ears, however, were the only resemblance to Mr. Spock. There was nothing logical or reserved about Rhonda at all. She always appeared to be in a frenzy, darting this way or that, never able to decide about the simplest things. Ethel watched as she stood on the other side of the glass entryway, shifting the laundry basket from side to side, scrutinizing the best way to open the door. Sam, of all people, came rushing up from behind and opened the door for her. Ethel gasped. She had not seen Sam since that day at The Emporium.

In one quick swoosh, like the Energizer bunny in that commercial (oh, to be young again), Sam went to a dryer, removed the contents, and deposited them into a plastic garbage bag without concern for wrinkles. He had his earbuds in. Ethel remembered him wearing them in his dad's shop. Turned to full volume, a loud jumble of music spilled out, a blur of inharmonious sounds.

"Hello, Mrs. Sharma," he shouted. With the plastic garbage bag slung over his shoulder, he made his way over to her.

"Hi, Sam. It's so nice to see you again. Please, don't feel you have to call me Mrs. Sharma. Ethel is fine."

His face turned a little red.

"Well, I have to get back. I just wanted to say hello."

"Sam, did you take your trip to France?"

"Yes, I did. I've only been back a week."

"I want to hear about it when you have the time," Ethel said.

"It was great. Do you come to this laundromat much?"

"On Saturdays, until I get my washing machine fixed."

"Well, maybe I'll see you here next Saturday. I usually come to do my laundry this time. I can tell you all about it then," he said before rushing out the door.

"I look forward to it," Ethel shouted after him.

"Probably has to get to his girlfriend," Rhonda said to Ethel while setting her basket of dirty laundry on a nearby table.

"He has a girlfriend?" Ethel asked. He seemed too shy to

have a girlfriend, but Ethel didn't offer this opinion to Rhonda. Maybe Rhonda didn't have her facts straight.

"Pretty young thing. I saw them together in the park the other day."

Rhonda twitched her nose, a habit Ethel found most annoying. "Has Thor been here?" Rhonda had an uncanny sense of smell. But then, it was an easy deduction, considering Thor's cologne was as thick as the laundromat air.

"He and Hiram left right before you came. I'm surprised you didn't see them on your way out," Ethel said while thinking, no doubt, that upon seeing Rhonda, they hurried off in the opposite direction or ducked into an alleyway. Rhonda elicited that reaction from people. Ethel waited for Rhonda to comment about them, but surprisingly, she offered none.

Ethel watched Rhonda sort her laundry.

"Ethel, if I knew you would be here, I would have brought you some jam. The strawberries in my garden did great this year," she said with a slightly embarrassed grin while segregating her delicates. Ethel, blushing, looked away at seeing the black lace. Rather risqué for Rhonda, Ethel thought. Maybe she had a man on the side. Whatever happened to Mr. Jones was unclear. Rhonda had several children. Four, she thought. Ethel couldn't keep up, even though Rhonda constantly whipped out her cell phone to display their pictures. They were all grown-ups, none of whom lived in Seattle. Most strange, Ethel thought.

Rhonda continued to talk, her usual run-on sentence. "I had a surplus of carrots, left a lot in the ground, and mulched over them. Most people don't know you can keep them that way."

A rabbit, that's what Rhonda was, those long ears, the way she hopped about, and the constant sniffing, honing her already superb olfactory sense, the way a concert pianist stretches his fingers. Or maybe she was using cocaine. No, ridiculous, Ethel told herself... Although she did have an excessive amount of energy.

The dryer with Ethel's clothes suddenly stopped. She removed her clothes and placed them in her basket, along with her purse, book, and earbuds, before saying goodbye to Rhonda.

CHAPTER 16

Mid-July 2018

"Drat," Ethel said, disgusted with herself, looking at the clock beside her bed. She had fallen into an awful habit of oversleeping. If Raja were here, he would attribute it to stress, and he would be right.

As much as she wanted to roll back over and drift into another world, one more inviting, she forced herself to put her feet on the floor and move to the bathroom before heading to the kitchen for possibly an entire pot of coffee.

She and Luce had stopped by the bookstore the day before. The agony on Cornelius's face was apparent. His whole body seemed to absorb the burden of Ola's illness, like he was trying to siphon it from her body into his.

"No, no, we must not interfere. We must respect her wishes," he insisted.

"But Cornelius," Ethel pleaded.

He shook his head vehemently with closed eyes while pushing the air in front of him with both hands.

They left the bookstore defeated and sat in Luce's car, not saying anything for at least five minutes.

"Luce—"

"Ethel," Luce stopped her friend, "we must go along with what she wants. She said that even with surgery and radiation, it would extend her life to six months at the most. My brother's wife went through a similar experience. Her treatments resulted in endless nausea and drained both her and my brother. The thing is, she had every desire to live. Ola has resigned herself to this fate for reasons we're not aware of. Not to mention the financial toll. Santiago helped my brother with the medical bills for my brother's wife."

"It's more than that, Luce. It's almost like she sees death as some relief."

"Maybe she does, but all we can do is support her. She's a mature woman. I think we both know she's perfectly sane. It's her decision." Luce took Ethel's arm, reached over the console, and embraced her.

Ethel pushed back a tear as she did.

Back at her apartment, Ethel fell onto the couch. Fluffing up the pillow, she told herself an afternoon nap would do her good. She was drifting off to sleep when an awful commotion coming from downstairs startled her.

She looked out the window but could see nothing. Whatever was happening was taking place under the breezeway. She strained to make out the voices. One belonged to Rhonda. Another was Billy, the super of the apartment complex. He handled almost all jobs that needed tending, including pruning, trimming, painting, and minor repairs. No one knew his last name, but someone called him Billy the Fixer, which later evolved into Billy Fixer, and the name stuck. He was young, intelligent, and wise beyond his years. The other voice belonged to Mr. Thaddeus Murdock, the oldest resident. Ethel could hear Billy trying to calm him down.

"I saw one, I tell you," Ethel heard Thaddeus exclaim.

What on earth did he see? Thaddeus shouldn't be living alone at his age, almost one hundred. He had to be a little senile.

Rhonda was shouting. Everyone talked loudly around Mr. Murdock. "Now, Thaddeus, there are no rats here. The exterminator came only last week. He assured me we live in one of the nicest apartment complexes in Seattle." Also, one of the oldest, Ethel thought, but it had a good reputation. Most of the tenants had been here for years. There had been only a few rent increases over the years. Still, Ethel sometimes wondered how Rhonda could afford it. She didn't appear to have a job. Was Mr. Jones footing the bill?

Ethel deliberated whether to go down, try to help, or suggest they call his daughter. Rhonda had her number. She grabbed her key and walked down the stairwell. Everyone was going back inside, one by one, first Thaddeus, then Billy. Rhonda was about to, but saw Ethel standing on the steps.

"It's all okay now," she said. "Billy got Thaddeus settled down. Sad, he's on his own so young." She laughed. "Billy, that is. Certainly not Thaddeus. What kind of parents take off like that?" Rhonda looked doleful before brightening. "Billy's a real fixer. Somewhat of a psychologist, the way he calmed Thaddeus down."

It wasn't exactly true that Billy was on his own. His uncle owned the apartment complex and checked on Billy a lot. Billy reminded her of a badger with a white streak running over the top of his brown hair and darkened eyes. Ethel suspected he wore mascara. She had seen males of his age wearing it these days.

She would miss the diversity when she had to move. What

she wouldn't miss would be the bickering and arguing. The couple, two apartments down, were always arguing. At least she and Raja had been civil to each other. Why can't people get along? Ethel's thoughts lingered on the inhabitants of the apartment complex. They were such a peculiar lot.

"Ethel, why don't you come in for a cup of tea? I've been experimenting with some herbal blends, and I think I've found the right combinations." Rhonda looked at Ethel with imploring eyes.

Ethel would have begged off. She always found a reason to decline Rhonda's invitations. This time, it somehow seemed wrong to do so.

All these years, she had never been inside Rhonda's apartment. Nor had Rhonda been in hers. Shame spread through Ethel like a hot flash. Rhonda had asked her countless times to stop in. Ethel forced her lips into a smile, not wanting Rhonda to read her humiliation.

"I'd love to."

Ethel gasped upon seeing the interior of Rhonda's abode. Even though Ethel was one floor up, the layout of Rhonda's apartment was completely different. The kitchen looked like one that Martha Stewart, Rachel Ray, Julia Child, or a combination of the three might have. It was bright and cheery, with copper pots and pans hanging down from the ceiling, a bowl of fruit on a soapstone counter, and glass cabinets displaying colorful cups and dishes. Herbs hung everywhere. Her kitchen had a life of its own. It was a siren, a culinary seductress.

As remarkable as the kitchen was, it had nothing over the living area. The light hit the open space at just the right angle. Ola might have compared it to Stonehenge or Chichén-Itzá. The picture window on the backside overlooked the garden. An old, antique desk, with its paint partially peeled, emitted a Shabby Chic feel. On top of it sat a laptop and various books and magazines in an intentionally designed disarray, a snapshot that could have been featured in *Architectural Digest*. A plush couch with hand-woven cloths draped over it, accented with just the right amount of throw pillows dispersed in the appropriate spots, invited one to sit and decompress. Two alluring armchairs, made of different fabrics, sat off to the side. They were all gathered around a table with a teapot and cups perfectly laid out.

The decor took Ethel's breath away. She stuttered, flabbergasted. Everything was so different, yet perfectly coordinated, coming together as one—what Fritz might refer to as Shambhala. Rhonda's apartment was a small chunk of Shambhala.

"Rhonda, your apartment is beautiful." What would Rhonda think of *her* home with the couch all askew and messy piles of books and papers everywhere?

"Oh, well, it's work." Were her ears blushing?

"Yes, I can see this took a lot of thought."

"No, I mean, this is what I do."

"I don't understand?"

"I work from home. I'm a better living consultant."

Ethel squeezed her entire face into a question mark.

Rhonda laughed. "No one quite understands it. It involves a lot of different things. Most of it is about food. That's more or less my forte—food and gardening. I love gardening, but without my allergy shots, I'm afraid it can become torturous. I'm afraid I missed my last shot." She sniffed and reached for a tissue from a nearby table. "Anyway, I test various combinations for restaurants, develop new recipes, write articles for food and horticulture magazines, and occasionally for interior design magazines. I am a consultant to numerous businesses in this field, including some high-tech companies in Seattle. All from my little apartment. They never even see me. I could wear a business suit and go out in person to do this. However, working from home satisfies me. I'm near my garden. No one complains about my anonymity. Plus, it's one big tax write-off."

"Really? Do you care to name a few of those you advise? What magazines do you write for? I don't believe I've ever seen your name in any."

"Oh, you wouldn't. I use a pen name. I like to keep my personal life separate."

"Are you famous, Rhonda?"

She laughed and curled up her nose, which reminded Ethel of how she had compared her to a rabbit that day in the laundromat.

"Maybe I am as far as the business goes, but as far as little ole' me goes, I'm just Rhonda, a middle-aged woman whose husband left her and whose kids never come to visit. How about you, Ethel?"

Momentarily, upon seeing Rhonda's apartment and her apparent double life, Ethel's worries dissolved, replaced by curiosity.

"Rhonda, I love your apartment. But..."

"But what, dear?"

"I thought our rental agreement said we couldn't do any extensive renovations. If I'm not mistaken, you've knocked out walls. I would call what you've done extensive."

Rhonda gave Ethel a 'duh' look before answering. "You probably didn't put two and two together, considering Jones is such a common name, but my ex owns these apartments. I can make any alterations I want, and I also live here rent-free as part of the divorce agreement. Oh, and I still have some influence over him. He's afraid I'll make waves for him and his new family if he doesn't listen to me now and then. I'm the one who suggested he hire Billy. Of course, Billy and I are no longer related, but I've always had a soft spot for him. He had such a rough time growing up. Well, enough of my stuff. I believe it was you who needed to talk."

Ethel tensed. All the worries Ethel had temporarily shed came rushing back in.

"Now, dear, it can't be all that bad. Come. Sit," Rhonda said while patting the couch. "Let me get us some tea. This morning, I made lavender cookies. Superb, if I do say so myself. The tea is a special blend of herbs, something a restaurant here in town offers. All organic and from my garden. Well, they won't be coming from me per se, just the original batch and the recipe, and I only whip up the preliminary creations."

Over tea and cookies, Ethel poured out her heart to Rhonda. Despite the run-on sentences she was so famous for, Rhonda proved to be a good listener.

In two hours, Ethel had told her about Raja taking off for India three years ago, how she had stormed out of Mr. Densworth's office jobless, and about her two best friends, Ola and Luce. At this point, Rhonda interjected, "Ethel, I hope you will count me as one of your best friends."

How could she not? She had bared her soul to Rhonda, spilling out all the dirty little secrets she had been too proud to tell Ola or Luce and crying about how helpless she felt about Ola's cancer and how purposeless her life had become.

Nearing the end of the conversation, Ethel stated, "There is one bright note. Christine, my daughter, has some exciting news, and she'll be coming home for Thanksgiving."

"That's good news," Rhonda said, pushing the tray with one remaining lavender cookie toward her.

Ethel couldn't believe they had eaten the whole plate, besides consuming two pots of tea.

Ethel sighed. "I don't know how much longer I'll be living above you after losing my job. I need to look for a new place, but with everything going on, I haven't had the time."

"Didn't you say Luce's husband was in real estate?"

"Yes, I'm sure Santiago will be more than willing to help."

"These things have a way of working out. Please don't worry, Ethel. The first thing is seeing to your friend Ola."

"Yes, you're right."

Ethel didn't know when it happened, but her shoes were on the floor, and her feet were on the couch, covered by what looked to be an expensive hand-woven throw. She sighed, reluctantly moving her feet back to the floor and slipping on her shoes.

"Rhonda, I can't thank you enough."

"What are friends for, dear?"

Rhonda walked over to the window while Ethel came to her feet. "I see Thaddeus is out enjoying my garden. He loves to sit out there. I don't know how much longer he has. I've talked to my ex. I might take his apartment for an office after.... Well, I don't mean to sound callous. I hope you don't think me awful. I'm running out of room. I need a storage area for linens. My collection keeps growing. I hope more than anyone he sees his hundredth birthday and beyond."

"Thank you again, Rhonda. And, of course, I don't think you are in any way horrible concerning Thaddeus."

"Come back anytime, Ethel. My door is always open to you."

Ethel climbed the stairs to her apartment. She felt shame at the difference between hers and Rhonda's. "I will do better when I find a new place," she said out loud. She was only glad she hadn't accused Rhonda of cocaine use, when it was only allergies. Mr. Filbert came to her mind.

She spent the rest of the day on the couch, drifting off while watching old black-and-white movies. She switched channels to a Bollywood movie, which made her smile. Other than a few times during her conversation with Rhonda, it was her first smile since their day out with Ola. The movie reminded her of Raja—how their marriage had been in the beginning.

CHAPTER 17

Ethel and Raja

I t had been three years since Raja walked out the door, and not a day passed that Ethel didn't think of him, mostly analyzing what went wrong with her marriage. There were days when she surmised the union had faded quietly into the sunset, the way some brightly colored fabric left out in the sun too long loses its intensity.

Their courtship and early days of marriage were nothing less than a magic carpet ride. She smiled, thinking back to when they were dating. It was like something out of a Bollywood movie. As newlyweds, it turned into *Cats on a Hot Tin Roof.* They had a fierceness in the beginning, something akin to a Klingon mating ritual.

They met at Anika's uncle's house. Ethel was completing her master's degree at Columbia University and wanted to travel before committing to a job. She had followed the counterculture, exploring everything related to Timothy Leary, Ram Dass, and scores of Hindu gurus. So, when she saw a flyer in the student center about a talk on Saturday night by a visiting swami, she eagerly went.

Although Ethel had read numerous books about Eastern religions, she was ill-prepared for what she encountered. There were small nuances, a world of customs she wasn't privy to. Half of the attendees at the talk were Indians. Ethel recognized one girl as being in her Psych class, even though she wasn't wearing her usual faded jeans. Instead, she wore a sari. Most of the Indian women there, as well as some of the non-Indian women, wore them.

The girl smiled and approached her. She whispered, "Please remove your shoes."

"What?"

"It's custom to remove your shoes before seeking a blessing from a swami."

"I'm Ethel," she said, extending one hand while slightly bending to remove her sandals.

The girl took her hand. "Yes, I know. You talk a lot in class. I'm Anika."

"Pretty name," Ethel replied.

Ethel looked around.

Anika pointed. "Just put your shoes over there with the rest of them." She paused, smiling at Ethel's perplexed look. "No one will steal them."

Ethel returned to her place in line. "I've read much about Eastern religions, but experiencing this in person...."

"Yeah, I know. Culture shock. Happened to me when I came to America." Anika grew quiet. Then suddenly, she said, "We are having a Satsang at my uncle's house in Long Island on Wednesday night. You are welcome to come."

"Yes, I think I would like that." Ethel paused. "I don't have a car. Is there a bus line that goes to your uncle's house?"

"We can give you a ride," Anika said, smiling. She had pearly-white teeth, set off by her flawless, light-brown complexion. She wore a red bindi on her third eye. The red smear rested slightly above the spot between her piercing brown eyes. Anika always wore her long, dark hair pulled back into a ponytail during class. Tonight, it was down. Anika put her finger to her lips, indicating they should be quiet. The line to the swami was shortening.

"I don't know what to do," Ethel whispered.

"Just follow my lead," Anika whispered back.

Outside, an Indian guy wearing a white tunic and loose white pants to match strode up beside Ethel and Anika.

"This is my brother, Sanjiv. Sanjiv, this is Ethel. We have a class together."

Ethel extended her hand, but Sanjiv did a slight bow with hands in a prayer mudra in front of his chest, which she recognized as the Namaste sign. Ethel returned the gesture.

"Sanjiv will drive us to my uncle's house on Saturday night," Anika said.

Ethel had it in her mind that those who followed a swami would all be carrying rice bowls, begging for food, or, at the least, be living moderately in lower or middle-class neighborhoods. Sanjiv drove up to a guard station. The man in a blue uniform recognized him, opened the gate, and motioned them through. They pulled up to what Ethel would term a mansion, a somewhat downsized version of something a Vanderbilt might own. Low-end cars, as well as Cadillacs and Mercedes, lined the street and driveway in front of the four-car garage. Was this how the Brahmin class lived in the States?

She wanted to ask what Anika's family did for a living, but hesitated, thinking it rude. She looked at the massive stone structure with the immense columns on the front porch and looked back at Anika, smiling in delight at Ethel's awe.

Unsurprised by Ethel's reaction, Anika said, "My uncle deals in the gold trade."

"Oh," Ethel said, gulping.

Anika and Sanjiv removed their shoes and placed them in the marble entranceway with dozens of others. Ethel followed suit.

Upon entering through the tall double doors, pungent smells immediately invaded Ethel's nostrils.

"A slew of women is in the kitchen preparing a feast to be served after Swamiji's talk. You will find Indians love to feed you," Anika said.

The enormous room was a sea of almost solely Indians, men in comfortable tunics and loose pants, women in colorful saris, sitting cross-legged on the floor. Off to the side, a circular staircase lined with Indians led to a second-floor balcony, where others leaned against the railing. While the men wore primarily white, the colors of Van Gogh's palette would best describe the women's attire. Even Ethel was colorful in her loose, flowered-print dress. Anika had advised her to wear something both comfortable and respectful.

"Swamiji, of course, won't judge you based on your clothes. He only sees your soul. But even so, it wouldn't be fitting to wear something we might wear to class," Anika had told her.

Following the Satsang over a cup of chai, Raja approached Ethel. "I make an excellent cup of chai." Maybe it was because of the face she made while tasting it. Chai was an acquired taste, much like Chinese food. Initially, one was unsure about it, but after the third time, you were hooked.

Raja, a guest of Anika's aunt and uncle, who hailed from the same city back in India, was testing the job market in the States.

"I'll be returning in two weeks. We should make them count," he said.

Ethel had marveled at his audacity, but those two weeks were extraordinary.

"We will write, and I will call you," Raja promised. He was true to his word.

By Ethel's graduation, Raja had arranged for a couple of disciples of the swami to sponsor Ethel's trip to Raja's homeland. The couple was modernistic in their ways of thinking. They ignored Raja's presence, often retiring early, leaving them unchaperoned. When he wasn't making advances, he made chai, and Ethel made popcorn, which he bragged about endlessly.

"This popcorn is so light and fluffy; it could sprout wings and take the bowl with it, as effortlessly as a vimana."

Raja always said such ridiculous things.

"Now, why would the popcorn want to take the bowl with it, and what is a vimana?" Ethel asked.

What Ethel didn't know was that Raja was promised—an arranged marriage, something he confessed to Ethel after they made love on her last night in India. Would she still have slept with him had she known? Probably so. What had started as a tense attraction blossomed into a full-fledged relationship, even though they were thousands of miles apart. To his parents' chagrin, he broke off the engagement.

Raja aspired to teach at the college level. Several years older than Ethel, he had already obtained his doctorate in England. Ethel's goal was to steer young people on the right path. After careful consideration, teaching middle school—when pubescent minds can veer off in any direction—was the only choice.

Since Ethel's parents were dead, she consented without hesitation when Raja wanted to have an Indian wedding.

Knowing little about Indian weddings other than they were elaborate affairs, Raja's cousin, Gita, volunteered to oversee her education. Gita was more than eager, and Ethel was more than appreciative.

"Remember, for Indian weddings, the brighter, the better. None of this white-dress-American stuff."

Gita did a circle around Ethel, eyeing every aspect of the bride-to-be. "You would look best in blue, I think. Yes, a bold blue." She hesitated a moment, her fist to her chin. "You don't wear jewelry?"

"No, I guess I've always been rather practical. Not much for ornamentation."

Gita wobbled her head back and forth the same way Raja did. To this day, Ethel could never decipher if it meant yes or no.

"Indian weddings are all about ornamentation. I will lend you my jewelry."

"That's two down."

"What?" asked Gita.

"There is a saying in America: something old, something new, something borrowed, something blue. You must have these things for luck. The dress is blue, and the jewelry you lend me will be borrowed."

"Oh, I see." Gita shook her head from side to side while speaking.

"That takes coordination," Ethel said.

"What?"

"The way you move your head and talk."

"Ethel, you say such funny things."

"That's what Raja says."

"On the first night, a priest will perform the *Ganesh Pooja*. This will take place at Raja's home and will be the most private part of the ceremony. You, Raja, the bridal party, and only close relatives will be there."

"But Gita, I have no bridal party or relatives."

Gita put her arm around Ethel. "I have sisters, and we have

plenty of cousins. They can be your bridal party; we are your relatives now."

"Gita, is your family angry that Raja is marrying me?"

"You mean because Raja was promised?"

"Yes."

"Mmm." She shook her head back and forth again. "At first, but they have grown to like you. I am glad. I didn't like her at all. I much prefer you." She laughed.

"We begin with a *Mehndi* ceremony on the second day. This is only for females. We will draw intricate henna patterns on your hands and feet."

"In the evening, the *Sangeet* takes place. We invite every wedding guest. That's when we usually introduce the couple's families. There will be mingling, a meal, dances, and performances."

"Then the big day, the third day, is for the main ceremony. We have a cocktail hour and reception.

"Oh, the *Baraat*!" Gita exclaimed as if remembering.

"What is the *Baraat*?" Ethel asked.

"It is the best of all. It is the groom's procession. Raja will arrive on a white elephant."

"An elephant?"

"Yes, and it will be decorated. Everything at an Indian wedding is decorated. All the guests dance around him to the beat of a *dhol*, an Indian drum. Then you will greet him and exchange floral garlands, a symbol to say you accept each other."

"Then you and Raja, the priest, and Raja's parents sit beneath a *mandap*. It's a canopy. Since you have no parents to do so, my uncle will give you away. You have met my uncle."

"Yes, he seems quite nice."

"This is called *Kanya Daan*. You will join hands and circle a small, enclosed fire. It's called an *Agni*. The actual ritual is called the *Mangal Phera*."

"This is so much to remember," Ethel said.

"Oh, no worries. I will be there for you. And Raja, of course."

Ethel smiled.

"One more thing before the reception."

"Another reception?"

"Yes, the ending reception. However, before that, there are seven steps, known as *Saptapadi*. You vow to support each other and live happily together. Raja will apply a red powder, a bindi, to the center of your forehead and tie a black beaded necklace around your neck."

"Does this ever end?"

"*That* is the end of the ceremony. You are now husband and wife. Then the fun begins."

Ethel blushed.

"No," Gita laughed. "Not that fun. First, the reception. There will be all kinds of music and dancing. There is the traditional *Bhangra*, a Punjab folk dance."

"But I don't know how."

"It's easy enough to pick up. The food will be fabulous with four stations of chefs preparing food for guests."

The wedding was everything Gita said it would be and more. They honeymooned in France along the French Riviera.

Ethel might have been content to stay in India, but Raja was insistent about going to the States. He had grown accustomed to Western culture while studying in England and during his brief stay in New York, and, like many other Indians before him, he wanted to work in America.

He applied for a visa and sent applications and résumés to several universities in the States. He heard back quickly.

"Seattle?"

"What's wrong with Seattle?" he asked Ethel.

"I guess I was thinking more of the Eastern coast. I know New York, after all."

"But it's the University of Washington that wants me."

"I will go wherever you go, Raja."

On their twelfth anniversary, they left Christine with Luce and Santiago and traveled to Paris. This trip was partially to recapture what they had lost in the interim, and it seemed as if they had. But after returning, Raja suggested the three of them move to India.

She knew Raja's fascination for the States was waning and that he missed India. "But you have achieved tenure, and Christine is established in her elementary school. How can we uproot her like that?" Ethel asked.

"Christine will adjust."

"So many of your students look up to you. I think you are the most popular and respected professor in your department. And what of my job?"

"You're right," he said reluctantly. Ethel knew he was thinking of the time she had said she would go wherever he went.

CHAPTER 18

Early to Mid-August 2018

Venturing out on her own had become more demanding for Ola. Cornelius took her to her doctor's appointments, those she didn't cancel. She continued to refuse treatments. Ethel and Luce took her on small, subdued excursions to art exhibits, where they sat on a bench and reflected upon a painting, or to parks, where they sat on a bench and marveled at nature. At her insistence, they always picked her up and dropped her off at the bookstore. They sometimes visited small, out-of-the-way cafes or coffee shops. Ola picked at her plate, never taking home what she didn't eat, which was most of it. She said the bandage across her face made it hard to eat, but Ethel and Luce knew the cancer had robbed her of her appetite.

Words had become unnecessary for the three of them. The outings were brief. Ola tired quickly and spent a good deal of time sleeping. The bookstore's hours were sporadic since Cornelius prioritized spending the last precious days of Ola's life by her side.

After each excursion, Ethel cried. It was as if Ola willed herself to die. It took all the restraint Ethel could muster not to lecture her friend on what she deemed a morbid course of action.

"Ethel, it is her life and her decision. Don't you think she has thought deeply about and meditated on this decision? I'm sure she's discussed the whys of it with Cornelius, and he's honoring her wishes. We have to, too."

"Oh, Luce, but how can she just give up like this without a fight? I think it was the experience she had in Egypt. If she had only had the surgery and treatment *before* going. Maybe it would have made a difference."

"Maybe, Ethel, but she is an adult, and maybe she has reasons we don't know about."

Even though Luce was known for her wacky, rational way of viewing things, Ethel had known her for too long and suspected there was more to it. But what?

"Cornelius knows her better than anyone, and he seems to have come to terms with it," Luce continued.

"Cornelius," Ethel retorted. She reared back. "Do you really think that?" Her voice was gravelly, a mixture of anger and desperation. "He just doesn't know what to do. You know how she listens to Cornelius. We should both talk to him again."

"Ethel, please. You know the man loves her deeply. She has made up her mind, and he is, I'm sure, more heartbroken than both of us. All we can do is offer our full support to them both." With tears in her eyes, Luce placed her arm around Ethel.

"It's all we can do. Ola has resigned herself to this. Can't you see it written all over her face? I've honestly never seen her more at peace. It's as if some heavy weight has been lifted from her. I only hope when it's my time, I'll be able to face it with such acceptance and composure."

Since Ola announced she had opted not to have the surgery

or radiation, Cornelius went from a loyal friend to a tender, intimate caregiver. Whatever bond they shared went beyond what marriage might have given them. It was spiritual. Ethel guessed twin souls. According to Ola, twin souls go beyond soul mates.

"A soul mate is someone who comes into our lives to teach us a lesson," she had said. "A twin flame or soul has much more significance. You are entwined in the same lessons, trying to overcome the same difficulties."

Why in the world had they never married?

By mid-August, Ola walked with the support of both Cornelius and Ethel into the hospice center. The maximum was eight patients. Although designed to resemble a house that would blend in with the surrounding greenery, the bold signage, perfectly groomed flower beds, boxed shrubbery, and winding paths leading to small stop-offs with benches and picnic tables gave it away. It was not the home-sweet-home promoted, but more like a resort for those taking their last breaths. The three walked into a spacious lobby, another thing conspicuously absent from actual homes.

Ethel and Cornelius stood arm in arm with Ola while the administrator explained that each patient had a comfortable, private bedroom, allowing their loved ones to remain at the bedside around the clock.

"Time is precious," the administrator said as she helped move Ola into a chair.

Cornelius, his face grave, gripped the back of the over-stuffed, upholstered chair. Ola's expression was one of complacency and ethereality. She seemed to drift between worlds as the administrator explained the amenities. Ethel reached over, placing her hand over Cornelius's, whose droop had become more pronounced, his former erect posture erased from existence.

The slightly overweight, middle-aged administrator with rosy cheeks, a significant contrast to the patients who resided here, continued, "The setting is quiet, homey, and tranquil. We try to make it like a home away from home, nothing like a hospital or nursing home." Her words sank into the soft, serene background music in the lobby. She redirected her gaze downward toward Ola. "Maybe we can show you your room, Mrs. Sisko?"

Ola nodded.

An attendant offered a wheelchair, but Ola, with feebleness, waved him off. Cornelius held onto Ola's waist, who insisted on walking over to the window.

"It's beautiful, *almost* like home," Ola said. Her voice was as feeble as her body.

Ethel could not help noticing Ola mentioning her home.

"Yes, well, we have a beautiful woodland walking path. Both our patients and their loved ones use it a great deal. Our gardeners ensure it's always well-maintained, regardless of the time of year. We keep it wheelchair accessible. Some patients prefer to be outside, even during the colder weather."

"Yes, there is clarity to colder weather," Ola said. "Do you have deer?" she asked.

Ethel and Cornelius gave each other surprised glances.

"We *do* see deer from time to time. Lots of squirrels, of course. Some patients have pets. You are perfectly welcome to bring your pet."

Ola said nothing.

"She doesn't have any pets," Cornelius said.

"Well, there is a meditation garden." She paused. "I think that is about it. Do you have questions?"

"No, I don't think so," Cornelius said after looking at both Ola and Ethel.

"We will need to fill out some paperwork. I will have a nurse come and make Ola comfortable while one of you..." She looked at Cornelius, then Ethel. "Who is responsible?"

"We both are," Cornelius said.

The nurse entered, and Ethel and Cornelius walked into the hallway with the administrator.

"The typical stay is three weeks. I hardly wanted to say that in front of Mrs. Sisko, or does she prefer Ola?"

"Ola will be fine," Ethel said.

She handed the clipboard with the form attached to Ethel, who handed it off to Cornelius. "He has a power of attorney. I'm merely here for support. For both of them," she added.

Cornelius found a table in the far corner and commenced the paperwork.

"She seems to be accepting," the administrator said to Ethel. "That's a good thing. Some patients beg to go home. Many homes lack the essentials they need in these situations. Family bathrooms rarely accommodate wheelchairs. We have nice walk-in showers. Additionally, families, due to job commitments, often can't be full-time caregivers. Nor do most have the resources for around-the-clock care. We try to make this as much like home as possible."

"Yes, I can see that," Ethel said, even though she thought they emphasized the word home a little too much.

"This is a good time of year. If you can say there is a preferred time of year for something of this nature. The gardens are at their prime. Does Ola like the outdoors? She asked about deer."

Ethel hesitated.

"Yes, she does very much," Cornelius said while extending the clipboard with the paperwork toward the administrator.

"There are benches and tables outside, private areas, so families can stay together without mingling with the other patients. Sometimes, seeing how others have progressed in a disease can be a real downer." The administrator made a droopy lip that made Ethel think of an emoji. "However, there is a community room. We have as many activities as possible. Whatever Ola wants, and can participate in. It's totally up to her. You never know. Some patients have gotten better and walked out of here."

"Miracles do happen," Ethel said in a shaky voice, smiling as best she could. However, she and Cornelius knew Ola's recovery would require not only divine intervention but a change of attitude.

CHAPTER 19

Mid-August 2018

Luce, in a tizzy, paced from room to room. She could use Santiago's shoulder about now, but he was at work, and the boys, who might offer some distraction, were in the basement playing video games. She blamed herself for allowing them so much screen time. It was a relief on most days, but she could have used their company today.

She looked at the time on her phone. Ethel and Cornelius would be at the hospice house by now. She had considered going but begged off. She gave the boys as the reason, her usual cop-out. "Besides, the three of us hovering around her will be a crowd—too much for Ola to handle at once. You two get her settled in, and I will act as your relief," she had assured them.

She heaved a heavy sigh as she pushed back the door to the boys' room. She picked up their dirty laundry, scattered everywhere amid the Lego toys. She calculated each step as if maneuvering a minefield. She had learned early on always to wear shoes in their room. She should demand they come upstairs, clean their room, and take their soiled clothes to the laundry, but she didn't feel like struggling with them today.

How long would Ola last? Luce saw her yesterday.

Cornelius brought her into the bookstore briefly and asked that she or Ethel come by to keep her company while he tended to some things that couldn't be put off any longer. Seemingly uninterested in her surroundings or their efforts to make her comfortable, Ola sat silently in her office chair, an ethereal glow emanating from her fragile body as she stared into space.

Possibly, Cornelius thought she might want to see the bookstore one last time. But Ola seemed already to have moved beyond the trappings of the earth plane.

It would be so strange without Ola. Luce knew she acted as a buffer between Ethel and Ola. Their conflicting views, on more than one occasion, resulted in somewhat heated debates. She also knew they both characterized her as somewhat flaky, an airhead of sorts, or at least that had been what she had always surmised. During this crisis, she realized how much both relied on her. Santiago had always told her it was the case, but she had dismissed it.

Not because Ethel was a control freak, but because beneath it all, she was one of the most sensitive people Luce knew and could be easily hurt, something Ethel tried to hide. Luce could never let Ethel know what she found out by accident.

She could never forget that day. It was in May, near the end of the school year, right before Ola announced she had cancer. She was at the library doing research for one of Lou's school projects. Even though she promised Santiago that she would insist he do his own homework. It was always Lou who was falling behind. It would devastate Lou if he had to repeat a grade while his two siblings advanced. Santiago kept telling her she was making it too easy for him, but he wasn't with the boys as much and didn't understand how hard it could be.

"We should hire a tutor," he said.

She wanted to discuss it with Ethel when she called her on

that last school day. The secretary, announcing that Ethel no longer worked there, had thrown Luce for a loop. Then, on top of that, Ola confided in her, not Ethel, that she had been diagnosed with cancer and was leaving for Egypt.

The triplets weren't identical, a blessing. They wreaked enough havoc; being identical would have created more insanity. Lou, the youngest, was smaller than Martin and Dewey. When it came to his brothers, he was a follower, but when it came to his parents, he knew how to turn on the charm—a quality his brothers lacked. Lou had Santiago's eyes and the same alluring mannerisms. But smarts—well, he took those after her. She was never that great in school, but could handle middle-school assignments.

While looking at old newspaper clippings at the library for Lou's research paper, she came across Ola's name. Who would have the same name as Ola? Ola Sisko? But there it was, in black and white. Luce almost fell out of her chair. What she read was horrific. The article mentioned Ola's husband. *Her husband*? The article wasn't particularly long, but what it said was shocking. She read it four times, devouring the words. Ola had lost her only daughter. It was all Luce could do to hold back the tears. She searched for any follow-up articles but found none. There was no question it was Ola. Who in the world would have the same first and surname? Ola must have been thirty when it happened.

Cornelius was the detective on the case. Maybe Ola is still married. Perhaps that is why she and Cornelius never tied the knot. She would never have imagined Cornelius as a detective. And now, the two of them running a bookstore together? Why was he no longer a detective? She wanted to delve more into it, but the time on her phone said she couldn't linger any longer. She had to pick the boys up at a friend's house and start dinner.

She left the library, her mind abuzz. Life takes funny

twists. *More like tragic twists.* Also, there was no way she could let this slip to Ethel. Ola had chosen not to tell either of them. To say anything would be like divulging a best friend's secret —a secret she wasn't even privy to. People handled loss in different ways. Ola's way was private, and Luce must respect that.

Ola had a daughter, a little girl named Amelia, a family, and what appeared to be a good life. The death of a child changes everything. She could only imagine how life would change if she lost *even* one of her boys. And now, the death sentence of cancer.

CHAPTER 20

Mid-August 2018

It was one of those rare days when a glimpse of the sun came through the window of her room at the hospice house. It dripped yellow like melted butter across a piece of toast. Being too nice a day to be confined inside, Ola asked that the attendant wheel her outside. It was one of those brief moments when Cornelius and Ethel were absent and not hovering over her, as well as one of her more lucid moments. She knew her time was near, and they knew it too—why they hardly left her side. She had sent them both on frivolous errands. She asked Ethel to bring her a particular book from her office. There was something in it about her trip to Egypt that she wanted to show her. As soon as Ethel left, she sent Cornelius on an errand to her house for a children's book that had belonged to Amelia. They doted on her, casting aside any other purpose in their lives. Luce was more measured and sensible in her approach to Ola's deathbed watch. Unlike Cornelius and Ethel, Luce had a family who needed her.

So many memories were flooding back. The buttery sun and heat on her body made her think about toast and how Amelia had to have her toast light while Lloyd insisted on almost burnt. Simple moments from the past flooded her mind.

She hoped Lloyd was living a full life. She was often tempted to look for him on the internet, but at the last moment, she couldn't bear to hit enter after typing his name into the search bar. Cornelius used his connections at the police department and found that Lloyd had moved to Sacramento and had a new family, including two children, who were probably now parents themselves. She counted up the years on her bony fingers that were once plump. He could be a grandfather. Did he still think about Amelia? Did he think about her?

Maybe she could have found them online, but even now, she didn't know if she could look through family photos of her former husband, witnessing a life fate or one karma had deprived her of. There was no one to blame but herself. For so long, she refused to move on. She supposed things might have been different if she could have snapped out of her depression. She must ask Cornelius to contact him—to let him know how sorry she was, but not until after her death. There was so much she regretted.

There were some days she regretted not telling Ethel about her past. Or Luce. They would both find out soon enough. She had already asked Cornelius to make arrangements to leave Ethel her cottage. She would find Amelia's room, the journals, and the family albums. Who better than Ethel to unravel and analyze her past? She would share her findings with Luce, who would distill them into a concise statement, something of a Taoist nature. Luce was both the most pragmatic and spiritual of the three, although she didn't realize it.

Luce had made it a point to stop by every other day. Sometimes, she brought the triplets on Sundays when there was nothing else they were into, and once, Santiago came with her. He was a good man—a lot like Cornelius. However, during his visit, the painful expression on Santiago's face belied the fact that he had never experienced seeing a loved one sick or dying firsthand, having left his family behind in Cuba.

Ola didn't understand why Luce felt the need to bring the boys. Perhaps to give her some sense of life's continuation, or maybe as an excuse not to sit for so long. She couldn't fathom bringing Amelia to such a place. A hospice house was no place for children of that age, especially not for such rambunctious kids as Luce's.

Ola could only imagine what she looked like. There was a conspicuous lack of mirrors for a place that boasted about being home away from home, more like a realm for pale, zombie-like creatures taking their last breaths. She was sure she looked the same. She almost laughed. If only she could. Laughing would become a cough, resulting in the loss of control of one or more bodily functions. These days, only the most disquieting sounds came from her body, a grunt here and there, a groan, sometimes a fart, and those were the more pleasant things. At first, they were embarrassing, but she learned to accept them. It was as if the body was disengaging itself from her soul, which would soon be free. It would fly away and rejoin Amelia's.

Ola turned her head ever so slightly, feeling the bones creak as she did. From the corner of her eye, she could see the attendant—close enough should she topple over or merely request to be wheeled back to her room—at the same time, far enough away to give her room for her thoughts. Ola studied him. Mid-thirties. She wanted to ask if he had a family, but lacked the energy. She yearned to know what went through his mind, seeing death up close the way he did day after day.

Three house finches perched themselves in a nearby tree.

They chattered away and broke into song. Their song ceased, and they erupted into what sounded like bickering. Then, the song resumed.

Amelia loved birds. Lloyd had put feeders all over the backyard. Finches were regular visitors. Amelia jumped up and down and clapped her hands whenever Lloyd let her put out feed for the birds.

A bluebird flew almost in front of Ola, landing in a bush. She didn't know what a finch's appearance meant regarding spiritual omens, but she knew a bluebird meant happiness—something good was about to come into your life—in her case, something good *after life*. An involuntary smile flickered across her lips for a moment. She might not have even realized she was smiling if it were not for her cracked, parched lips hurting.

The sound of a woodpecker's steady hammering was in the distance—so much life all around her. The hammering reminded her of the addition, the one never finished. Both she and Lloyd wanted another child. In anticipation of getting pregnant, Lloyd had started constructing a bedroom. "Another project to add to the one of trying to get pregnant."

Both projects stopped when Amelia died. They couldn't just replace Amelia with another child, the way one might replace a dying automobile with a new car.

CHAPTER 21

Late August 2018

Within days of being at the hospice house, Ola was in a wheelchair, and within a week, she was bedridden. Being at Ola's side almost constantly, Cornelius hung a sign on the bookstore door: Temporarily Closed. Although the sign bore no explanation, the regular customers were aware of the situation.

"Did she decide to stay in Egypt?" one of their most dedicated customers asked Cornelius during a rare moment when she caught the bookstore open.

In a moment of stress, one of many, Cornelius confided the reason for Ola's absence to the woman who had spent a small fortune in the metaphysical section of the bookstore. She always insisted on Ola being the one to help if she had questions.

Since Ola had entered hospice, Cornelius was hardly ever at the bookstore but by Ola's bedside. Ethel stood by and watched as he changed the dressings on her face, washed and bathed her, and fed her when she would eat. Feeling her contribution was minuscule in comparison, Ethel busied herself with menial tasks, such as running errands for both of them. At Ola's request, Ethel visited the bookstore daily to check messages.

"We have a lot of customers who depend on us." Her voice was a mere whisper.

Even in her deteriorated state, Ola thought of the bookstore. Or was it Cornelius she worried about? He would need the bookstore after Ola was gone.

Ethel went out for food. She brought lunch and sometimes dinner for Cornelius. Sometimes, Ola craved a particular food. Eager to please, Ethel would run out and get whatever she requested. It was always the same. Ola took one bite and shoved it aside, claiming it tasted nothing like she remembered. The way Ola was wasting away, Ethel feared only a skeleton would be left to bury.

Ethel read to Ola, mainly about Egypt. Ola would break in occasionally, explaining her theories about Egypt. She declared the pyramids were much older than history made them out to be, and the Sphinx even more so. Ethel read everything Edgar Cayce had written about Egypt. He was Ola's favorite.

Once, Luce's boys' antics temporarily cheered Ola. Ethel saw it as a slim beacon of hope. However, the progression of Ola's demise was undeniable, as much as she fought it. Ethel's grandmother had died of cancer, but she was eighty-four. Ethel had read that cancer spreads more slowly in people of advanced age.

There were long stretches when Ola was completely out of it. Ethel surmised that the faint smile on Ola's parched lips meant she might again be a star resting in Source's divine oneness. Then, without warning, she would return to the realm of Earth.

"Ethel, what day is it?" she asked, her eyes popping open wide, as if she just remembered something important.

"Tuesday," Ethel answered. There were days when Ola

might talk a lot and others when she said nothing. Even though she was in pain, she refused morphine.

"No, I mean the date." Ethel had to bend down as close as possible even to hear Ola.

"August 29."

"Doesn't school usually start by this time?"

"Not until next week," Ethel lied.

Ola lay there, not speaking for ten minutes. Then, with a raspy voice, "Ethel, I know better. Please get my purse."

Ethel went to the bureau, opened the drawer, and took out the leather bag.

"Please get my house keys out."

Ethel did as she said. "Ola, do you think you are going home?"

Ola almost laughed but coughed instead. Ethel put the purse on the top of the bureau and rushed over, placing the cup of water to Ola's lips. Only a dribble went in, the rest oozing from her mouth, trickling down her chin. Ethel reached for a tissue beside the bed, blotting her chin and a few wisps of sprouting gray hair.

"Amel…" Ola uttered, staring toward the half-opened door where a shaft of light entered the dimmed room.

"Ola, I don't understand." Ethel looked at the doorway. No one was there. "Do you want something?"

Ola had shut her eyes and drifted off to sleep. Perhaps it was an end-of-life illusion. She remembered her grandmother had those. The nurse said they were common.

Ethel slipped the keys back into Ola's purse and returned the bag to the drawer. She sat by Ola's side but jumped up when Cornelius entered the room. "I just thought of something—Ola's birthday present. Christine sent it from India. I don't know how it slipped my mind. I should have given it to her long before now. I must run home and get it."

"But her birthday is not—" Cornelius stopped short. "It's

almost midnight, Ethel. Stay home and get some sleep. Come back in the morning and show her."

"No, it can't wait. You must see it, Cornelius. It will make her so happy. I'll be back as soon as I can." She kissed Ola on the cheek. "Ola, I'll be back."

Ethel rushed in, carrying a bag. "I got back as fast as I could."

Cornelius was by the bed, holding Ola's hand. The nurse stood on the other side of her, writing on her clipboard.

"No!" Ethel cried.

"She never woke up, Ethel."

Ethel walked over and put her arm around Cornelius. Tears were gushing from her eyes. "I thought I was prepared," she said.

"Yes, I did, too," Cornelius said with reddened eyes and tears streaming down his cheeks.

"It was a good way to go—in her sleep," Ethel said. She remembered the death rattle of her grandmother as she took her last breaths. She was glad Ola was spared that.

CHAPTER 22

Early September 2018

Ola transitioned on August 30. The funeral, which was more of a visitation, took place on the following Monday and was small and intimate. It mainly consisted of bookstore patrons—professors, researchers, and regular customers who had become more like family over the years—an atypical bunch. There were no long-lost relatives who only all came together on sad occasions. Ethel had hoped there might be someone, but there were none. The final count of those who signed the register was forty-three, including herself, Cornelius, Luce, and her family.

The boxes of tissues discreetly placed throughout the establishment mainly went untouched. The tears shed were light. The only reddened eyes were those of Cornelius, Luce, and herself.

If Ethel could sum up the assembly in one word, it would be respect. Ethel recognized a few attendees, those who had visited the bookstore while she was there, the ones Ola knew by name. For the most part, those paying their respects were a ragtag bunch who buried themselves in their research, giving little heed to appearance, much like Ola. They huddled in small groups, discussing their projects, often mentioning how Ola had led them to a rare text.

One woman came in late. She walked up to the casket. Unlike the pale attendees who buried their noses in printed pages beneath artificial lights, wiling away the hours studying books, the healthy, vibrant, slender, tanned, well-kept woman, who looked to be in her sixties, belonged outdoors.

Ethel made her way over to her. "Hello, I'm Ethel Sharma. You knew Ola?"

The woman turned and smiled. Her physique suggested that she maintained a regular exercise program, possibly including yoga.

"I'm Peg Jenkins. I met Ola on the Egyptian tour. We were roommates. You must be Ethel. Ola talked about you. And Luce. Is she here?"

"Oh?" Ethel's eyebrows arched as she motioned for Luce to join them. Peg Jenkins stood, admiring the three lotuses in a large water bowl atop the casket.

"We thought this would be most appropriate. The lotus was Ola's favorite," Ethel said.

"Yes, I know. I take it there are three representing yourself, Luce, and Cornelius."

"Yes, you're very perceptive."

"Not really. Ola talked about the three of you a lot."

"They were cut less than an hour ago," Ethel said.

"Their life force diminishes quickly," Peg said. "In Egypt, the lotus symbolizes the sun and creation because it disappears at night only to re-emerge in the morning. In many hieroglyphic works, the lotus was depicted as emerging from Nun, the primordial water bearing the Sun God. But I guess you know that. She told me she planned on a closed casket." *Had Ola confided her dying wishes to this woman?* The woman spoke as if she had known Ola for as long as she or Luce had.

"Luce, this is Peg Jenkins. She was Ola's roommate in Egypt." Luce extended her hand.

"Considering how she wasted away, it was the only option. I'm surprised Ola didn't request cremation," Ethel said.

"I'm sure she wanted to be buried beside—" Before she could finish, Cornelius walked up. He extended his hand. "I'm guessing you are Peg."

"That's correct, and you must be Cornelius."

Cornelius knows who this woman is?

"It is so nice of you to drive here from Portland."

"I only knew Ola briefly, but the people we meet on these tours are like family. The experiences we share bind us for eternity."

Ethel did her best to hide her disappointment at not being privy to Ola's friend Peg and that Cornelius knew about her. The four stood there, passing thirty minutes, mostly talking about Egypt.

"We should sit down," Luce said.

"No, I sat in my car on the drive here. I want to get back before dark. I had to come and pay my respects."

From the corner of her eye, Ethel saw a tall, slender, gray-haired man, possibly around Ola's age or older, enter the chapel and sit in the back. She intended to make her way back after saying goodbye to Peg, but when she looked again, he had disappeared. He couldn't have been inside the chapel for over fifteen minutes. Cornelius excused himself and went to the back, where the man had been sitting. She thought he intended to talk to someone Ethel recognized as one of the bookstore's customers, but instead, he went through the chapel doors in pursuit of the mysterious man.

With Cornelius's exit, Peg said her goodbyes, hugging Luce and Ethel before leaving. She was still walking toward the door when Ethel called, "Mrs. Jenkins?"

Peg turned. "Peg, please."

"Peg, the man in the back? I saw him, but he left. Was that possibly your husband?"

"No, I came alone." She smiled and waved to Ethel one last time.

Ethel sighed. He must have been a book vendor or possibly an author. She would ask Cornelius when he returned, but the mysterious man slipped from her mind at the sight of Christine and Raja entering through the double doors. For a moment, she thought she might faint.

She met them halfway up the aisle. She embraced her daughter and stood back, taking her in. "Christine," she gasped. Her gaze went to Raja, who gave a half roll of his eyes and shrugged slightly.

"Is this your exciting news?" she asked Christine.

"Yes. I said I would show you."

"Yes, you certainly did."

"Well?"

"Did you marry and not tell me?"

"No."

"Ethel, we can talk about it later," Raja said.

"Yes, not here," Ethel agreed, looking around to see if anyone else had noticed her former husband and very pregnant daughter walk in.

"Raja, I don't know what to say. When I emailed you about Ola, I hardly expected you to attend her funeral."

"We both knew Ola, too, Mom," Christine said.

"We wanted to come. Is it all right if I hug you?" Raja asked.

Ethel smiled. "Yes, I can't get enough hugs at the moment."

"Your hair is green," he whispered in her ear while embracing her.

"Not green. Matcha tea."

Luce walked over. "Christine, Raja! It is so nice that you

are here. Santiago left a little while ago. I'm so sorry you missed him. But then, I'm sure you will see him and our boys while you're here. And Christine? Ethel didn't tell me," she said, staring at her swollen belly. She hugged them both. Breaking the embrace with Raja, she asked, "How long are you staying?"

Raja and Christine both looked at each other. Ethel's eyes grew wide.

"For as long as Ethel needs us," Raja said.

"I quit my job, Mom. So, I'm here for a while."

"I'm so glad you are here. Ethel, why don't the three of you go on? I will wait for Cornelius. The two of us can take care of any last-minute details with the funeral home," Luce offered. "And you can fill me in on everything later," she whispered to Ethel.

"What about the burial?" Christine asked.

"Ola requested there be no graveside service," Luce said.

"Are you sure, Luce? I wanted to say goodbye to Cornelius," Ethel said.

"Yes, I'm sure. The three of you have a lot to talk about." She looked at Christine's belly again and then at Raja.

Luce hugged Ethel. "Call me in a couple of days to catch up, okay?"

While embracing Luce, Ethel said, "Yes, we'll talk later."

CHAPTER 23

Early September 2018

Cornelius stopped at a liquor store on his way home from Ola's visitation. His hand shook the way some underage teenagers might when handing his credit card to the clerk.

He told himself just one drink, maybe two—enough to take the edge off.

Luce had invited him and Ethel to her house for a late lunch, but he begged off. He heard Ethel tell Luce, "All of this, such a strain on poor Cornelius," as he walked away from them to greet one of the bookstore's customers who had come. If they knew the truth, they would hate him.

And Lloyd? He hadn't expected him to come. How did he find out?

He opened the door to his drab apartment. Other than the books surrounding him, it was as empty as his life. He positioned himself in his easy chair and took a sip of whiskey. He hadn't had a drink in decades, not since that night. What happened on that night, what he remembered of it, had shocked him into sobriety.

He wanted to tell Ola on her deathbed, but she had been peaceful since returning from Egypt. How could he disturb her tranquility? She knew now. He was sure of it. She was in the place of forgiveness, but could she forgive him?

CHAPTER 24

Early September 2018

"I'll drive," Raja said.

"Okay, my car is in the chapel lot."

"We can take mine," he said.

"Yours?"

"Yes, you remember my car?"

"I thought you would have sold it. You've been gone for three years."

"I was going to, but decided at the last minute to leave it in Dr. Hartford's garage. He offered."

"For three years?"

"I know—a little long, but I *did* plan to return. We'll swing around and get your car on the way back from lunch."

"You should have told me you planned on coming back."

"Is pizza okay? I've been craving some from that wood-fired pizza place we used to go to for the longest time."

"You don't want Indian food?" Ethel asked.

Christine laughed.

"God, no, Ethel. What do you think I've been eating for three years? We need some wine. To celebrate Ola's life. None for you, Christine. Sparkling water."

Christine glowed. Pregnancy suited her.

"It appears you have a lot to tell me," Ethel said.

"I do, but we'll save it for when we're back home if that's okay?" Christine said.

Raja cleared his throat, and they were silent on the drive to the restaurant.

"Well, at least tell me when the baby's due," Ethel said after they were seated and had given the server their drink orders.

"Mid-November."

"When you said you had exciting news, and you would show me, did you mean you would hand me a newborn and say, 'Surprise, you're a grandmother?'"

"No, Mom. I mean, I don't know."

"Ethel," Raja reprimanded. He put his hand on Ethel's. "Please, let's let it rest for now. How about we take a moment to appreciate being together again? In fact, let us toast to that," he said, holding up his wine glass.

"Yes, you're right," Ethel said.

The topics of conversation over lunch included Raja's family and their health, the politics in India, and various events happening at Raja's university in India and the university here. Raja had kept in touch with a few of the faculty members he used to work with.

"You're not thinking about returning to U Dub, are you, Raja?"

"That depends on whether I stay here. Not full-time." He did that back-and-forth thing with his head.

"And you, Christine. You said you quit your job. It will be hard to find a job here with—"

"Being pregnant, being a single mother?" she finished.

"Well, yes."

"Actually, I already have a job."

Ethel's eyebrows raised in surprise. "You do?"

"Ola wrote me, and she said I had a job at the bookstore if I ever wanted to return to the States." Christine hesitated. "She felt bad about how she broke the news to you about her cancer and about your disappointment in her not going forward with the treatments. She was worried about you and Cornelius. She said he would need someone to help in the bookstore, that I would be the one she would most trust to do it."

"But—"

"My condition? Mom, women work while pregnant and after they have babies. You did."

"I'm sorry. I don't know what I meant. This is all such a shock. I mean, seeing both of you here like this."

"The three of us have a lot to talk about," Raja said, looking at his wife.

"Yes, we do."

"Why don't I take us home, and we can figure it out in a more private setting?" He signalled the waiter for the check.

"Yes, that would be good," Ethel said. "Plus, I'm so tired after the funeral. After everything."

"And I'm tired after the flight," Christine said.

"Just one more question?" Ethel looked at Christine.

"What?"

"Do you know the sex?"

She smiled. "A boy."

"A grandson." Ethel smiled.

"Sam!" Ethel exclaimed. He entered the restaurant as they were leaving. The athletic-looking blonde hanging beside him would not have been the type of girlfriend Ethel would have expected Sam to have. Rhonda had said she was a pretty young thing.

"Mrs. Sharma!" He exclaimed. "And Dr. Sharma."

"Hello, Sam. I don't believe you have met my husband or my daughter. This is Raja, and this is Christine."

"This is Susan," he said.

There were no explanations offered. Sam stood at her side, not holding her hand or showing affection. Possibly due to his shyness, Ethel thought.

"I see you're going to be a grandmother?"

"Yes, I am. A little boy."

"Well, congratulations!"

"Thank you, Sam." Deterring any possible questions about the father's whereabouts, Ethel said, "I still want to hear about your trip to France. We can compare notes."

"And I still want to tell you."

"You're not teaching today?"

After sidestepping the issue for so long with Luce and not telling Ola, she didn't have the fortitude to do the same with Sam. Maybe it was his large, soulful brown eyes that begged honesty that prompted her to say, "Actually, Mr. Densworth and I didn't see eye to eye on much of anything. Since I was at retirement age, I retired."

"Mom, what?"

"We'll talk about this later, Christine."

Raja stood there with a blankness.

Ethel sensed Sam's awkwardness, but being the wordsmith he was, he said, "Mr. Densworth was a real grizzly bear. All the kids were afraid of him."

More like a lion, Ethel thought, but she accepted Sam's analysis of a grizzly bear.

"Mrs. Sharma, I could see you starting a school."

She laughed. "That's a peculiar notion. I don't think starting a school would be so easy, Sam."

"True." He smiled.

"Well, it was so nice to run into you. And nice to meet you, Susan. Enjoy your lunch."

"You retired and didn't tell us anything?" Raja said after the three of them were in the car.

Ethel shook her head in disgust before looking at both of them. "Since we were dropping bombshells today, I thought I might drop one of my own."

CHAPTER 25

Early September 2018

"Christine—"

"Mom, I can hardly hold my eyes open. Can we do this tomorrow?" She held her hand over her bulge. "Besides, you and Dad have a lot to talk about."

"I understand." She kissed her daughter's forehead. "There are clean sheets in the linen closet. Do you want me to change your bed?"

"No, I can do it. I think I'll take a bath first. I could use one."

"Everything is where it was. Nothing has changed around here."

"I can see," she said, eyeing the living room furniture.

Christine wheeled her luggage into her old bedroom. Raja, clearly not knowing his status, pushed his small suitcase into the corner of the entryway.

"It's a pleasant night. Do you want to go out onto the balcony and talk? That way, we won't disturb Christine."

Ethel nodded.

"Do you have any wine?"

"I think there is a bottle of red in the cupboard."

"I'll get it. Same place?"

"Everything's the same," Ethel said.

"I am not used to sharing my bed."

"Neither am I," Raja replied.

"When you walked into the funeral chapel along with Christine, I thought you had come back to ask me to sign divorce papers."

"Ethel, do you think I am thinking of divorce after what happened between us a moment ago? And why would I bring Christine?"

"Moral support. What *are* you thinking, Raja?"

"I think you are as beautiful as the day I married you."

"Oh, Raja." She laughed. "We both know that's not true."

The white sheets emphasized his dark skin. Christine, like her, had a pale, almost ruddy complexion. Christine's thick black hair, always unruly, came from Raja. What little hair that clung to Raja's scalp was gray.

"I notice you are not saying I'm as handsome."

"You know I married you for your brains, and that part of you is intact."

"I assume you are referring to the complete absence of hair now."

"You're not completely bald, and you have other attributes." Ethel looked downward.

"It's been a long time. I wasn't sure if I still had it in me."

"Raja, are you saying you have not been with another woman in our three years apart?" A chill ran through her at the thought.

"No, Ethel. How about you?"

"Do you mean, have I been with another man?"

"Yes. A younger one."

"Why would you say that?"

He tugged at a strand of her hair.

"Oh, the green hair. Not green, but Matcha Tea. That's what the hairdresser called it."

"You're not seeing that weird-looking kid we passed on the sidewalk downstairs? The one with the mascara. Did he talk you into dying your hair like a teenager?"

"Billy! Don't be silly, Raja. He's younger than Christine. You sound jealous."

"Maybe a little."

"Didn't you notice the cobwebs down there?"

He laughed. "Ethel, you still say the funniest things."

"So, Raja, why *are* you here? Do you plan on staying?"

"Since retiring, the thought crossed my mind that we might come to an arrangement—like you could teach for nine months, and perhaps you would consider spending your three-month vacation in India with me. That was my thought before I found out Christine was pregnant, and now that I've found out you're retired... Well, a grandchild on the way changes things. We could still travel after the baby is older. I want him to know my parents."

"Yes, Christine's condition changes everything. She is next door. Do you think she can hear us?"

"I think she has conked out. She's at that stage where she wants to sleep all the time. You remember that, don't you?"

"I remember being sick, mostly. Does Christine have morning sickness? I feel so bad, and I haven't asked her anything."

Raja massaged Ethel's shoulders. "There was no time. Seeing both of us appear without warning was a surprise, plus the stress of Ola's memorial. The restaurant was hardly the place to delve into it. You can talk to her in the morning."

"What time is it?"

Raja looked at his phone on the nightstand. "It's midnight."

"I guess we should get some sleep, but my thoughts are a contradiction. I want to fall into your arms and sleep, but I also want to know everything that's happening with Christine."

"I will tell you what I know, but first, tell me why you are no longer teaching."

"That man is intolerable."

"I take it you are talking about Principal Densworth?"

"Who else? It was the last day, and only the teachers were present. It was the end of the day. I had prepared all this data about meditation and how to incorporate it into the school's curriculum. Do you think he would even listen? I don't remember exactly what I said, but he was yelling. I was, too. I do remember saying I couldn't work under such a rigid dictatorship or something like that. Then he said, 'Do you mean you quit?' I said, 'Yes, I do.' We might have both looked at each other for a moment. Both of us were in shock. Now that I think about it, I half expected him to smile, but he didn't. Possibly, he did a little. I'm no longer sure. I stormed out of his office before he could."

"Oh, Ethel." Raja put his hands on his wife's face and kissed her. "Maybe it's for the best."

"Raja, why now?"

"Why now?" he repeated.

"Yes, why did you come back after three years? Was it only because of Christine? Is it because she is having a baby out of wedlock? Do your parents know? Does any of your family know?"

"They know and thought it would be best if she had the baby here."

Ethel drew away from him.

"But Ethel, please don't think that was the only reason. I

wanted to come back. I have thought about it for the last two years, even before that. I don't know. My parents are getting up in years. I didn't want to leave them. And the way I left you…" He looked down. "I was ashamed. I wasn't sure how to approach you about returning. I was afraid that things would be worse if I came home. I knew you were doing fine without me."

"You said home."

"What?"

"You called this home."

He smiled. "I've always thought of this as my home."

"You are a dutiful son, Raja." Ethel looked away. Tears rolled down her cheeks.

"But not such a good husband."

"I've always tried to remember the good times."

"You are being kind, Ethel, but I know how your mind operates."

"You do?"

"Of course I do."

"Then explain it to me, because sometimes I don't know what is up or what is down."

He drew nearer and heaved a heavy sigh. "I know I hurt you, but I also know you hid it. Because hiding things is what you do."

"No—"

He put his fingers against Ethel's lips.

"Ethel, let's be honest with each other. How I left has plagued me, and when we were first together—"

"We talked," Ethel finished.

"Yes, we talked. Oh, maybe not about the deep things like our innermost feelings, but we skimmed their surface. And then, I don't know when it happened, but we stopped doing even that."

"You were all wrapped up in your lectures and studies, and I, my students."

"And neither of us seemed to pay all that much attention to Christine," he said.

"I know. It was as if she didn't need us," Ethel said with a hint of sadness.

"Oh, but Ethel, she did."

"Yes, I know. Somehow, Christine turned out pretty good, didn't she? Well, I guess despite what has happened."

"Yes, she did," he said, placing his hand over Ethel's and smiling. "Despite what has happened," he repeated. "I have thought and thought about this, and I think it is for the best. Her pregnancy made it easy for me to come back. Would you turn the grandfather of your grandchild away? We can be a family again. Except now, there will be four of us instead of three. She is going to need us."

He laughed.

"Why are you laughing?"

"I'm old. I'm going to be a grandfather."

"Raja, you are not old."

He gave a slight roll of his eyes.

"When you emailed me about Ola, I thought you would need a shoulder to cry on."

"Do you know what you are, Raja?"

"What, Ethel?"

"A cuddly polar bear."

He laughed. "A white bear. Interesting. I would have thought a black bear or a brown bear."

"Polar bears are regal. I see you that way," she said.

"You have never compared me to an animal before."

"Lately, I've been comparing everyone to animals."

"Oh?"

"I don't know why. But I think it means something."

"What animal is Christine?"

"I don't know. I must give it some thought."

"Back to getting older. Even though you still have plenty more years to go until old age, I don't want us to be apart. Do you, Ethel?"

"With Ola's death, I have been thinking about that," she said.

He laughed.

"Now, what is so funny?"

"I think we just made some progress. You said something you felt inside. You didn't cover up your feelings. Tell me, Ethel, what *do you* feel?"

"I suppose I feel lost."

"Because of Ola's death?"

"That, but because of so many things. Losing my job is another reason. I don't know. I sometimes feel so helpless and hopeless." Tears burst from her eyes.

Raja pulled his wife closer and held her. When Ethel's tears subsided, he pulled away from the embrace.

"Let's look on the bright side of life. We are going to be grandparents."

"Yes, you're right. Raja, I'm glad you're here. I'm glad you both are here. I don't know if I could bear it if Christine had her baby in India without me."

Ethel leaped from the bed with renewed energy and paced around the room before coming to a halt. She noticed Raja ogling her with the same lust in his eyes he had displayed an hour ago. Ethel had temporarily forgotten her nakedness. She reached for her robe at the foot of the bed, but Raja grabbed her hand.

"Why do you need your robe?" he implored.

His hand was tight around her own. For a moment, she felt like a young woman without a belly bulge, cellulite, or angel-wing arms. And Raja, as if in a mirage, appeared like he did when they were first married. She smiled. She hadn't felt sexual in years—until tonight.

"Remember, Christine is in the next room." She tugged on her robe, and he released his grip. "Follow me," she said while tying the belt around her waist.

Raja obeyed, following his wife into the living room.

She sat on the couch and looked at the two saris on the chair. Ola's was beneath the other two, in a bag on the floor where she set it after returning from the hospice center. Raja stood behind her, his hands on her shoulders. Ethel reached up with one hand and grasped his.

"Did you know Christine sent me those saris? Three—one each for Ola, Luce, and me. Here they still are. I should have given the one meant for Ola to her before she died. I tried, but it was too late. I should have thought of it sooner, but so much was happening at the time. I either kept forgetting, or the time wasn't right. I don't know what to do with it now."

Raja rubbed Ethel's shoulder with his free hand.

"It will be okay, Ethel. I'm sure you'll think of something marvelous. Meditate on it."

Raja always told her to meditate. She tried, but she never could silence her thoughts. She used to watch him sometimes. He often looked like an angel sitting cross-legged in his white linen pants, his brown chest glistening.

"Do you want me to make you a chai?"

She smiled and turned. "Should I make some popcorn to go with it?"

He laughed. "This might have been a good idea in our twenties. Chai and popcorn this late? I would get indigestion." Raja moved his head from side to side. "I think we should get some sleep, don't you? You and Christine will have a lot to talk about tomorrow. Maybe you could go out together and shop for things to decorate a nursery."

"Yes, we will have to do that. Tell me about the father."

"Aw." Raja shook his head in disgust. "He's older than

Christine, has grown children, plus a wife in London. He has ties with the shipping company where Christine worked. One reason Christine quit, although I dare say they would have fired her eventually."

"He's not Indian?"

"No, he's British."

"I take it he doesn't plan to divorce his wife and marry Christine."

"From what little Christine has told me, I don't think so."

"Does his wife know about this?"

"Christine hasn't said. I highly doubt it, though."

"Does Christine love him?"

"I think she *did*."

"Raja, do you remember that discussion we once had when Christine was a senior in high school?"

"Can you be more specific? We had lots of discussions about Christine, as I recall."

"The one where we worried about Christine not having a boyfriend."

"I think there were plenty of those."

"Once, you said you wished she might try to sneak a boy into her room at night. Then you would at least think she was a normal teenager."

"Aw, yes." He smiled. "If I remember correctly, you replied, 'How could she? We live on the second floor.'"

"And you said, 'Leave it to Christine to pick a boy with no initiative. Couldn't even grasp the idea of a ladder." Ethel laughed.

"I guess our daughter is what you call a late bloomer. We could talk to her together. Do you remember the bed-and-breakfast we visited in Portland once? Betsy's?" Raja asked.

"Yes. I believe Christine was five when we went."

"At the airport, I made reservations online for Thanksgiving for the three of us. Or rather, the four of us. I wasn't sure what would transpire between us when I came home, but I was hoping we could at least be together as a family for Thanksgiving."

"That was thoughtful of you, but that may be too early to take the baby out," Ethel said.

"You're right. The baby could be late. Christine was. I wanted to save you the trouble of cooking, but I can cancel."

"It won't be trouble. It will be nice. I haven't cooked for anyone other than Ola and Luce for the longest time."

"Whatever you want."

"Do you remember when we thought something was wrong with Christine because she was always such a dutiful child?" Ethel asked.

"Yes."

"It's strange she waits until she is twenty-six to sow her wild oats."

CHAPTER 26

Early September 2018

One o'clock in the morning. All was quiet at the apartment complex except for the faint sound of croaking bullfrogs coming through the cracked window. The frogs were making their last pleas of the summer to attract females. Would they succeed? No seduction was needed on Raja's part, as she had fallen under his spell as soon as he walked through the funeral home doors. Ethel reached over and touched her husband. Perhaps the strain of losing her job, Ola's death, and her longing to be connected with them again made her delusional into thinking both he and Christine were back for good. Raja turned over on his side and began snoring. When did he start snoring?

While the rest of the apartment dwellers slept, Ethel lay there, thinking about all that had changed over the course of the summer—her dear friend, no longer in physical form, her estranged husband of three years, once again, lying next to her in bed very much in bodily form, and their daughter, sound asleep in the room she had grown up in, carrying a new life within her womb.

Ethel had given up on grandchildren long ago. Now,

Christine was two and a half months shy of making her a grandmother.

Three years after she and Raja took the seven vows while taking *Saat Pheras* around the sacred fire, Ethel had her first pregnancy symptom, waking up to dry heaves. You name it; Ethel had it—nausea, vomiting, aversion to certain foods such as tea and chocolate, foods she once loved. During her first trimester, the mere sight of most foods would send her at breakneck speeds to the nearest restroom. As the pregnancy progressed, cramps set in, and Charley horses woke her up in the middle of the night. Thank goodness, Christine seemed to have been spared the pregnancy woes she had endured. She could never have withstood an intercontinental flight while carrying Christine.

During her pregnancy, Raja and Luce did their utmost to comfort her, bringing pillows for her back and massaging her elevated feet. Luce stopped by almost every day after work to check on her. When she wasn't fussing over Ethel's diet and hydration, she was making sure the nursery was in order, something Ethel had little energy for after making it through a day of teaching—that is, on the days she *could* teach.

Five years younger than Ethel, Luce's desire for children grew strong. She had only begun dating Santiago, a real estate developer by day and a womanizing bongo player by night. Santiago had a charm Ethel couldn't deny.

Luce, who had read every book published on pregnancy and child-rearing, said the baby they knew would be a girl, whose name would be Christine, after Ethel's grandmother, would either be late or early.

"Babies rarely come on the due date," Luce said.

Luce was right. The baby arrived two weeks late. When children for Ethel and Raja were still in the dreaming stage, Ethel had planned on natural childbirth, cloth diapers, and breastfeeding, but after such a roller coaster ride of carrying a child, all of Ethel's grandiose plans fell by the wayside. She applauded the use of epidurals, disposable diapers, and formula.

It would be twelve years later when Luce finally got pregnant.

Ethel suspected Christine would breastfeed. A boy. Had she picked out a name yet? A chill went through Ethel's body in anticipation of all they would do to prepare for this baby. Raja had suggested preparing a nursery. Would they stay here? At one time, this apartment would have been big enough for three, but three adults plus a baby? One bathroom wouldn't do. Christine needed her own space. Now that she and Raja were back together, *they* needed space, too. Ethel touched her husband's chest. He turned, and his snoring ceased.

Christine would eventually move out, but for now, she would need their help. There was childcare. Had Christine considered any of this? If she knew her daughter, no, she hadn't. She hadn't even thought about using birth control. Ethel had to admit she was kind of glad she hadn't. The more Ethel thought of a grandson, the more she smiled. And Raja. It was apparent he welcomed the idea.

"A perfect, healthy baby," the doctor announced. "Weighing in at seven pounds and twenty inches, all perfectly normal," he said, handing Christine off to the nurse.

Both Ethel and Raja breathed a sigh of relief.

"That's all I want, a normal child," Ethel said as the nurse laid the infant wrapped in a pink receiving blanket, compliments of Luce, into Ethel's arms while Raja, the typical proud father, hovered over them.

Years later, Ethel remembered what she had said in the

delivery room. Her grandmother would have said, "Be careful what you wish for."

Christine was a delightful baby, so good that Ethel and Raja walked on eggshells, neither believing their good fortune. Immediately after returning home with her from the hospital, Christine slept a solid eight hours at night and a good portion of the day. Even after two years, she had not woken up once during the middle of the night, and as far as childhood illnesses went, they were virtually nonexistent.

"Just wait until the terrible twos hit," one teacher at her school said smugly. "She will make up for it."

Both she and Raja waited. Nothing. Even the daycare workers were perplexed, thinking at first that Christine might have a form of autism. After several doctor's appointments, they concluded she was normal in every way—normal to the point of being abnormal.

All of their friends who had children were envious. "You are so lucky," they said, relating their parenting horror stories.

Was Christine taking vitamins? She had taken none at the restaurant. And seeing Sam there. What must he think about her losing her job? But then he believes it was her choice. Technically, it was. She was, after all, the one who said, 'I quit.' Well, those weren't her exact words. It was getting fuzzy now. And seeing her daughter knocked up at twenty-six. No, no, Ethel thought. Sam doesn't know that. For all he knows, Christine could have a husband. Is he sleeping with that girl? What was her name? Susan. More than likely, he was. Everyone slept together these days. How old was Sam? Ethel counted up from when she had him in class. Twenty-two or twenty-three. She remembered the other teachers always bragging about Sam. Such a model student. Why was she thinking of Sam, of all people?

Throughout grade school, Christine's teachers consistently praised her. "She is the most caring, kindest child, always polite," they would say.

When Ethel and Raja asked at the teacher/parent conferences how she was doing academically, the answer was always the same—normal—normal to the point of being the centermost point on a graph. While they were pleased that she was such a well-mannered and courteous child, they had hoped the school would advance her to the gifted class. Simultaneously, they sighed heavily as the school counselor shook her head. She added, "You should be proud. There are few students like Christine, so well-behaved and never any trouble."

"Yes, yes, we know," they replied in unison.

One teacher, a devout Christian, had even commented, "Such an apt name. She is so Christlike."

On their way home, Raja grunted and said, "Even Krishna got into mischief as a child."

After attending one such meeting, Ethel, in the car seat next to Raja, put her hand to her chest in a sudden panic. He almost stopped the car. "What's wrong?"

"Puberty. It's all building up and will hit during middle school. You know the students I have. She will go Goth on us, defiant in every way. Smoking, drugs. Oh, dear, Raja, what will we do?"

"Ethel, calm down. I can't see that happening. Not our Christine." But Ethel saw how he gripped the steering wheel more tightly as he tried to reassure both himself and her.

They drove home the rest of the way without speaking, stopping at Luce's to pick Christine up. "Did everything go okay?" Ethel asked.

"You're joking?" Luce said with a raised eyebrow. "Christine is the perfect child. I asked if she wanted to watch a movie, but she saw the dust cloth and furniture polish I had abandoned on a table and insisted on dusting my entire house. So, I handed them to her and said, 'Go for it.' I hope you won't call Child Protection Services on me, but you know how insistent Christine is about being helpful."

"Yes, I know," Ethel said.

Talk about having a second child was non-existent. After such a dull and monotonous first child, they both feared the worst—juvenile court, leading to a life of crime. Lacking the typical challenges of child-rearing, Ethel and Raja grew lazy regarding Christine. They dedicated themselves to their careers, growing lethargic in parenthood. Unfortunately, their love life had also grown lethargic.

The years passed. Christine never once deviated from the middle line on that normalcy graph. Ethel sometimes regretted blaming Raja's three-year departure on Christine's normalcy. Christine reminded Ethel of an automaton or android, someone with perfect programming, possessing flawless self-sufficiency. Also, on the physical graph of normal, Christine again flatlined in the middle. Not skinny. Not fat. Not exceptional in the looks department—not homely, but not beautiful.

As far as boys went, there were no worries, no admonishing Christine of a curfew or how to behave with them. There was no need. The opposite sex, the ones Christine called friends, Ethel knew no better word for. Calling them steady boyfriends would have been pushing it. They were unexceptional, nerdy, ho-hum, nothing exciting.

Ethel and Raja pushed down the wish that Christine might develop a wild streak at some point. "Are we terrible parents?" Raja asked Ethel with a guilty look.

But no, there was never any crisis regarding their daughter in which she and Raja might be thrown off-balance, a scenario where they both would have to draw upon all their strength and parental love to move mountains for their child. Having never been tested as parents, perhaps there was no longer a practical need for their union, resulting in the gradual disintegration of their marriage over a quarter of a century.

Christine attended the University of Washington, graduating with a degree in business, with no aspirations beyond an office job. As far as Ethel and Raja could surmise, there were no prospects of a son-in-law or grandchildren for them. With a trust fund set up by Raja's family, there was no need for any steady job or husband.

Raja once joked, "One thing we can be assured of is that we won't have to worry about being taken care of in our old age."

Ethel responded, "I regret not breastfeeding."

She whispered a prayer for Ola, Christine, Raja, herself, and their grandchild, closed her eyes, and slept.

CHAPTER 27

Mid-September 2018

The following week, Ethel and Christine shopped for the nursery while researching numerous obstetricians in the Seattle area. Luce suggested Dr. Langley.

"You must have him deliver the baby," Luce said, grasping Christine's hands. "He delivered the triplets and was fantastic. I will have Santiago call him. He sold him his house."

Raja spent his days conferring with the university about the possibility of teaching online classes, something he could do from home. Only one or two, he told Ethel. "I want to spend as much time with you, Christine, and my new grandson as possible."

"Ethel, could you come by the bookstore the first chance you get?" That was the message on her cell phone.

"Oh, dear. I hope Cornelius is okay. We've been so busy preparing for the baby's arrival that I'm afraid I've neglected to check on him."

"I need to talk to him about the job," Christine said. "I want to work some before the baby is born."

"We'll go together."

Ethel couldn't help but wipe away a tear upon seeing Ola's name on the sign above the door and hearing the familiar tune from *Somewhere in Time* playing as she and Christine walked over the threshold into the bookstore. Ever since Ola's prognosis, Ethel's tear ducts had worked overtime. Luce said the crying was a little of everything—Ola, Raja, and Christine coming home, the fact she was going to be a grandmother, and maybe menopause.

"Menopause?" Ethel screeched over the phone. "I've never had a hot flash in my life."

Cornelius was at the cash register finishing up with a customer. Ethel glanced at Ola's closed office door. She and Christine browsed the new releases while he thanked the woman and bid her a good day.

"It's good to see Cornelius is keeping up with things," Ethel said while picking up a contemporary memoir, perusing the cover.

"Yes, that's encouraging," Christine replied.

"It's been so hard without Ola here," he said, walking toward them and shaking his head, but his demeanor quickly lightened at their presence. "Christine, I haven't seen you in ages. You look well. A little bigger through the middle. Of course, I saw you at the memorial service, but we didn't get a chance to talk. Are you coping with pregnancy? And the little one? How is he doing?"

Ola must have told Cornelius, but how could Ola have known? He even knows it's a boy.

Christine smiled, placing her hand over her baby bump.

"We're both doing fine. I have my first doctor's appointment scheduled for the end of the week. Then perhaps we can talk about my hours?"

"Yes, yes. I could certainly use you."

She looked around. "The place looks the way I remember it."

"We don't change things around much." He shook his head, realizing what he had said. "An old habit, saying we."

Cornelius's once-perfect posture slumped more than ever. At least he had a family. Ola mentioned a younger sister who was married with grown children.

"What did you want to talk to me about, Cornelius?" Ethel asked.

He reached behind the counter, pulled out a set of keys, and extended them toward Ethel. "Ola left you her house and her car. There will be a formal reading of the will. Ola said you probably wouldn't want her car, but Christine might."

Ethel stood in shock while Cornelius dangled the keys before her. "Why would she do that?" Ethel changed her gaze from Cornelius to Christine, who didn't appear surprised. Did she know about this?

"She had no one else. You were her best friend."

"What will I do with it?"

"Whatever you want. Live there. Sell it. Rent it. The deed is clear."

"But what about you?" Ethel asked.

"She knows I couldn't live there."

"I don't understand."

"I think it will all become apparent soon enough. Ethel, please take them," he said, holding them out to her.

Ethel reached for the keys attached to the carved wooden Egyptian ankh, a symbol of life. Cornelius retrieved a pad from behind the counter, scribbled something on it, tore off the top sheet, and handed it to Ethel. "Her address."

"The keys. Ola tried to give them to me before she died. She asked me to get them out of her purse. I did, but I put them back when she fell asleep. I thought it was her way of asking me to take her home."

"I believe she *is* home."

Ethel smiled. "Yes, Cornelius, you're right."

"You'll receive a call from the lawyer for the formal reading of the will, but feel free to check the house out beforehand." He paused. "Everything left in the house is yours. I already have what she wanted me to have.

"I had the utilities turned off while she was at the hospice house, not knowing how long it might be. I'll call and have everything turned back on. You know how that is. It may take a few days."

"That's fine. I don't know what else to say. This is all such a shock." She hugged Cornelius. "You take care. I'll still be in occasionally, but call if you need anything. Ola would want Luce and me to look out for you."

He smiled as they parted from their embrace. "Both of you, I mean the three of you, take care too."

"I will come by after my doctor's visit, Cornelius, and you can go over things with me and set my hours. Is that okay?"

"Yes, that would be great."

Ethel and her daughter walked up the street, Ethel in a daze, toward the car. When seated, she turned to Christine. "Did you know anything about this?"

"Mom, Ola, and I corresponded several times before she went into hospice. Yes, I knew she was going to leave the house to you. Also, when she asked if I might come home, more to help Cornelius and you out than anything, I told her I was pregnant. I felt it was something she needed to know before taking her place in the bookstore."

Ethel was silent for a moment.

"Mom?"

"No, Christine, it's okay. I understand." Ethel pushed the start button on the Prius. She turned to Christine. "So, if you take Ola's place, I guess you will be Cornelius's boss now?"

Christine looked embarrassed. "No, Mom, he'll be my boss. It's Cornelius who owns the bookstore."

"What?"

"It took me by surprise, too."

"But the sign says OLA'S WISE OLD BOOKS. And it's Ola's office, not Cornelius's," Ethel said, utterly stunned. "I always assumed...."

"So, did I. Listen, according to Ola, we will discover everything in time."

"Christine, is there anything more you should tell me?"

"No, that's everything I know."

"Well, I have the keys to her house and the address." She pulled the slip of paper from her pocket. "I don't recognize this street. It appears to be located outside the city. Your doctor's appointment is not until Friday. Tomorrow is Thursday. What do you say we go have a look?"

"I don't know, Mom. Since I've been home, we've been running here and there, deciding what I need for the baby. I want to take it easy tomorrow before my doctor's appointment."

"Probably a good idea. Maybe I'll call Luce and see if she wants to go with me."

CHAPTER 28

Mid-September 2018

"She left *you* her house?" Luce exclaimed as she buckled her seat belt on the passenger side of Ethel's Prius.

"Yes. And her car, but Cornelius suggested Christine might need the car, which she does. Luce, you're not—"

"Jealous? Really, Ethel? What would we do with another property?" Luce reached her hand over the console, placing it on Ethel's.

Ethel punched the address into her phone's GPS app. "Are you familiar with this area?"

"No, but Santiago probably knows it," Luce said.

"We'll finally see where Ola retreated to when she wasn't at the bookstore. Are you nervous?" Ethel asked.

"I don't know if nervous is the right word. Maybe apprehensive eagerness—like when you are coming to the end of a good mystery novel," Luce said.

Ethel touched the button to start the engine.

Luce asked a few miles from the city, "Do you think we are going in the right direction? There have been no cars or houses for the last mile."

"If you can trust this app, it says we're on track."

"Turn right in a half mile," came the female voice from the phone, as if in defiance that her directions be questioned. Ethel squinted in the sunlight coming through her windshield before taking a sharp turn onto the sideroad, nearly obscured by a thicket of fir trees. Keeping to the right side of the narrow road, she inched forward until she came to a slightly dented, rusty mailbox. The name, although faded, read Ola Sisko. Ethel heaved a sigh of relief, almost slowing to a complete stop.

"Probably gets all her mail at the bookstore," Luce said.

"Got all her mail," Ethel corrected.

"Yeah, I forget sometimes. Everything that's happened seems surreal."

"Yes, I know what you mean."

"So, we passed her mailbox. Where is the house?"

"Couldn't be too much further," Ethel said.

"Rather ominous, don't you think?" Luce said.

"I hope we're not coming to the end of a horror novel. Maybe Ola never invited us to her house because of the location. We've been driving for an hour," Ethel said.

"True, but you picked me up, which took at least fifteen minutes, and we've been driving slowly because we've been talking and weren't sure where we were going. You could shave thirty minutes off the time as long as we avoid rush hour."

"I didn't think we were going so slow."

"Ethel, whenever you talk, you slow down."

"I don't."

"Yes, you do."

"Well, I didn't know I did."

"No matter. How long is this driveway, anyway?" Ethel exclaimed.

"It only seems long because we're practically walking instead of driving. No, more like limping. You could hit the gas pedal a little harder."

Ethel rolled her eyes, continuing her measured pace over a bed of pine needles. She maneuvered through twists and turns to avoid the evergreen branches scraping against the side of her car. The mileage gauge said one-fourth mile when they pulled up in front of a small ivy-covered stone cottage.

"Yes," Ethel said. "I can see Ola living here."

"Well, it's too quaint for a horror novel. A good sign, don't you think?"

As they walked up the shaded slate walkway, Ethel nuzzled her chin inside the collar of her lightweight jacket. "Do you feel the cold?" she asked Luce.

"I suppose a little. Typical Seattle September."

"For a moment..."

"What?" Luce asked.

"For a moment, I thought the chill might mean Ola's ghost hovers over us."

"I think a ghost is around when you walk through a spot of cold air," Luce said.

The yard, more like a jungle, obviously neglected for most of the summer, was void of ornamental plants or flowers. Ethel placed the key in the lock. A sliver of paint fell to the ground as she did so. Only traces of cobalt blue remained on the door. Ethel turned the key, then the doorknob. The door screeched in arthritic pain.

Luce followed Ethel over the threshold to a large open area. A worn, red leather couch and matching chair faced a stone fireplace set between wall-to-wall bookcases. A small side table, holding a single candle holder with a white candle, sat by the chair, and a narrow coffee table, overflowing with books, was in front of the couch. "Typical Ola," Ethel commented.

The only technology was a small flat-screen television above the fireplace's mantel.

Luce walked over to the bookcase and ran her fingers

across the titles. "They're all about ancient sites and religions and of a self-help nature."

The room spanned across the width of the house. They directed their attention to the opposite side, bathed in shadow, where a large desk sat.

"Let's pull back those curtains, Luce."

Afternoon light streamed through a large bay window, revealing an antique mahogany desk cluttered with papers and *more* books. Ola's laptop peeked from their midst.

"I love the openness of this. You could do a lot with it. If you decide to live here," Luce said while perusing the surroundings.

Ethel, now standing in front of the fireplace, said nothing.

Luce put her hand to her nose and walked back to the desk. "I'm going to see if I can open this window."

The congregation of odors and general mustiness from a house shut up too long had merged into something indistinguishable. The only definable smell was the smoky trace lingering from those fires Ethel imagined Ola in front of on chilly nights, sitting in her plump red-leather chair with a book and a glass of wine on the table beside it.

A bundle of seasoned wood lay on the floor—a box of matches next to it. A poker leaned against the hearth. Ethel smiled.

"Ethel, I hope you're not thinking of lighting a fire. We don't know what shape that fireplace is in. These things have to be checked first."

"No, no. I was thinking Ola *would* use matches instead of a butane lighter."

"Definitely old school," Luce said.

The kitchen, hardly the dream of someone practicing culinary arts like Rhonda, was small, practical, and logically arranged with the bare necessities. Luce ran her hand along the doorway's frame leading into the dining room.

"I wonder if this is a load-bearing wall. If it isn't, I would knock it down."

"Hmm, I'll think about it," Ethel said as they walked back into the kitchen.

The window over the sink looked out over a portion of the backyard.

A gurgling noise preceded a gush of brown water from the gyrating, noisy spigot. Startled, Ethel closed the tap. "*At least we have water.*"

"Could be the remainder left in the pipes," Luce said.

Ethel snarled.

"Or maybe Cornelius has been paying the water bill, and it's still on," Luce countered.

"Let's see what's out here," Luce said, unlatching the sliding glass door. Both women walked out to a partially screened-in, weathered deck. The deck ended with an addition to the house, which appeared to have been long abandoned before its completion.

"Ola never mentioned she was adding on to her house," Ethel said.

"That, plus the fact she mentioned nothing about her house," Luce added.

"Yeah." Ethel half-rolled her eyes.

"Anyway, this construction was started long ago and never finished," Luce said.

Luce relaxed in one of the Adirondack chairs in the screened-in area, and Ethel followed suit.

"Ethel, do you notice all the inside furniture and areas outside are conducive to reading?"

"Yes, now that you mention it. It was Ola's favorite pastime, her only pastime, and passion as far as we know, except for traveling."

"Yeah, if only she could have done more of it," Luce offered.

"Do you see what I see, Luce?"

"Do you mean the hammock hanging between those two oak trees?"

"Yes. Can you imagine Ola lying in a hammock?"

"No, not at all," Ethel said.

"What about Cornelius?" Luce asked.

Ethel snorted a laugh. "You're being silly, Luce."

"Yes, but that is what you like about me."

Luce wiped her finger over the counter as they reentered the kitchen, leaving a trail through the dust. She stopped at the stove and lifted the iron grill. "Ooh, sticky. We could bring back some cleaning supplies, and I could help you with the cleaning. This place has gone untouched, I bet, since Ola's illness."

"I love gas stoves. I had one back in India." Ethel turned the knob—only a hiss.

"Cornelius obviously didn't pay the gas bill."

"Oh, well, I thought we might make ourselves some tea. I'm sure Ola has a stash somewhere." Ethel opened a cupboard, and a mouse ran down the side and scurried off.

Luce screamed. With her hand to her chest, she said, "Sorry, I don't like creatures."

"I know," Ethel said. "The fish in the fish market."

"Mice are much worse than fish. You need to get a cat. They work better than traps."

"You're right. I hope the baby won't be allergic."

"Sounds like you *are* thinking about moving here."

"I don't know what I'm thinking right now. Raja and Christine would have to agree." She paused. "Do you remember once when Ola was talking about cats?"

"No, I don't believe so."

"She said, 'Cats are the perfect psychopaths.'"

"Oh yeah, I remember that now."

"I asked her how so, and she said they experienced no

guilt. She said, 'You can tell a lot about an animal from its body language. Dogs are very open, always wagging their tails, grateful for everything. They care so much about what humans think. Its whole body droops in shame if you even look at it wrong. A cat, on the other hand, couldn't care less. People think they're cuddly, but they're self-serving.' Then we both told her we had neither. You told her you couldn't have pets because Lou had allergies. And I said, 'You seem to know a lot about them. She said she owned both dogs and cats and that cats were from parallel worlds, although they somehow interact with *our* world."

Luce's eyes widened in remembrance. "Yes, and I asked her if she had any now, and she said she wasn't home enough to tend to them. And when I asked her what happened to the animals she had, she said Brandi, the dog, died of old age, and the cat, whose name she had forgotten because the cat didn't care for it, never answering to it, wandered off."

"I remember how she related all of this to us. So matter-of-factly," Ethel said.

"She said everything matter-of-factly. No matter how far-out the subject was," Luce said.

"Fritz, my yoga instructor, said cats were enlightened."

"Your yoga instructor sounds like a nut job to me."

Ethel laughed. "Do you feel like the three of us are together having this conversation?"

"Yeah, it feels like Ola is here with us," Luce said, tilting her head to the side and smiling.

"I would say all of Ola's esoteric knowledge has been vindicated now," Ethel said.

"Do you think she was talking about childhood pets, Ethel? We never asked her that; if we did, I can't recall."

"I don't know. Ola never talked about her childhood, only that her parents divorced when she was in high school and that neither was still living."

They walked back into the living area. Ethel walked over to the bay window.

"What on earth? Come here, Luce. Look."

Luce gazed out the window but offered no explanation.

"It's four o'clock already, Luce," Ethel exclaimed, looking at her phone. "We must inspect the rest of the cottage before darkness sets in. There's no electricity, remember?"

"Yeah, we can use the flashlights on our phones."

Ethel checked her battery percentage. "We'll have to use yours. Mine is almost dead."

From the hallway, Ethel opened a door leading into an antiquated bathroom.

"These are all the rage now," Luce said, her hand on the rim of an old clawfoot cast iron tub. Most things in this house look like they're from the fifties or sixties. Do you know when it was built?"

"No, I don't have the deed for it yet."

"Might date back to the forties. Santiago says they built houses better then."

"The commode looks new," Ethel said.

"I think you will need to make a lot of updates if you live here."

They entered a bedroom, no doubt Ola's. A cherry blanket chest rested at the foot of a brass bed. Ethel opened it to find stacks of books and papers rather than blankets. Ethel opened the top drawer of the chest against the opposing wall.

"Panties and bras. All purely practical," Ethel said.

"Were you expecting to find something risqué?" Luce asked.

"No, I suppose not. I guess the secrets of her life weren't sexual."

"You know, Ethel? This is getting weird. I feel like a voyeur or Peeping Tom or something. Let's move on." Luce opened the door on the right wall of the bedroom. "Wallah! You have another bathroom—one more modern."

Ethel peeked in and smiled her approval.

The next door they opened led to the unfinished addition. The drywall had only been started. Joint tape, drywall knives, and dust masks lay beside a bucket of drywall mud—all shoved to the corner. A table saw and various other tools occupied the rest of the room.

"Why would workmen leave their tools?" Ethel asked. She shook her head. "Oh well, so many unanswered questions."

"There is one more door off the hallway," Luce said.

"A child's room," Ethel said in shock. A Cabbage Patch doll rested on a patchwork quilt atop a maple twin bed. Other toys, some of the same ones Christine had while growing up, were displayed throughout the room. A bookcase overflowed with children's books—those a young child would read—both picture books and early chapter books. Ethel pulled one from the case—*A Million Cats.*

Ethel held her hand over her chest while gazing around the room. Drawings, appearing to have been executed by an eight- or nine-year-old, were tacked to a bulletin board. Ethel opened a closet to find the clothes of a small girl. They were predominantly yellow.

"Luce, what in the world? Did Ola have a child? Why did she never mention this child? Where could she be now? Why did I inherit this house according to the will and not her? This would explain the old rusty swing set pushed against the trees we saw from the bay window. None of this makes any sense." She turned to Luce. "Is this why she never invited us to her house?"

"Ethel, she had a child and a husband. The child died in a horrible auto accident."

Ethel sat down on the twin-size bed. She saw the sun

disappearing over the horizon through the thin lace curtains. Only a sliver of light revealed the pain on Luce's face.

"Did Ola tell you this?"

"No, no, she didn't. I found out by accident." Luce related how she had come across the article in the library.

"And you said nothing?"

"I didn't know what to say, nor who to say it to. I wanted to tell you, but I felt like I came upon something Ola didn't want either of us to know. For that same reason, I never approached Ola about it, especially since I found out only days before she announced she had cancer."

Luce sat down beside Ethel and put her arm around her.

"I think we've seen enough for the day. It's getting dark, and I know you need to start dinner," Ethel said, her body rigid.

"Yeah, we should go. I haven't even texted Santiago."

"Luce, did you know we would find this here when you came with me?"

"No, Ethel. I had no idea. I only knew that the child had died in an auto accident. Her father was driving. Initially, they thought it was a hit and run, but they closed the case, saying the father was driving too fast around a curve on a rainy night."

"This is so horrible. A mystery and horror novel rolled into one. Where is the father?"

"I don't know, Ethel. I'm assuming Ola and he divorced. That happens a lot when a child dies. It's too much for the parents to handle. Oh, and there is one more thing. Cornelius was the detective handling the case."

"Cornelius? A detective? This is all too strange." This reminded Ethel of what Raja had said about Ola and Cornelius's relationship: that he was hiding something.

Ethel let out a heavy sigh. "Before we go, tell me, does Cornelius know you know about this?"

"Oh, my gosh, no! If I had gone to anyone, I would have gone to Ola first—or maybe you. I was so horrified when I read the article. I thought about going back to the library to see if I might find out more, but I felt like I was betraying some confidence that I shouldn't have been privy to in the first place. I didn't even tell Santiago."

"It's okay, Luce. I'm not sure what I would have done. Well, actually, I do know. I would have come straight to you."

Even though the light in the room was waning, Ethel could see the look of hurt on Luce's face. She reached for her and hugged her. "I'm sorry, Luce. It's been a rough three months for both of us. You did what you thought was best. We have been friends for a long time. Promise me we'll always be honest with each other from here on out."

A tightness spread across Ethel's chest as she suddenly remembered she hadn't told Luce she was no longer working at Densworth Academy.

"Luce..."

"Yes, I know about you losing your job."

"How?"

"I called the school on your last day, looking for you. I figured you had forgotten to charge your phone."

"Why didn't you say anything?"

"Because I knew you would eventually tell me."

Tears carrying past deceptions cascaded down their cheeks. In an act of renewal, Luce wiped her wet eyes and reached over to hug Ethel. "I'm sorry."

"No, *I'm* sorry," Ethel said.

"Listen, the road out of here is dark. I need to text Santiago and tell him we're on our way back."

"Yeah, I should do the same with Christine and Raja with what power I have left on my phone."

"Come on, Ethel. You can charge it in the car. You've got

more pleasant things to think about. Tomorrow is Christine's doctor's appointment."

When rising from the bed, Ethel kicked her shoe backward. "Wait, I lost my shoe under the bed."

"Here, let me see," Luce said. She knelt, shining the phone's flashlight under the bed. "I see it." She reached her hand under the bed. "I don't know how you managed to do it, but you caught your shoe on the box staple. I'll pull the box out along with your shoe. I bet it's more books."

"These are not books, Luce. They're journals." Ethel picked up the top one and opened it. "In Ola's handwriting."

"What does it say?"

"Give me a moment." Ethel read the first page. "Hold the flashlight steady. This one is talking about Lloyd, her husband."

"Do you think we should be reading these, Ethel?"

"You just asked me what it said."

Luce rolled her eyes.

"Besides, if Ola didn't want us to see them, why didn't she destroy them?" Ethel said.

"Maybe she meant to, but was too drained near the end."

"Possibly, but my intuition tells me otherwise."

"I think you're right," Luce said. "It's too dark to read them now. Do you think we should take the box with us?"

Ethel breathed in and let out a heavy sigh. "No, I'm not up for this at the moment. We can come back during the day and read them. Somehow, I think reading them here might make more sense."

"Yeah, you're right."

CHAPTER 29

Mid-September 2018

"Everything looks fine," Dr. Langley said, looking pleased.

Raja put his arm around Ethel's waist as he, Ethel, and Christine looked at the ultrasound. Feeling a tingling sensation, Ethel looked to see chill bumps on her pale arm and Raja's dark arm beside hers. He reached for her hand and clasped it tightly with his other arm.

The doctor studied the questionnaire that Christine had filled out so meticulously. Pregnancy had not deterred Christine's obsession with documentation.

"So, no morning sickness?"

"No."

"What about cramping?"

"Cramping?"

"Charley horses in your legs or feet."

"I thought you meant my stomach. No, no Charley horses."

"I see you are a vegetarian."

"Have been for most of my life."

"Well, your weight is good. Being a vegetarian doesn't necessarily mean you're eating well, though. I see many vegetarians and vegans eating processed fake meats, chips, and sodas."

"Hardly ever, Doctor," Christine said.

"Still, I want the nurse to review your diet to ensure you get all the necessary nutrients. Are you taking any vitamins?"

"Mom, will you get my vitamins out of my purse?"

Ethel handed them to the doctor.

"I got them at the health food store when I returned to the States," Christine said. "They're vegetarian. It's what the lady working there recommended."

"What did you take when you were in India?"

"An Ayurvedic blend."

Ethel expected him to say something negative. Instead, he said, "Well, they must have been good for you."

He carefully examined the label on the vitamin container. "I think you can continue with these for now, but if any problems arise, I'll prescribe more heavy-duty ones. Don't worry. I'll make sure they're vegetarian. Several of my mothers are vegan."

He returned the vitamins to Ethel and placed the chart under his arm. "I'll see you in two weeks. My nurse will talk to you about your diet before you leave. You can pick up your appointment card on the way out. If you have no questions, your parents can wait outside while you dress."

Christine looked at her parents, who shook their heads in response. "I guess not," Christine said.

"Call the office immediately if something out of the ordinary happens. If it's after hours, please call the emergency number on the appointment card. Hopefully, everything will be fine, and I'll see you in two weeks." He smiled and proceeded out the door.

"Such a nice man," Ethel said.

"Yes, I like him," agreed Raja.

"If anyone wants my opinion, I think he'll do just fine," Christine said.

CHAPTER 30

Mid-September 2018

A week had passed since Ethel and Luce had visited Ola's cottage. It was as if entering Ola's home and reading her private journals had opened up one of those parallel universes Ola liked to discuss so much. While most people might be eager to tear into the journals, Ethel harbored mixed emotions.

"It's like finding out your husband is a bigamist or living an entirely different life. I only want to remember her as the Ola we knew her as," Ethel told Luce over the phone.

"There are a lot of layers to people, Ethel. Concentrate on Christine, Raja, and the grandson you'll soon have," Luce said.

Luce was right, of course.

"Ethel, are you there?"

"Yes, I'm here."

"You're going to have to decide what you're going to do about the house."

"I know."

"Discuss it with Raja and Christine."

Another parallel universe. Raja, the husband who was

now back in her life after a three-year absence, and Christine, the daughter she thought might never have a boyfriend, ended up having an affair with a married man with whom she was now pregnant.

But what would she do with Ola's house? The memories within its walls cast a dismal shadow over the new turn of events: Raja's return home and their daughter's gift of a grandchild. Yes, the positive aspects.

It wasn't so much that Ola had a whole other life she had kept hidden from them; it was the out-of-the-blue way Ola left her the house, the house containing secrets she had never confided to either of them while she was living.

"I haven't told Christine what we found. What if she had gone with me instead of Luce? Finding out Ola had a child who died? How might that have affected her? Considering her condition?" Ethel said to Raja.

"I'm sure Christine could have handled it. Also, it happened a long time ago. You need to calm down, Ethel. Are you still doing yoga in the park?"

"Yes, well, no. I've let it slip by most of the summer." Ethel looked at the time on her phone. "It begins in about fifteen minutes."

"Then, hurry. Grab your yoga mat and walk over to the park."

"But I'm not ready."

"What do you need to do to get ready? You're wearing sweats."

"I won't be here when the new washing machine arrives."

"I'm here. You think I can't handle instructing the delivery men where it goes?"

"I suppose..."

"Go on," he said, kissing her. When you get back, we can do some loads of all this piled-up laundry and perhaps meet Christine for lunch," he yelled as she walked down the steps.

Ethel had only made it a few steps when she ran into Rhonda.

"Off to yoga?" she asked.

"Yes."

"What's wrong, Ethel? You look down."

"I honestly don't feel like yoga today."

"Then why don't you come in and sit for a while?"

All those times, Ethel would have brushed Rhonda off, devising excuses the moment she came into view, but remembering their last and only talk in Rhonda's inviting home made her hope Rhonda would ask her back. Rhonda wasn't how she had judged her at all, but then, neither was Ola. Ethel followed Rhonda through her garden into the living area, her yoga mat under her arm.

"I hope I'm not keeping you from your work."

"No, not at all. There are deadlines, but mostly, I set my own hours. I see your husband is back. And your daughter."

In the past, Ethel would have thought Rhonda was only being nosy, but no longer. It wasn't long before she had her feet up on Rhonda's couch, sipping her latest herbal concoction while pouring out everything that had transpired since the funeral.

After a pause of perhaps thirty seconds, which was highly unusual for Rhonda, she said, "You're a lucky woman, Ethel."

"Lucky?" she questioned.

"You have your husband back, and you'll be a grandmother. Your friend left you a house, and you said it had a nice backyard. It sounds like the perfect place to raise a child."

"Oh, no, Rhonda. I couldn't live there. Not now."

"Why not?"

"Because of what we found."

"Someone's past life? Ola must have treasured your friendship, not because she left you her house, but because she left you her secrets. It sounds like she was doing her best to hold it all together and start over." Rhonda's eyes watered up. "I lost a child once."

"Oh, Rhonda, you did?" Ethel jerked up from her prone position.

"Crib death. My little Carl was only three months old. My third child. It's hard, but I had two children who needed me. I didn't like talking about it. For the longest time, I thought it was my fault. I had two more children." Rhonda laughed. "Maybe deep down, I was compensating for losing Carl. Since my divorce, my youngest daughter, Angela, has been begging me to move in with her in Los Angeles, but I've established my business in Seattle. If I'm completely honest, the main reason is that Carl's grave is here."

Ethel stumbled for something to say.

"Everyone has some sadness in their lives; how I see it is that Ola didn't want to burden you. And with you having a living daughter and Luce having how many children?

"Three boys. Triplets."

"That's remarkable. As I said, Ola didn't want you walking on eggshells around her whenever you brought up your child. And trust me. You would have been uneasy talking about your child to her, knowing she had lost her only one. I've experienced how uncomfortable it makes people, even though I still had two others. Nor did she want to keep reliving it by talking about it. But, at the same time, because you were such a good friend to her, she didn't want to go to her grave not having confided in you."

"What do you suggest I do?"

When Ethel asked for her counsel, Rhonda's ears almost wiggled, conjuring up the image of a rabbit.

"You said there was no electricity. I would pack some cold cuts on ice and make a day of it. Sit down, read the journals, and discover who your friend really was. Usually, our friends are a reflection of us in some way. I think you will understand yourself better after having done so. And don't make any hasty decisions about living in the house yet. I would miss you greatly as a neighbor now that we've gotten to know each other, but it could be a move in the right direction." She laughed. "I didn't intend for that to be a pun."

Ethel felt her face turn red. She had misjudged Rhonda so.

Rhonda ran over to the window. "Looks like someone is getting a new washing machine."

"That would be me," Ethel said. "Rhonda, tell me. Why do you go to the laundromat? Since you are below me, I know you have a washer and dryer hookup."

"Oh, I have them. But I enjoy going to the laundromat. Such interesting people go there."

Ethel smiled. "I know what you mean."

CHAPTER 31

Mid-September 2018

"What's this?" Luce asked as Ethel handed her the gift bag.

"Happy Birthday, a day early. Did you think I would forget?"

"I certainly wouldn't blame you, considering everything that has happened. Do you want me to open it now?"

Ethel nodded with a smile.

Luce untied the ribbon that held the twine handles together and pulled out the sari.

"A sari?" Luce's eyebrows raised. "It's my color," she added.

"I have to give Christine credit for that." She paused. "It's a sorry gift when I think about it."

"No, Ethel, I love it. Why would you say that?"

"I got one for myself, you, and Ola. I was hoping we could all go together, perhaps to an Indian restaurant to celebrate your birthdays. But with everything happening and Ola dying before her sixtieth birthday, I forgot to give hers to her until it was too late. I left to go home and get it the night she died. I'll never forget the look on Cornelius's face when I returned. She died shortly after I left. I should have been there."

"Oh, Ethel." She hugged her friend. She settled into her seat, put the sari back in the bag, and placed it in the back seat. "We can still do it, the two of us, or maybe all of us, you, Raja, Christine, me, Santiago, and the boys."

"You know. That's a marvelous idea." Ethel pressed the button to start the vehicle and activated her GPS. "I don't remember if I know how to get back."

"No worries. I remember," Luce said.

They drove up to a freshly mowed lawn.

"Cornelius called the lawn service for me," Ethel said.

"I'll have to say the room looks much cheerier with the sun coming through the window," Luce said.

"So, maybe we'll find those answers today in her journals. Where do you want to do this?"

"We could both sit at her desk, where there is plenty of light. I'll pull up another chair," Luce said.

After retrieving the journals under the bed, Luce said, "We must clear this off first. It's a mess."

"Like her office." Ethel picked up a book from on top of the mess. "The Eye of Horus."

"She must have been writing this before she went into hospice," Luce said. She sighed. "This all seems so wrong. Prying into her life like this."

"No, Luce. I think she wanted us to. Rhonda thinks so."

"Rhonda? The one downstairs that you say is the talker you can't get away from?"

"I'm afraid I misjudged her."

"Woah, Ethel. Those are strange words coming from you."

"Seriously, Luce? I admit when I'm wrong."

Luce's eyebrows lifted slightly.

"I've discovered Rhonda is rather wise. She said she would like to meet you."

"Oh, then, I guess she is wise." Luce laughed.

Ethel's eyes did a half roll. "I told her the three of us could have lunch together one day, and she insisted on cooking for us."

"Oh? We're not trying to replace Ola, are we?"

"I hadn't thought of that."

"It's a subconscious thing," Luce said. "But maybe she might be what both of us need."

Ethel and Luce cleared off the desk, moving Ola's laptop to the edge and stacking the clutter of papers and books in the room's corner. Ethel moved the box of journals to the top of the desk.

"Okay. First, we have to organize the journals chronologically," Luce said.

Ethel laid the Eye of Horus journal off to the side while they sorted through the others, placing them in three neat stacks. Ethel opened the earliest, a leather-bound book with the word "Journal" embossed on it. The name, Dr. Roberta Asher, Psychologist, was stamped into the upper right-hand corner.

"Shall I?" Ethel asked.

"You're the teacher."

Ethel read aloud:

> September 22, 1988
> Dr. Asher says writing about this will help. She must prescribe this for all her patients since she pulled out two journals from a box filled with them. So, here goes:
> I had often thought about keeping a travel

journal, that is, if I were to travel one day. Now, any desire to even leave the house is gone. All passion for anything is gone, except wanting my life back the way it was before.

Lloyd left for work. At least he has that. I could no longer continue my job at the library. It's so awkward. People tiptoe around me like I'm a wobbly ballerina that might topple over at any moment or a volcano that might erupt. And they're right. Some do their best to express words of comfort. They are only abstract phrases that have no depth. None of them has ever lost a child. How can they know what it feels like? How can they say it will pass? On the day a children's group came in for the Reading Corner—a third-grade class, all Amelia's age—I couldn't hold it together any longer. I suddenly felt faint. I couldn't make my way to the restroom fast enough. I sat in a stall, my head on my lap, until there was a tap on the door. I don't know how much time had elapsed. I only remember phasing in and out.

"Ola, are you in there?"

It was Audrey. They must have sent her to check on me. More than likely because Audrey is older, old enough to be my mother. But Audrey never had children. Audrey always reminded me of the Potterville version of Mary in It's a Wonderful Life, the spinster librarian who never married.

I couldn't speak.

"Ola, please. If you don't answer, I'll have to

get the supervisor."

"No," I finally eked out when I heard her walking down the hall.

I opened the stall door, walked over to the sink, splashed water on my face, unlocked the door, stepped out, and told Audrey, who turned abruptly upon hearing me come out, "I quit." It wasn't the proper chain of command, but under the circumstances and given my volatile situation, I knew no one would care or dare say anything to me. Straight from the bathroom, I walked out onto the street. Droplets of snow stung my face. I walked out with only my purse. Luckily, out of habit, I grabbed it from beneath my desk before running into the restroom. My coat still hung in the cloakroom. That was nearly one month ago. Lloyd offered to return to retrieve it, but I said, "No need. Why do I need one? I don't plan on leaving this cottage."

"Never?" he asked.

"I don't know. Possibly," I said.

He walked into the other room. Since that day, I have only gone out for a counseling session with him. He runs all the errands and shops for groceries. We hardly eat anything these days.

The roads were slick when I left the library. I used to be so scared to drive in such weather, but on that day, I didn't care. I prayed to crash, but then I thought, what if I kill another child? I couldn't bear the thought of putting another mother through such torment. I eased off on the gas. The drive, which usually took thirty minutes, took twice that long.

Lloyd and I hardly speak to each other these days. Our only communication other than our counseling sessions is the sadness we relay to each other through our eyes. The counselor thinks it would be good if we kept journals in which we recorded the thoughts we could hardly voice during our sessions. Lloyd's journal has lain untouched.

Lloyd blames himself for the accident. Deep down, I blame him, too. There, I wrote on paper what I could never say out loud. So maybe this journal is a good idea. We'll see.

No, no. I know it wasn't his fault. It was the other person's fault. I'm convinced there was another car: a hit and run. Lloyd never told the police there was another car. He couldn't remember, but one night, he awoke from a nightmare, and in his nightmare, another car ran them off the road. I often wonder if it was a man or a woman—if he or she has an ounce of guilt. Why did that person never come forward?

Lloyd said it was only a nightmare. He wasn't sure if that was what had happened or not. I wanted him to tell the police, but he persuaded me it was a bad dream, nothing more. We both have bad dreams when we can sleep. Sometimes, I wish I could fall asleep and never wake up. I want it for both of us. We'll all be together again. We were once a happy family.

The only thing I can say was good about it was that Amelia died instantly. She didn't suffer. Lloyd suffered broken ribs, a concussion, and a broken arm. But worst of all—survivor's guilt. Even though Lloyd was at the wheel, and I wasn't in the car, I have it, too.

"Well, that's the first entry," Ethel said, tears streaming down her face. Luce grabbed her purse, pulling out tissues for both of them.

"If Ola's daughter had been eight around 1988, she would be thirty-eight today if she had lived. I was always rattling on about Christine to Ola. Can you imagine how that made her feel?"

"Same here. You know how much I talk about my boys."

"Maybe she should have told both of us to shut up."

Ethel heaved a heavy sigh and turned the page.

September 23, 1988
I hardly slept last night. Neither did Lloyd. Sleepless nights are typical. After an hour of tossing and turning, he put his arm around me and squeezed me tightly. His grip was firm. He feared I would push him away like I had on many other nights. Our faces touched, and I could feel the wetness streaming down his face.

He showed no emotion at the funeral. He had a blank stare throughout the entire memorial service, all the while holding me up. It was all I could do to stand erect when we did our final walk-by of the casket.

He wanted a closed casket, but I insisted it be opened. I wanted to see Amelia's tiny body until they lowered it into the ground. People who have not experienced this do not understand. Like any other mother, how often had I thought about losing Amelia? You know, one of those freak accidents or her getting sick. I see the kids with cancer with no hair, yet they are smiling. The children seem above it all, their minds off on some higher plane. I had never thought much about an afterlife until now. Why would I? We had so much life ahead of us.

Lloyd and I got married right out of high school. Everyone advised us to wait, but we were so much in love. Lloyd worked at a construction company, and I attended college during the day, pursuing a degree in library science. No sooner had I gotten my degree than I got pregnant. I waited until Amelia started kindergarten before I began working at the library. Nothing gave me greater pleasure than being a full-time mom during the first five years of her life. Amelia was the most delightful child in every sense of the word. Her rosy little cheeks, her curls, the way she always came into our room first thing in the morning when she woke up. She gave us so much happiness. Lloyd got a raise from the construction company he worked for. He said it was time for another child. We had always talked about having two or even three. We started trying, and he began the addition. We had proved *everyone wrong about getting married so young, that is, until the accident. How do other parents who lose children get through it?*

In the first days, I let Lloyd hold me. I'm not sure at what point I turned away. I shouldn't have.

This is all I can write today. My heart is not in it. We have a counseling session tomorrow. Maybe I will force myself to say something. I think, soon, Dr. Asher might refuse to help us if we don't help ourselves.

"This is like reading a melancholy novel. No wonder Ola had no novels on her bookshelves. Her life *was* one," Luce said, reaching for more tissues from her purse.

As Ethel and Luce progressed through the first journal, they found the entries to be a mix. Ola went back and forth; some days, she wrote only positive things about Amelia, and on others, she wrote about her grief. She suddenly remembered something Ola had said during a conversation. If she recalled correctly, it was during the first year she met Ola. That would have been in 2001. Ethel was complaining about how perfect Christine was. Ola looked at her. Her entire body appeared to be on fire. Flames shot from her eyes. "Better a perfect child than no child." What Ethel thought she meant at the time wasn't what she meant at all.

Amelia, it seemed, had a stubborn streak. Ola, who she no doubt took it after, found no fault in that trait. What mother could find any fault in their dead child? How could Ethel find any real fault with Christine? Or Luce with her boys. A chill went through her, realizing how lucky she was.

"Do you think it's getting chilly in here?" Ethel asked Luce.

"A little."

"We could build a fire."

"Do you think it will be okay?" Luce asked.

"It appears as if Ola was using it last winter. I'm sure it will be fine."

After placing some dried-out logs on top of the grate, Ethel lit a match. It took several attempts before a fire took hold.

"That's better," Luce said.

Ethel's phone buzzed. It was Christine.

"Mom?"

"Hi, Christine. Are you okay?"

"Yes, fine. Is everything okay with you?"

"Yes... Well, not really. Luce and I are still at Ola's cottage. We're reading some of her journals and going through some of her things."

"Depressing, huh?"

"Yes."

"I wanted to check on you. Dad said you weren't home yet. I told him I would call."

Ethel smiled. She looked at Luce and said to Christine, "We'll be home by dinner."

Luce nodded.

"Okay, Mom, I love you. Talk to you later."

"I love you, too." Ethel pressed end call.

"Is Christine okay?" Luce asked.

"Yes, she was just checking on us."

"Is she at the bookstore?"

"Yes."

"Still liking it?"

"Yeah, she said she helped a pregnant mom yesterday who already had a bookcase for the nursery and was looking for some starter books, pop-ups, and other simple ones."

"Did you tell Christine Ola had a child?"

Ethel shook her head.

"Considering she's pregnant, I think that was wise, but you must tell her at some point."

"I'll ask Raja what he thinks."

"That sounds like a good idea."

Ethel got up, placed another log on the fire, and opened journal number two.

> April 30, 1989
>
> I have avoided writing about Lloyd. He stopped seeing the counselor. There is this wall between us, and I'll admit I put it there.
>
> I asked him what he was going to do about the addition.
>
> "What would you have me do?" he yelled.
>
> I honestly thought for a moment he might strike me. I've never seen him like this—so angry. He was always such a kind man. Amelia's death has changed us both. I wonder how he sees me now.
>
> If only we could go back in time and change everything. I keep watching movies about time travel. I'm fixated on it. Also, parallel universes. Is my Amelia alive in another universe? Are we one happy family where none of this happened?
>
> Somewhere in Time is my favorite. Lloyd and I once loved each other like that.
>
> The other day, he asked if we might start again. I asked him what he meant, and he said we could still have another baby.
>
> It shocked me that he would say such a thing. I said, "No, Lloyd. How could we?"

"It wouldn't be disrespectful to her memory," he said.

Ethel and Luce stopped for lunch before continuing. By mid-afternoon, they had reached the fourth journal. It began in January 1990. Things had only worsened between Ola and Lloyd, and he was drinking heavily. They had both stopped the couples' counseling sessions. However, Ola had begun attending group sessions.

Ethel yawned. There were no more logs by the hearth, and the fire had died out over an hour ago. "What do you say we give this a rest for the day? It's all too depressing."

"I agree," Luce said. "I need to go pick up the boys from school soon."

After making sure the fire was completely out, they locked up.

CHAPTER 32

Mid-September 2018

After dropping Luce off, Ethel thought about picking up Indian food for dinner. Neither Raja nor Christine had eaten Indian food since being back. Before Raja returned to India, he had insisted on his native food almost daily, even if it was only a cup of chai. Being emotionally drained, Ethel opted for easy, calling in an order at the Chinese restaurant on the way home from Ola's house.

Raja had changed after returning from India. The changes were subtle. There were his eating habits. He was much more willing to try new things. The tenseness she remembered was absent. Even she had mellowed. Both Raja and Christine remarked on it. Perhaps they had both come to terms with retirement and were soon to be grandparents.

"You glow, Ethel," Rhonda said.

"Pregnant women glow, not the mother of pregnant women, Rhonda," Ethel said.

"I find Rhonda perfectly delightful. I don't know what you ever saw wrong with that woman," Raja said.

"I don't know either. Maybe I've matured."

"We both have," he said.

Since Raja had returned, their lovemaking had taken on a different aspect, perhaps something couples often find in advancing years—it was more tender and accepting.

"I've put on so much weight since you left," Ethel said while holding her towel up against her body in embarrassment after getting out of the shower while Raja stood unabashedly naked.

"Do you not see this bulge in my middle? Someone might think *I'm* pregnant, along with my daughter," Raja replied while pinching the flab between his fingers.

It was like getting to know each other all over again. Physically, they settled into each other's new hills and valleys. Emotionally, they offered advice and comfort.

"So much more convenient for you, my breasts being nearer to my vagina than when you left," Ethel joked.

Their pillow talk was essentially gossip. Ethel told Raja about Rhonda washing her delicates at the laundromat. He filled her in on which professors were sleeping with each other at the university. He hadn't started teaching online but was meeting weekly with the department in preparation. One of the assistant professors in his department was aware of everything that was going on behind the scenes, although most of them did little to hide it.

Ethel's orgasms were loud, to the point Raja often covered her mouth for fear Christine would hear. For this reason, they had taken to afternoon sex when Christine was at the bookstore. "Retirement isn't so bad," Raja had remarked.

Orgasms had become a drug to release the pent-up frustration because of all the changes over the summer. Raja told her he would happily accommodate any time she needed a release. Is this what three years' absence of sex did to a couple? More like six since it had dried up long before Raja left for India.

Ethel waited several days before returning to Ola's. Even though the house was now hers, she couldn't help but still think of it as Ola's. It was now in her name, and the car was in Christine's. Raja insisted on a thorough tune-up before letting his daughter drive it.

Ethel pulled into the long driveway. Luce told her she might join her later, but the boys all had different places to go, since it was Saturday, so she doubted it. "Call me later and give me the CliffsNotes version."

It was Luce's way of begging off. Ethel couldn't blame her. Who needed all of this surrealism in their life?

All the utilities were back on, and even though she brought cleaning supplies, it wasn't cleaning that was on her mind, but rather the journals. It was like she started a marathon at the beginning of June—a marathon of obstacles —and she was only at the halfway point. It was something she had to finish. Only then could she make sound decisions about the house and the rest of her life.

Ethel exited her car, leaving the cleaning supplies in the back seat. She opened the door, flipped the light switch, and smiled.

Going directly to the kitchen, she opened the cabinet door cautiously to give any rodents proper warning, pulled out a cup and saucer, retrieved the dish soap under the sink, and washed them. She filled the teakettle with water, set it atop the stove, and turned on the gas burner. It hissed for a moment before the flame appeared. She looked through the cupboards until she found a box of teabags, an Egyptian licorice blend. Filling the sink with sudsy water, she saturated a dishtowel and cleaned the countertop until the water came to a boil. Taking her teacup to Ola's desk, she began reading where she and Luce had left off.

Her concentration waned with the growls coming from her stomach. She reached for her phone. It was one o'clock. She had become so absorbed in Ola's life. It was like reading a novel. The main character was someone she didn't know.

She picked up her phone from the desk and called the same Chinese restaurant she had ordered takeout from the previous week, as it was the nearest option.

"Do you deliver?" she asked.

"Oh, Mrs. Sisko's house?" the voice on the other end said in broken English.

"Yes, Mrs. Sisko's house."

"Sure, but there will be a five-dollar delivery fee."

"That's fine."

She could either clean or continue to read until they delivered the food. Ethel opted for reading. She was only a fourth of the way through the journals.

She was on the fifth journal when the doorbell rang. The tantalizing aroma of the vegetable fried rice and spring rolls hit her with welcome relief. She tipped the delivery boy eight dollars, all the bills except for the twenty remaining in her wallet. He looked at her in surprise.

"Anyone who delivers up this driveway deserves it."

She poured freshly boiled water over the same tea bag and returned to Ola's desk. Ravenous, she tore open the duck sauce and poured it lavishly over the two spring rolls. After unwrapping the chopsticks, she opened the fried rice container and ate mindlessly while her eyes rapidly stalked Ola's past.

After scraping the container for the last bite of rice, she rose from her seat to return to the kitchen for more hot water and a fresh tea bag, but Cornelius's name caught her eye, or rather, Detective White's. She remembered Luce telling her Cornelius had met Ola while he was a detective on the case. The date of the entry was December 17, 1990.

I was having a terrible day, more so than usual. I was on the couch watching It's a Wonderful Life when there was a knock at the door. It's so rare for anyone to come up this secluded road. I was both startled and scared. I was in sweats, thank goodness. So many days, I never bother shedding my pajamas. Still, I pulled the blanket over my head and hoped it was only Jehovah's Witnesses. Our long driveway never deterred them. After a time, they would leave their pamphlet by the door and depart. A second knock. From the couch, I squinted my eyes and focused on the slit through the curtains. I should have been able to see a car in the driveway, but there was none. I had Lloyd park mine in the garage to keep it hidden from view, hoping they would think no one was at home if someone did come by. I prayed that whoever it was would go away. I was not up to facing anyone today. I remembered the television. Whoever it is, they must be able to hear it.

Usually, I would have been able to hear a car engine, but it had rained the previous two days, and our driveway was a mess. Even Lloyd had taken to parking halfway down the road to avoid some of the bigger mud holes near the house. I thought whoever was outside must have seen the ruts to the side of the road and parked there as well.

I willed myself up. I tiptoed over to the closed drapes and inched the side back enough to see that it was Detective White. I could only think, what on earth, and why is he here after all this time?

Could he have something new concerning Amelia's death? Almost two years later? Chills coursed through my body, and I wished Lloyd were here.

Another knock. This time, even harder. I knew there was no way I could pretend I wasn't home. Did he have news? Some recent development to report? I didn't know if I could face it alone.

I ran my fingers through my hair, attempting to look halfway decent, and answered the door.

"Detective White," I said. He appeared embarrassed.

"Mrs. Sisko, please forgive the intrusion. I promise you I'm safe." He held a book to his side.

Wet pellets of snow fell. I stared at the snowflakes falling on his black woolen coat. I watched long enough to see at least twenty or more melt as they came into contact with the fabric.

"Mrs. Sisko, are you okay?"

"Yes, I'm fine."

"May I come in? If not, I understand. I

brought you something. A book I thought might help. I can leave it here with you." He held it toward me.

I hesitated for an instant, but he came across so gently. "No, please come in," I said. I don't know what possessed me to do it. I think I saw something in his eyes. There was a pain I recognized. It was only a flicker. I can't say for sure.

I reasoned that if he wanted to harm me, there would have been nothing I could do about it, being so far off the road and having no neighbors who could hear me call out. All those times that I had wished I were dead, and now, I was scared for my life.

He looked over at the television.

"It's a Wonderful Life is one of my favorites. Christmas is tough," he said.

"Yes, maybe the hardest, except the anniversary of Amelia's death," I replied.

I didn't turn the television off, but reached for the control and muted the volume. Something about Jimmy Stewart and Donna Reed in the background reassured me.

"I don't understand. Why are you here? Did you find out something about the accident after all this time?"

He held his head down, then, as he lifted it back up, he extended his hand, which still held the book. "I brought you this. Have you heard of Edgar Cayce?"

"No," I said while taking the book and looking at its cover.

"He's known as the sleeping prophet. He writes a lot about reincarnation."

"Could I get you some tea or coffee? I think we have some. I depend on Lloyd to do all the shopping these days."

"Tea would be nice if you have it."

"Please have a seat," I told him.

I found some tea bags and got cups down from the cupboard. While waiting for the water to boil, I looked around the corner to see him still sitting in the chair, but his eyes wandered around the room. When I returned with the tea, he said, "You don't have bookshelves. Since you're a librarian, I'm surprised."

"You remember that?"

"Yes, I do."

"I'm a librarian, or rather, I was a librarian before all this happened. I always checked them out and returned them. There wasn't much time for reading with Amelia. She took all my time and energy. She was barely eight when she..."

I couldn't say the word. Pain registered across his face. I think it was his empathy that let me know I could trust him.

"We had plenty of children's books, though. Still do. I haven't been able to give any of her things away. She loved to read, and I loved reading to her."

"Yes, children that age do. When you checked out books for yourself, what did you read?"

"Oh, I guess classics, literary fiction, and a little mystery."

"My tastes run along the line of the metaphysical or esoteric, as well as spiritual, anything that might help me find answers." He looked solemn for a moment. "I guess not what you would expect for someone in police work."

"All occupations came into the library, and their book tastes might surprise you." I took a drink from my cup of tea and then said, "I forgot to ask you if you take sugar or milk. Well, actually, we don't have any milk. Neither Lloyd nor I drinks it, and I'm afraid no one comes by anymore."

"Black is fine," he said, although he had not yet taken a drink.

"And have you found answers?"

He hesitated. "There are times it all seems so clear to me, or at least I have momentary glimpses into peace. I've taken to meditating. It helps a great deal."

I said, "Please, Detective White, drink your tea. It's getting cold."

"Please, call me Cornelius," he said, taking his cup in hand.

After he finished, he said he had to return to work and asked if I would like to discuss the book after I had read it. I told him I wasn't sure, but he gave me his card, wrote his phone number on the *back, and said to call if I felt inclined.*

After he left, I realized some of the emptiness that occupied my days had departed during his brief visit. I watched him walk down the driveway. He left wet footprints in the snow. Even though everything was perfectly innocent, I worried Lloyd might see them and hoped that the snow would continue to fall, hiding the physical evidence of a visitor. I returned to the couch, and instead of watching the rest of the movie, I turned the television off and opened the book.

Ethel read on. Cornelius's visits became weekly, then twice weekly, and sometimes even more frequent. He brought new books, most of which had something to do with the afterlife. Not to arouse Lloyd's curiosity about how she acquired the books since she seldom went out, she hid them under Amelia's bed, along with each completed journal. She sat in Amelia's room for hours. Lloyd labeled it as her private shrine, off-limits to him.

According to what Ethel read in Ola's journals, the meetings were innocent. However, an undertone in her friend's writing gave her a sense that there was more, if not physically, emotionally. Tension was building between them, an underlying current akin to Elizabeth and Mr. Darcy. Although Ethel knew there was more than a platonic relationship, or at least there had been at one time between Ola and Cornelius, she couldn't imagine any deep longing between them. Not love. Ethel had always considered them friends with benefits. And she never would have guessed in a million years the circumstances of how they met until Luce told her about the article she had run across in the library.

Ethel put down the journal and reached for the next one, which began in March 1992. She sifted through the stack, all labeled with dates on the inside cover, to no avail. Odd, did she miss one? Had it somehow gotten lost in the far corner under the bed? She would ask Luce if she remembered one missing. For now, she needed to get home.

CHAPTER 33

Mid-September 2018

Ethel lingered at the window, staring at the sale sign. *Is Cornelius selling the bookstore?* The shock dissipated when she realized it was a sale on books. In all the years Ethel had been coming to the bookstore, she had never known Ola's Wise Old Books to have a sale. She smiled upon hearing the familiar melody from *Somewhere in Time* when she opened the door. Then, she remembered Ola's journal entry and understood why she chose that particular tune.

Instead of finding Cornelius shuffling about, categorizing, and placing books on various shelves, he was busy helping customers. And there were more customers than Ethel had ever seen in the bookstore at one time.

"I'm here to pick Christine up for lunch."

Cornelius nodded and said, "She's in her office."

Her office? It was hard to think of it as anything but Ola's office. She imagined Ola looking out from her open door. *"So glad to see you, Ethel."* That was Christmas past. Instead, she saw her daughter focused on her laptop. This was Christmas present. And it was only September.

Christine lifted her eyes from the computer screen. "Hello,

Mom. I'm just finishing up something before I can leave for lunch—that is, if I *can* leave. We're busier than ever."

"I can see."

The office looked nothing like it had before. The shelf along the three walls surrounding the desk was almost bare and polished to a gleam. An enlarged picture of Ola standing between the paws of the Sphinx, a fitting tribute to the one who occupied this office for so long, hung above the back shelf. A picture of Christine in a lotus pose at the ashram, the same size, with a matching wormwood frame, was on the right-hand wall. A mixture of Ola and Christine permeated the room, giving it an eclectic look. No longer a fire hazard, the electric teapot was visible on a special mat. Ethel gasped to see the red sari with the Egyptian hieroglyphs spread along the left-hand wall. Ethel froze at its magnificence.

"I didn't realize you had even taken the sari from the chair."

"I'm not surprised. You've been so involved with everything—Dad, me, and the cottage."

"Are you ready?"

Christine hit a key on the laptop, closed the lid, and said, "Yes, now I am."

"You're so busy today."

Before Christine could answer, Cornelius came up from behind. "It's your daughter's doing. The sale was her idea." He placed a load of new books on the biography table and was off again.

There had to be at least thirty people in the store, some with books in hand, most taking their sweet time—all but Cornelius, who was running back and forth, looking somewhat frazzled and unkempt. His hair, always neatly combed back, fell to one side. Ethel doubted he had been to a barbershop in months. The once-speckled gray took on a sheen of whiteness like new-fallen snow. Ethel remembered the journal entry about Ola staring at the snow falling on him as he stood in her doorway holding the book. A family parked in front of the check-out counter grew anxious. Cornelius shuffled over as fast as his arthritic legs would allow.

The woman rifled through her purse, looking for her most current Visa card. "This one gives me more points. If you could bear with me," she said to Cornelius. In the meantime, her two unruly boys, who appeared to be two and four years old, grew impatient with their mother and began rolling about on the floor. "Boys, get up," she demanded. They paid no heed. Ethel wondered if Christine's child might turn out like that—the total opposite of his mother. He might take after his father, a man she knew nothing about. Maybe at some point, Christine would open up about him.

"Boys, let me show you something." Christine directed the boys to the children's bookshelf. *No, Christine has a natural talent for motherhood.*

The woman finally produced the card, and Cornelius completed the transaction. The woman gathered her bag and the two boys and disappeared onto the street.

Ethel walked over to the cash register where Cornelius stood. Through the bookstore window, Ethel watched the woman walk down the street with her boys. Upon hearing Cornelius say, "It's been like this all day," Ethel jerked her head toward him.

"Yes, Mom, it has," Christine said, making her way to the front of the store. "I think we should order something and eat it here if it's okay with you. I don't want to leave Cornelius in a bind."

She was about to agree when a woman who had just entered the shop rushed to the counter.

"I'm looking for a particular book. I know it's a bestseller, but I can't think of the name. Something about a swamp."

Cornelius stumbled.

"I believe it has water on the cover. Well, maybe. I'm not sure."

"Might it be *Where the Crawdads Sing*?" Ethel asked, stepping almost between the woman and Cornelius.

"Why yes, that's the title."

Ethel reached for a book prominently displayed on the first shelf, directly under the BEST SELLERS signage, and handed it to the lady. If only the woman had looked right in front of her, Ethel thought.

"Is it any good?" the woman asked, examining the cover.

Ethel caught herself raising her eyebrow in disbelief. At mid-rise, she forced a smile. "I thoroughly enjoyed it." Ethel hadn't read it yet, but had planned to before everything in her world started crumbling.

"It's excellent. It's set in North Carolina," Christine added.

"Yes, my cousin is from there. She's the one who recommended it. And it's on sale?" Ethel looked at both Cornelius and Christine.

"All books are thirty percent off today only," Christine said.

"I'll take it, then."

"You know, you might also enjoy this book." Ethel picked one up from the local author table beside the best-seller section because Ola didn't believe in relegating local talent to the back. It also has water on the cover and is set in the swamplands of Louisiana."

The woman perused the cover, unsure. "Have you read it?" She looked up at Ethel. Most women looked up, considering Ethel's tall frame.

"Yes, it's a real page-turner." This time, she didn't lie. She *had* read it.

"Is it on sale?"

"All books except the rare edition section are on sale. Today only," Christine repeated.

"Okay, sold." She placed the two books on the counter, where Cornelius took over.

"You two go on. I can handle this."

"Well, only for thirty minutes, tops. We'll go to the cafe down the street and grab something," Christine said.

Cornelius looked relieved, even though the crowd had thinned when Ethel and Christine returned earlier than expected.

"I'll stay and help," Ethel said.

The three made sounds similar to orgasmic relief as Cornelius hung the CLOSED sign in the window.

"I need to get some things out of the office before leaving, Mom. Just a moment, and I'll follow you home."

Ethel watched as her daughter waddled back to her office, carrying the additional person she was now expecting.

"I think if you have any more sales, you may have to hire someone other than Christine, especially when she has the baby."

"It has crossed my mind. Several times, but I don't know."

Crow's feet surrounded the lingering sadness in Cornelius's eyes.

"Ola would want you to, you know. You'll run yourself ragged trying to manage this all by yourself when Christine takes time off."

"It's hard, Ethel. Your daughter has progressive ideas. When it was just Ola and me running everything, we kept things quiet. I can't even imagine training someone."

"Christine could teach them, couldn't she?"

"Yes, she's proven to be quite capable, but I don't know if we could afford anyone else at the moment. I'm sure they would be young. How many young people would appreciate the rare volumes we carry? And when would I find time to do interviews? No, no, too time-consuming." He shook his head.

"What about me?"

"You?"

"Yes, I've helped you and Ola out when things were hectic. I can certainly talk up a book. Having taught school, I've read and can recommend children's books. You need to carry more children's books, you know. A large dedicated children's section would be a good idea."

"Yes, your daughter has already brought that up."

"I'm only talking about replacing Christine while she's off, and only part-time. I want to spend as much time as possible with my grandson."

"Of course you do. Ethel, you're a godsend."

"Not every day, mind you."

"Agreed. You can even set your hours."

"Well, then it's settled," she said.

"No, not yet. We should seal the deal over dinner."

"Dinner?" Surely, Cornelius wasn't asking her out on a date. He knew Raja was back. She put her hand to her face, something absent-minded on her part. Was she blushing? Don't be absurd, she told herself. It's purely professional. He probably only wanted her advice about the bookstore or to tie up some loose ends regarding Ola's estate.

"There's a nice little Mediterranean restaurant up the street if that's okay with you. We can walk if Christine is up to it. Call Raja and ask him to join us."

"Oh," Ethel said. Jumping to conclusions again, she could hear Luce saying. She hoped she wasn't blushing. Cornelius was lonely. That was all.

"Sounds good," she said, regaining her composure. "We can talk about my responsibilities over some hummus and fattoush."

Christine appeared. "What's going on?"

"Cornelius has invited you, me, and your father to dinner. I'll text him and tell him to meet us at the restaurant."

Cornelius removed the cash from the drawer, placed it in a zip-up pouch, and said, "The bank's on the way. I'll drop this off." They grabbed their jackets. Cornelius locked up, and they walked down the street together.

"There will be four of us. We're waiting for someone else to arrive," Cornelius told the host.

"Would you like some wine, Ethel?" Cornelius asked as the server poured four glasses of water.

"Oh, no. Water will be just fine," she said.

"If you don't mind, I believe I'll have some," Cornelius said.

"No, not at all," she said. She had never known Cornelius to drink.

"Your house red will be fine," Cornelius said.

"Are you sure you want to give up your freedom?" he asked as he perused the menu.

"Freedom? With everything going on, I haven't had time to sit down and think about the luxury of freedom."

"Yes, I know what you mean," he said with the sad look that had dominated his face since Ola's passing. "I find myself in some vacuum. I walk through the bookstore's aisles, and it seems like some echo of the past without her presence. Oh, there were days when we went about our business, Ola in her office, me minding the front, without speaking so much as a few sentences to each other, except during lunch break. But I had the comfort of knowing she was there. Seeing her engrossed in some new find when I passed the doorway greatly pleased me. She was a librarian, you know, before the bookstore. Still, she had never even explored the realm of reading anything of a metaphysical or esoteric nature until I brought it up to her."

"Oh?" Ethel did her best to act surprised. Maybe Cornelius didn't know about the journals. What would he think of her if he knew she had been snooping into Ola's personal life, both of their private lives?

The server returned with the wine.

"Do you think Raja will want some when he arrives?"

"Possibly, I don't know."

"We'll just take the bottle, in case," he told the server.

Cornelius was already halfway through the bottle when Raja arrived.

"Wine, Raja?" Cornelius asked, holding up the bottle, ready to pour.

"No, none for me," he said, holding his hand up.

The server came back to the table. "Are you ready to order?" he asked.

"Hummus, pita bread, and a fattoush," Ethel said, handing him the menu.

"I'll have the same," Christine said.

"You, Raja?" Cornelius asked.

"Moussaka, please," Raja said, handing the server his menu.

"Kafta Kabob, and please bring me the check," Cornelius said.

"No, Cornelius, that isn't necessary," Raja said.

"I insist. It was a good day at the bookstore."

Ethel couldn't help but stare at Cornelius. There was something different about him. He still looked haggard from everything he had endured over the last few months, but his spirits seemed to be lifting. And to treat the three of them to dinner? She had never known him to be so extravagant.

"Excellent choice," the server said before turning and walking away.

"I don't know how they do it," Raja said.

"Do what?" Cornelius asked.

"Remember what everyone orders. They no longer use pads to write down orders. It's as if writing it down would imply the restaurant was of some lesser quality, merely a diner of some sort, the kind you see in movies—the kind you want to step into because they look so cozy. There are only booths or bar stools, and the food is simple. It's breakfast with sunny-side-up eggs, bacon, and toast, or hamburgers and fries, accompanied by apple pie for dessert. One wouldn't even need to record such simple choices, yet they do. Here, there are multiple menu pages to choose from, and the servers take great pride in remembering everything everyone orders, even for large parties, as if it were a final exam. Our order was simple. Still, I would forget before I got back to the kitchen."

"I guess I had never really thought of it," Cornelius said.

"And why do they say excellent choice?" Ethel asked. It implies that the other items on the menu are not up to snuff."

Cornelius laughed. "Something I would expect Luce to say," he said.

"Luce doesn't have the ownership of witticisms. Raja thinks I'm rather quick-witted."

Raja smiled and placed his hand over Ethel's.

"Oh, Mom, that boy, Sam, came to the bookstore before I left for my doctor's appointment this morning."

"He did?"

"Yes."

"Did he remember you?"

"From the restaurant? Yes, but also from school. Everyone I went to school with remembers me."

"But you're a couple of years older."

"Still, I'm Mrs. Sharma's daughter. That's how they see me."

The food arrived.

"Looks good," Raja said.

"Thank you," Cornelius told the server. He turned to Ethel. "Have you decided what you will do with Ola's house?"

"No, not yet." She looked at Raja.

"It would make an ideal home for a family. Has a great backyard. I thought the three of you, soon to be four, might move in."

"Raja hasn't even seen it yet."

"I haven't either," Christine said. "Funny how I practically grew up in the bookstore and thought of Ola as an aunt, Luce too, and yet we always went to Luce's house but never Ola's."

Ethel cleared her throat and took a drink of water.

"Sam said he remembered seeing me in the bookstore when we were young."

"Oh? Do you remember him?"

"I paid little attention. I guess because he was younger."

"You should take Raja and Christine to see the house. It's beautiful when the leaves turn. A pleasant contrast with all the evergreen trees," Cornelius said, changing the conversation back to Ola's house.

"Yes, it sits in its own private forest," Ethel said. "But I don't know. I had hoped to get it cleaned up a little first."

"I don't think how clean it is matters. Maybe you, Christine, and I can see it together on Sunday, Christine's day off," Raja said.

What was Raja thinking? He knew about Ola's child and that she was reading the journals. He even knew she had gotten to the part where Cornelius came into the picture. Ethel looked at her husband in disbelief. Last night, Raja repeated what he had said the one time Ola and Cornelius came to their house for dinner, about their strange relationship and his suspicion that Cornelius was hiding something. It was before having sex. Gossip seemed to turn her husband on.

When Ethel texted Raja to see if he wanted to join them for dinner, she expected him to beg off, but he was eager to come. She realized he was studying Cornelius. Luce always said men were more interested in gossip than women. And encouraging the three of them to go out to the house this weekend? Did he want Christine to see Amelia's room? Raja was playing along with Cornelius, trying to trip him up. It wouldn't be hard. He had consumed all but a drop of the bottle of wine.

"What will you do with Ola's furniture?" he asked.

"I don't know. I haven't given it much thought."

"You could sell it, give it to Goodwill. You should keep the desk," he said.

"Yes, I love the desk."

"Ethel told me about the desk. Mahogany? Right, dear?" Raja asked.

"Yes."

"I always loved the big picture window that looked out over the backyard. Yes, very nice for a little girl, I mean, boy," he said, looking at Christine. "The desk, and where it sits, in front of the window. I can see it as the perfect spot for writing. You can finish that book you started."

"You started a book, Ethel? You never told me about that," Raja said.

"What's this book about, Mom?"

Feeling ganged up on, Ethel said, "It's about nothing."

"Oh, come on. *Seinfeld* is about nothing," Raja said.

"I only wrote one chapter. I don't even remember now. I might have thrown it away."

"A shame," Raja said. "I would love to have read what you wrote."

"Peace and quiet. Yes, Ola's cottage, I mean *your* cottage, is tucked just enough away from the main thoroughfare to give you solitude. The perfect place to write a book." Cornelius was babbling. So unlike him. "Yes, when you're settled. Or maybe you can convert the child's room to an office." He took a sip of water.

"Child's room?" Christine put the fork full of fattoush, almost up to her mouth, back down on her plate.

Cornelius didn't give Ethel a chance to say anything, not that she knew what to say.

"Ola felt bad that she never confided in you about losing her child. She never could bear to change the room. She left it as a shrine to Amelia. When she told me she wanted you to have the cottage, I asked her if she wanted me to give the room a makeover, remove Amelia's things, and give them to a charity, but she said, 'No, Ethel will know what to do with them.' I suppose leaving everything intact was her way of letting you know she regretted not telling you."

He paused. Ethel, Raja, and Christine sat flabbergasted. Cornelius was tipsy, if not drunk.

Why had he invited the three of them to dinner? To talk? Some type of closure? A crowded restaurant was no place for such complexities of life. Maybe, as far as Cornelius was concerned, it provided a protection of sorts.

"Amelia was almost eight when it happened. Her father was driving. It wasn't his fault, but Amelia's death destroyed both of them. It caused a rift in their marriage that couldn't be repaired."

"And you came along?" Ethel said.

"Yes, I came along." He took a bite of the food he had hardly touched. "You shouldn't wait to move. Moving in the winter is not advisable. It would be much easier now before Christine has the baby." Cornelius poured the remaining wine into his glass and raised it. "To new beginnings for all of us."

The three of them looked at each other, astounded. Time

froze as he held his wine goblet in the air. Raja made the first move, holding his water up. "Agreed," he said. Ethel and Christine followed suit.

Abruptly, he called the server and asked for the check. He paid and said, "I believe I'll walk back home. It's been a long day. You three stay. Finish your meal." Cornelius's meal had barely been touched.

The three watched as he teetered toward the coat rack, retrieved his coat, and walked out the door.

"At least he took the right coat," Raja said.

Christine laughed. "I'm sorry. I couldn't help it."

"It was as if he were deciding our lives for us," Ethel said.

"I want to see the cottage," Christine said.

CHAPTER 34

Mid-Late September 2018

Compelled to learn as much as she could before visiting the cottage together on Sunday, Ethel took the opportunity to drive back while Christine was at work.

She shed her coat and purse on the red leather couch, went straightaway to the kitchen, and put the water kettle on the stove to boil. She was learning her way around Ola's kitchen while envisioning how to make it look like Rhonda's.

She took her saucer and cup of tea, set them on a coaster on the mahogany desk, pushed the journals she had already read off to the side, and picked up the next journal from the declining stack of unread ones.

March 31, 1992
Lloyd is drinking more. We rarely ever keep wine in the house, just on special occasions, but the other day, I found three bottles of hard liquor in the top corner of the cupboard. Being so short, he thought I wouldn't see them.

On some days, I blame myself. I am confident he knows nothing about Cornelius's visits. His drinking started before Cornelius began coming around.

I pushed Lloyd away. Our counselor warned us of many scenarios with couples after the death of a child. It was a myth that most marriages end in divorce. She said the death of a child instead polarizes the existing factors in the marriage. A marriage could get worse, better, or end in divorce. Some couples go along as before. It depended on the couple's coping mechanisms. My coping mechanism must be non-existent.

She said our marriage would have the same valleys and peaks as other marriages, just that in cases where a couple has lost a child, those valleys and peaks are more exaggerated. 'But be assured, no matter what happens, your marriage will never be the same.' When she said that, I asked about the couples who kept going as before. But I didn't wait for her answer. I demanded to know how anyone could keep going on. I guess I lost it. I remember Lloyd telling me to calm down, at which point I turned on him and asked him how he could ask me to calm down.

Doctor Asher gave me a sedative and had me lie on the couch before we left. Lloyd said nothing on the drive home.

We might have made it work if we had kept attending the sessions. I'm the one who wanted to quit. But then Lloyd didn't encourage me to keep going.

Amelia's death ripped us apart. I know marriages change over time, but the death of a child is not supposed to be one of them.

From the moment I became pregnant, everything changed. The marriage was no longer two but three. Amelia became the glue that held us together. Things would have been radically different if we hadn't had a child. Not knowing what it's like, many couples are complete with just two. But a child, or children, changes lives. We lost both our future and posterity when Amelia died.

I feel so isolated. I know Lloyd does, too. He quit reaching out to me. He only reaches for the bottle now. If I were to reach out to him, he might stop drinking. As hard as I try, I can't.

I say I don't leave the house, but that's not entirely true. I visit her grave once a week and place yellow roses on it. Yellow was Amelia's favorite color. Cornelius took me last week and the week before that. I think this will become a ritual for us.

I remember when my parents died. I thought of my mother daily, but those thoughts faded with marriage. I wish that my parents could have met Lloyd. When I got pregnant, I missed my mom more than ever. When Amelia was born, I wondered if my mom was looking down on us. I even wondered if Amelia might be my mother's reincarnation. She had my mother's blue eyes. I had given little thought to reincarnation until then. I think of it a lot, especially since I met Cornelius.

Lloyd also has blue eyes, but not the same shade of blue. My mother's eyes were distinct, a cerulean blue, while Lloyd's eyes border on navy.

We expect our parents to die. Not early, but at some point during our adult life. We even expect a spouse to die. But not our children.

I wonder what Amelia would look like now. She would be twelve, and I imagine she would be thinking of boys. I miss the small things that transpire between a mother and a daughter, such as picking out that first dress for a school dance or getting her a pet. We had planned to get her a puppy for her next birthday. Brandi, our black lab, died of old age while I was still pregnant with Amelia.

In the group sessions, the leader stated that females tend to grieve more deeply and intensely, and for longer periods. She said that mothers are usually involved in their children's daily activities, while fathers tend to have a more passive role.

Amelia used to spell words with the letters of Alphabet cereal. She floated the words like boats in the middle of the milk. I used a cookie cutter for her peanut butter and jelly sandwiches. She detested the crust and would cross her arms and pout in protest if I asked her to eat it. She pretended to feed the food to her Cabbage Patch doll, who sat at the table with her when she ate. I miss all the things I won't experience with her, even the fights I knew would happen in mother-and-daughter relationships when she reached puberty.

I'm tempted to have a glass of that bourbon I found in the cupboard, but I know it's not the answer.

Ethel read much of the same in the following entries.

April 3, 1992

Lloyd doesn't cry. Last Tuesday, both Cornelius and I cried. He held me. Lloyd has stopped trying. I recall the counselor saying that males tend to focus more on tasks than relationships. Being defined by their work, their grief is far more inward.

Sometimes, I suspect Lloyd expects me to suffer for both of us. No, no, how can I say that? I found more booze in the upper cabinet. I believe he knows I know. Neither of us brings it up.

I have rarely seen him noticeably drunk until the other night. He tried grabbing me. It's been over four years since we've had sex. I know it is just a matter of time before he finds it elsewhere. Lloyd always had a powerful sex drive. It's just every time I look at him, I see Amelia.

With Cornelius, sex is for comfort. I don't see our child. With Lloyd, all I can see is Amelia. I should get it over with and ask for a divorce. I believe he would be happier.

Cornelius has been looking over papers for me.

He said Lloyd's insurance is good, and I need not worry financially if anything were to happen to him. At first, I thought nothing of it. I thought he meant because Lloyd drinks. An alcoholic's life is precarious. All sorts of things flittered through my mind after Cornelius left. Amelia left my mind for a brief period. Cornelius is such a kind-hearted man. I don't know how I could think such thoughts.

May 2, 1992

Lloyd came home the other day in such a good mood. I accused him of being over Amelia's death. His mood changed instantly. I thought he was going to hit me. It's not the first time I've thought that.

The counselor told us that grief in males declines more rapidly than in females. Grief in females after the death of a child tends to be particularly intense for about two years after the child's death, but mine is still going on just as fervently after four years. She also said that while a husband's grief decreased, the wife's might increase or remain constant. She said it was a normal phenomenon.

I resent Lloyd for this. He doesn't understand why I can't even try to resume a normal life. Cornelius understands. Lloyd says I overreact. He says our grocery bill consists mainly of Kleenex.

"I have to deal with reality every day, Ola. Do you think I want to? But one of us has to. There are still bills to pay. What good does reflecting on

Amelia's death every moment of the day do for you? You are old before your time. Do you think this is what Amelia would want?"

He walked around, waving his arms in the air. He said, "I'm going out." I knew he was going to a bar.

After he slammed the door behind him, it hit me that, as bad as things were, things could get even more so. I wasn't sure if Lloyd's drinking was affecting his performance at work. I never brought his drinking up. It was one more thing I couldn't deal with. But what if he lost his job? I have shut myself up in this house for so long. What if we lost the house? Where would we go? How would we live? I know I'm being selfish. Lloyd provides for me while I waste my life grieving, not being a proper wife to him, while I'm having sex with another man.

I know Cornelius feels the guilt as much as I do.

May 29, 1992
Lloyd packed his bags. He's gone. He is leaving it up to me to file for divorce. He has someone else, someone who works in his office. I don't blame her. I'm not jealous. I blame myself.

I wanted to tell Lloyd about Cornelius, but couldn't bring myself to. I'm not sure how he would have taken it. I only told him I was glad for him. He said that maybe we both could move on. I said, "I hope so."

    Lloyd walked out the door. When that door closed, I was tempted to run after him, but I stood paralyzed. I stood there, watching the door for, I don't know how long. All the memories came flooding back: our first date, our falling in love, our wedding, my becoming pregnant. It was another world, vastly different from the one we know now.

    I know Lloyd was grieving in his way. The few times we were out together in the beginning, mostly taking care of arrangements and the burial plot, people would ask how I was doing. No one ever inquired about Lloyd. Why is that?

    Maybe Lloyd saw his grief as less important. I can't blame him for leaving. I'm sure he felt helpless in so many ways. He failed to protect his child and me.

    The counselor gave us a profile of a grieving couple. She said there were four major issues. The first is sexual problems. The second is emotional distance. The third is conflict or fighting. The fourth is that the couple needs to establish a new marital foundation, one that is not centered on their child.

    She also said grieving is like labor, yet one that bears no fruit.

Ethel kept reading and found it was Cornelius who found Ola a lawyer so she could file for divorce. He handled all the details that Ola couldn't cope with. The house was now in her name. Lloyd even paid it off. He contested nothing. Lloyd was a good man. His life had been four years of misery. They were both hurting, and in the process, hurting each other.

> *June 20, 1992*
> *Cornelius came by. It's strange for him to come by on a Saturday. He had some good news he wanted to tell me.*
>
> *"I've rented a building downtown and plan to open a bookstore. How does the name Ola's Wise Old Books sound?"*
>
> *I think it was one of the few times I smiled in months.*
>
> *"We will both run it. I will own it, but it will bear your name."*
>
> *I asked him if he could afford it on his salary. He said he and his ex-wife profited from selling their house, enough for a hefty down payment.*
>
> *A bookstore has always been Cornelius's dream. I'm thrilled he wants me to be a part of it, and the name—well, I can't believe it. This, at least, gives me some purpose.*
>
> *He says we can do much of the work ourselves, such as painting and arranging the placement of the bookshelves. There is only one office, and he wants me to have it.*

It was the last journal in the pile.

Ethel called Luce to tell her what had transpired over the last few days and told her not to worry about helping her with the cleaning. "Raja is bringing lunch and plans to help me."

It was hard gauging Luce's reaction over the phone, but

Ethel imagined her sitting there with her earbuds, mouth open.

"We will talk in person after Christine looks at the cottage. I want to know what she thinks." Ethel hit end call, took her saucer and teacup back to the kitchen, left them in the sink, grabbed her coat and purse, and drove home.

CHAPTER 35

1988

It had been raining, which was not unusual for Seattle. He had fought with his wife, also not unusual. Storming out of the house, he headed for the nearest bar. Again, not uncommon. His drinking was out of control, the principal reason for their fights, along with the long hours he put in at work.

He should have called his wife to come and pick him up. Everything was a blur. He bumped into someone on his way out. A fistfight could have quickly ensued, but the man glimpsed his badge and backed off. He didn't know how he had even managed to start his car and drive it out of the parking lot.

The rain had started up again. He had taken a wrong turn. He realized it, and at the same time, it registered that he was driving on the wrong side of the road. Headlights came up suddenly, and both he and the other car swerved. He thought he heard something—a loud bang, but he shrugged it off and kept driving.

The following day, he woke with a throbbing headache.

He looked over to see that his wife's side of the bed was empty.

"I was getting ready to wake you, but I thought it might be better to let you sleep. Rough night?" She said it with a scowl when he walked into the kitchen, still in his pajamas. He didn't even remember undressing last night and putting them on.

Nancy was wearing moderate pumps, and her navy pantsuit, the jacket covering a white camisole. His wife always dressed immaculately, even though her job didn't require it most days. She was in the tech industry, and as far as dress codes went, almost anything was acceptable. However, since she met clients, she had come to prefer a more professional appearance. He also loved to dress well, one of the things that attracted her to him. It hadn't been a cop's salary. She made triple what he did.

She stood by the back door, collecting items into her matching navy purse. It had been her routine since landing her promotion. She looked up only long enough to say, "I went to the store yesterday, and there are some bagels in the bread box and cream cheese in the refrigerator."

He followed her to the door, wanting to grab her, but his reaction was slow. She walked out the door, leaving a trace of perfume in her wake. The fragrance he once loved invaded his sinuses, intensifying his headache. It was some primal desperation. He wanted her arms around him, offering an embrace that provided security from the world outside. He couldn't bring himself to call out for her. Fear of rejection. They had stopped kissing each other before leaving for work. He wasn't sure when it happened.

Feeling the urge to throw up, he dismissed the bagel and headed for the bathroom.

He showered, lingering for longer than he should have. He was already late. After getting dressed, he put on his watch, grabbed his wallet and badge from the bureau, and placed them inside his coat pocket. He approached his car with trepidation. He wasn't sure what he might see, but the car was in the exact spot where he always parked it. The next-door neighbor, bending down to get his paper, looked up at him. The headline, DEADLY HIT AND RUN, POLICE DETECTIVE MAIN SUSPECT, flashed through his mind. He waved and did his best to act as if everything were normal while making his way around the vehicle. He saw no dents or scratches. The tires appeared okay. His mind was playing tricks on him.

Despite being late, he drove to work at a snail's pace. The fear of being caught, of the consequences of his actions, was palpable. His mind raced with possible excuses, but the dread of being handcuffed and read his rights loomed large.

There were a few nods when he walked in. This horrible feeling he had—was it written on his face? In his body language? Cops automatically looked at people's posture, mannerisms, and any sign of guilt.

He only imagined that something had happened last night. He grabbed a cup of coffee and sat down at his desk. The headache still had not subsided. He pushed some rare edition books he had found the previous week off to the side of his desk. He had intended to review during his lunch break, which he usually took at his desk. He treated himself on Fridays, getting lunch at a small cafe near his favorite bookstore. His life was predictable. Nancy commented on that. No, she complained about that.

Books were his love. Detective work was in his genes. For as long as he could remember, it had been a given that he'd follow in his father's footsteps and join the police force.

He reached for some aspirin inside his desk drawer, something he knew he shouldn't do on an empty stomach. He would grab a donut in the break room if it weren't too late. If it was, there was always the vending machine. He looked at the wall clock. It was pushing ten. Glazed ones were always the last to go. He wasn't hungry, but he needed something on his stomach. He rose from his chair to head toward the donuts when his boss, Jake, came by.

"Happened sometime between eight and nine last night, as best as we can determine," Jake said while handing him a file. "A vehicle clipped a guardrail. An ambulance took the man to the hospital. Rushed to surgery. Still in recovery. So, can't ask questions yet. His little girl was with him. She died upon impact. The man's wife is at the hospital, too torn up to talk. You can imagine. The only thing we got was that the father was picking her up from some practice. It's too early to tell, but it could have been a hit-and-run. Be prepared when you look at the pictures." Jake sighed. "This kind of thing never gets any easier. Especially when it's a child. Alex was called to the scene, but he left for vacation this morning. I was hoping you would take the case. Probably just driving too fast with the rain and all. There was no sign of impact with another car, no differing paint marks on the auto."

"Sure," Cornelius said. His hands trembled when he took the file.

"You okay, Corn?" He hated the nickname, but everyone in the department called him that.

"Terrible headache. Woke up with it. I just took some aspirin. It'll be okay."

Jake slapped him on the shoulder and walked back to his office.

If his boss suspected a hangover, he didn't let on. A lot of the guys drank. It came with the job, but he never let it interfere with his duties until now.

He heaved a heavy sigh as he opened up the folder. Then he ran to the restroom. Luckily, no one was there. He closed the stall door behind him and threw up what little must have been in his stomach, followed by dry heaves. He flushed the toilet and left the stall.

He splashed cold water on his face and looked into the mirror. The eyes of a raccoon stared back at him. He searched in his pocket for a mint. He popped the only one left into his mouth. After patting his face dry, he walked almost in a daze back to his desk to see a man in dockers and a navy jacket.

"Mr. Cornelius White?"

"Yes," he said with a stutter. This was it. Maybe a witness or a relative. No, couldn't be. He was being paranoid and irrational. But then, he hadn't had a rational thought since last night—only insane, nightmarish ones.

The man handed him an envelope and said, "You've been served." He pivoted around on his leather loafers and headed toward the door.

Cornelius opened it to find divorce papers. *What else could go wrong?*

The thing with Ola started for so many reasons. Number one was guilt. The little girl's funeral was delayed until after the hospital released the father. He went to see the Siskos two days after the funeral, on the same day he had moved out of the house and into a motel, somewhere to stay until he could find a cheap apartment.

"I hope you won't put up a fight," Nancy said when they met for lunch at a restaurant near her work.

The love she once felt for him had been replaced with pity. He was tempted to beg, but he didn't deserve her. He didn't deserve anything or anyone. Whenever he looked at anybody, the picture of the little girl in the pink, blood-spattered ballerina costume popped into his mind.

"Cornelius?"

Had she said his name more than once? It sounded as if it came from another realm.

"No, no fight. You can have everything. I'll pack a few things and move into a motel until I find someplace."

Puzzlement replaced the look of pity. "You're different today."

He looked down at his uneaten sandwich. He wanted to hold her, cry like a baby in her arms. Tell her he would never touch another drop of alcohol, convince her he meant it this time, even go into a different line of work. Instead, he said, "I guess divorce changes a man."

Cornelius knocked on the bright blue door of the cottage. The father answered.

"I'm Detective White. I'm the one assigned to your daughter's case."

"Oh, yes, come in."

Mr. Sisko looked at him with vacant eyes, his arm in a sling.

"Please have a seat." Cornelius looked around, evaluating the surroundings. It was a habit of detectives to take in as much information as possible and sum up the situation, but in this case, these people were innocent victims. His victims. If only he could remember. He chose not to.

The house was in total disarray. On the coffee table was a half-eaten pizza and some red plastic cups, the kind you use at picnics.

"I'm sorry for the mess," Mr. Sisko apologized. "My wife hasn't felt like cooking or eating."

Cornelius looked down. "That's perfectly understandable."

He saw a remembrance card for their daughter lying on

the coffee table. Amelia Sisko. He didn't want to give her a name. He willed his hand not to tremble as he picked it up. A picture of her in a pink ballerina costume was on the cover. "She was exquisite." He saw Amelia was just shy of eight. Her birthday would have been in another month. He read the date of death, August 30, 1988.

It turned out Mr. Sisko couldn't remember what had happened. Not clearly. His head had hit the steering wheel hard. Partial amnesia, the doctor told him. The doctors said his faulty memory could be the trauma of the head injury or not wanting to deal with it, one or both. This man didn't deserve this.

Six weeks went by—six excruciating weeks. Cornelius woke up with dread each morning. He bit his nails, something he had never done. No witnesses had come forward, and still, Mr. Sisko did not remember anything. Each time his phone rang, he took a deep breath before answering. His co-workers noticed a change in him but attributed it to the fact that he was going through a divorce. Divorce would have been nasty enough, but it was nothing like this other weight he carried around. Besides, the last five years of his ten-year marriage had been rocky. Divorce was inevitable.

Janice, the secretary, was always consoling him. "Corn, can I get you something? Why don't you take some time off?"

He might have thought she was making a move if it were anyone else, but Janice wasn't the type. Not to mention, she had one of those storybook marriages, incessantly talking about her husband, Ben, as much as she did their two boys, whose pictures she was always showing off. If Janice knew the actual truth, she would despise him.

So many times, he thought about confessing. More than likely, they would charge him with manslaughter. He guessed second degree, given his experience on the police force and his scrupulously clean record. Not even a ticket. It would mean a ten-year prison sentence and a fine of $20,000.

On the other hand, a jury might convict him of first-degree manslaughter because he was a police officer who failed to come forward and was the very detective assigned to the case. That would mean life imprisonment and a $50,000 fine. And what would Nancy think? And his poor parents? His father retired from the force only last year. It no longer mattered what Nancy thought. But this would kill his parents, especially his father.

He still could only have been imagining it was his fault. There could have been another vehicle. After all, he had drunk a little more than usual, but not that much. Yes, there had to have been another car. It couldn't have been his fault. He drove home okay. He was a cop, not a bad guy. He was the one who caught the bad guys. What was he telling himself?

He was ready to quit detective work. He now had some money put aside. It turned out Nancy didn't want the house. She said they would sell it and split the money down the middle. She felt nothing but pity for him. He saw it in her eyes, the big brown eyes that had first attracted him to her. She thought the change in him was because of the divorce and the affair she was having, something she told him about only after signing the divorce papers.

The house sold within two days of being on the market. Property values had skyrocketed in Seattle since they had purchased it, and there was a high demand for a house like theirs, particularly because of its location.

Cornelius had done nothing but reflect since that night. It wasn't just the long hours and the drinking that killed his marriage to Nancy. It was the disappointment of not having a child. He had a low sperm count, and Nancy had endometriosis. The odds were against them. It didn't help that trying to conceive made sex stressful and often resulted in Cornelius being impotent. He couldn't envision having a child now, not after what he took away from the Siskos.

He hoped Nancy would be happy and have a child with her new lover. He might have been jealous, had it not been for his guilt—the guilt that was consuming him, the guilt over something he couldn't remember, but his gut told him was his fault.

He visited the Siskos several times, giving them updates—no leads, no witnesses. Lloyd was still hazy about that night. He thought he saw another car on the road, but couldn't remember. Cornelius saw what this was doing to their marriage. He knew marital troubles when he saw them, long before his own. The signs were all too obvious in police work.

Lloyd received a clean bill of health and returned to work. The case was officially closed. A year and a half had passed. After one of his many sleepless nights, he went to their house. It was a snowy afternoon nearing Christmas. Mrs. Sisko was taken totally off guard, to the point of fright at seeing him. She was scared to open the door. He saw movement through the slit in the curtains and could hear the television. *It's a Wonderful Life* was playing. He recognized it because he could hear "Hee-Haw" spoken by the character Sam Wainwright. It was the scene where Jimmy Stewart's character first realized he was in love with Donna Reed's character while on the phone.

What was he doing? He almost walked away. The door opened—only a crack.

Cornelius had a stack of books in his car, ones he hadn't yet carried into his new apartment. One was *The Egyptian Book of the Dead,* and the others were about reincarnation based on Edgar Cayce's readings. He figured he had several lives of atoning ahead of him.

Mrs. Sisko was a librarian. It was odd that there were no bookshelves in the living room. Probably in another room, he thought. To his surprise, books of an esoteric nature had mostly escaped her radar. She handled the book with an unsteady hand.

"Keep it. It may not be to your taste. If not, I can retrieve it sometime."

He waited a week before checking back. She had devoured the book and asked if he might recommend more.

He made subsequent visits, each time bringing more books along the lines of the occult. She expressed a keen interest in anything that would give her answers concerning Amelia's death.

She confided in him, and sometimes he would even break down and cry with her. She would never have conceived of the real reason.

"You must call me Ola," she said.

He knew Lloyd was seeing another woman. The death of a child does all sorts of things to marriages. He found himself loving Ola. He didn't think it was the typical falling in love that happened to most couples. It was a protective love, one borne of guilt. He knew he must do what he could to ease her burden. Call it his penance for not going to jail. Marriage to her was out of the question. Not with what would always hang over his head, and what, if she ever found out, would be the final blow.

Ola needed something in her life. After Lloyd moved out of the house, Cornelius presented his idea to her. "We should start a bookstore together. I have enough money saved up."

❧

Early September 2018

Cornelius picked up the remembrance card for Ola.

No survivors were listed, not even Ola's daughter, who

had preceded her in death. She had said reading it on an *In Memory* card would be too much of a shock for Ethel.

"Maybe not for Luce, but definitely for Ethel," she said.

Ola was always thinking of others.

Did Ola somehow will herself to die on August 30?

He burst into uncontrollable tears, crying himself to sleep on the couch.

CHAPTER 36

Late September 2018

Christine stood in the doorway of Amelia's room. Ethel wrapped her arm around her daughter as far as it would reach. "How are you doing?"

"Okay," she said with a blank stare on her face.

"It worried me this might affect you... the baby."

"It was a shock. But the baby and I are doing okay."

Raja came up behind them. "Eerie, isn't it?"

Christine turned. "I think we should live here."

"You do?"

"Cornelius said it would be a perfect place for a child. I think it was what Ola had in mind when she gave you the house."

"But the apartment is so close to everything. It's within walking distance to the university, close to the hospital, across the street from the park, and my yoga class."

"Yes, but Dad's classes are online. It's not such a far drive from the bookstore. Ola did it every day. Mom, you haven't been going to the park for yoga much. You know the postures well enough; you don't need a class. The deck or backyard would be a perfect spot for morning yoga. Dad, maybe you could finish the addition that Ola and her husband started. I think it would be a good thing. I want my child to have a big yard to play in. It was something I missed."

"You had the park. That's big," Ethel said.

"It's not the same as having your *own* yard."

"Sounds like you have decided *for* us," Raja said.

"No, it's your decision. I'm only giving you the pros."

"The hospital is clear across town."

"You said yourself the first baby isn't quick."

Raja looked at Ethel. "Maybe the three of us should discuss the pros and cons."

"One pro is that Sam has a pickup truck and will help us move. He said for free, but I insisted we pay for his gasoline."

"You've been talking to Sam?" Ethel questioned.

"He comes into the bookstore a lot."

CHAPTER 37

Late October 2018

"Christine, don't lift any boxes, even small ones."

"Don't worry, Mom," she said, looking out the window. "He's here."

"Then, I guess we are all set for this new adventure," Raja said.

"Don't let me forget to give Billy our keys before we leave."

"Lucky for us, he wanted the furniture," Raja said.

There was a tap on the door.

"Come in, Sam. It's open," Christine said.

"Is this it?" Sam asked, looking at the boxes inhabiting most of the living room.

"Yes," Raja said. "The moving people took the big things we had to move. What's left is odds and ends."

"I wouldn't call them odds and ends. They represent thirty years of marriage and a child growing up here," Ethel said.

"Yes, dear, you're right." Raja put his arm around Ethel.

"If we pack the boxes tightly in the back of your pickup,

and Ethel and I stack the rest in our vehicles, we might get this in one trip."

Sam looked skeptical. "Well, there's only one way to find out." He picked up the largest box and went down the stairwell with it.

After two hours of carrying boxes and loading them on the truck under Christine's supervision, Sam said, "They're all squeezed in and tied down, considering her talent for organization and spatial arrangement."

"You've done this before, haven't you?" Ethel said.

"Yeah, I moved Susan into her new apartment."

"How are you and Susan?"

"Me and Susan?" he questioned. "Oh, no, no," he shook his head. "There's no me and Susan. Well, there might have been a little something. It was all casual. I haven't seen her since that day when we ran into you in the restaurant."

"Oh?" Ethel said.

Raja glared at Ethel, preventing her from saying more.

"I felt so useless watching everyone else doing all the work," Christine said, handing them bottles of water as they sat down for a breather.

"No, Christine, you meticulously organized and marked all the boxes."

Sam let out a heavy breath and got up from the couch. "We'd better get this load over there. Will you and Mr. Sharma be following us?"

"Yes," Ethel said.

"I knew that boy was interested in Christine," Raja said after Sam and Christine left.

"What?" Ethel said, shocked.

"Ethel, a man can see what's going on when another man looks at a woman."

"But Raja, she's eight months pregnant with another man's baby out of wedlock."

"Doesn't matter. He's more than interested."

"You don't think they've...."

"No, no. I don't think he's even said anything to Christine. It would be a little strange at this point under the circumstances, don't you think?"

"I don't know, Raja. I don't see it."

"Really? I thought for sure you were going to say something when he said he and his former girlfriend broke up."

"No, the thought didn't cross my mind."

"Ethel, don't lie to me. Why has he been coming into the bookstore so much?"

"He's a writer. He loves books."

"And volunteering to help our family move for free?"

"He has a pickup truck."

Raja rolled his eyes.

"Well, Christine has said nothing," she said.

"Has she ever confided anything about her personal life to us?"

"Okay, well, why would Sam want an older woman carrying another man's baby?"

"Ethel, I'm surprised at you. You've always been a liberal thinker." He shrugged. "She's not that much older. Okay, there might be a few hindrances to a normal relationship, but if they are fated to be together, they will be together. Some past life has brought them to this point."

"I hope what you are saying is true. I like Sam. He's a good and responsible boy, but I think you are totally off base on this one."

"We had better get going. They will wonder what has happened to us."

"I'm a little hungry after carrying all those boxes down to his truck. Is there anything left in the cupboard to eat?"

"You want to eat before we go?"

"Yes, I'm hungry."

"There is a half loaf of bread and some peanut butter."

"That will do."

Ethel watched Raja take his time, spreading the peanut butter with the precision of a bricklayer.

"Do we have any jelly?"

"No, we don't. I didn't buy groceries since we were moving. Raja, what are you doing?"

"I'm giving them some alone time."

"Unchaperoned?"

Raja let out a boisterous laugh. "Ethel, seriously, our daughter is, well... What more could he do?"

"Okay, okay," Raja said after taking the last bite under Ethel's glare.

"We packed the paper towels," Ethel said.

Raja wiped his mouth with the edge of his sleeve.

Both stood in the doorway.

"So many memories," she said.

"I know," he said, wrapping his arms around her. "But it's a new start for the four of us; another family will make fresh memories here."

They locked the door, much in the same way Raja painstakingly spread the peanut butter over the bread. Ethel dropped the keys off to Billy and was about to open the door to her Prius when her phone rang. It was Christine. She looked to see Raja in his vehicle with his hands on the steering wheel. She held up her hand, signaling for Raja to wait.

She answered, "Christine? Is everything okay?"

"No, this is Sam. Her water broke, and we're on our way to the hospital."

"We're not going to make it," she groaned, clutching her bulging belly.

"I'm driving as fast as possible, considering the truck is loaded."

"No, Sam, stop the truck."

"What? False labor? Should we head back to the apartment?"

"Oh, no, it's real."

"Oh, gosh, I was afraid you would say that."

"I can feel the baby's head. It's coming. I mean, now!" she screamed.

"No, no," he shouted. "This is a first baby, right? First babies take longer."

"Pull over," she screamed.

"Okay, okay!"

He screeched the truck to a stop on the side of the road, grabbed his phone from his back pocket, and keyed in 911.

"Yes, we're having a baby. I pulled off on the side of the road."

"Okay, sir, you can't make it to a hospital?"

He looked at Christine, who was shaking her head.

"No."

"Okay, don't panic. We've dispatched an ambulance to your location. Birth is a natural process. Stay calm and tell me how far apart the contractions are."

Sam put the phone on speaker and laid it on the dashboard.

"I don't know. Seconds?"

"Sir, you have to calm down. Look, tell me what you see."

"She's holding her belly and screaming,"

"Yes, sir. I can hear her. No, look to see if you can tell how far she has dilated. Can you venture a guess?"

"Down there?"

"Yes, sir. You've seen it before."

"No, I haven't. I'm not her husband."

"Oh, well, it doesn't matter at this point. You're going to have to woman up and look."

"Christine?"

"Yeah, I know." She lifted one leg from the floorboard, barely reaching the seat. Sam took it and placed her foot on the seat in front of him.

"I can't get my pants off. You're going to have to."

"Okay, okay." He began tugging.

"Gently," she said. "Just pull my pants and panties off."

"What do you see, sir?" The voice on the other end asked.

"A head of dark hair making its way out. What do I do? What do I do?"

"It's going to be okay. The body knows how to do this naturally. Do not stop the process."

"No, no, okay. Christine?"

"Just keep your eyes on the baby. You have to. Please don't be squeamish," she said.

The voice on the phone said, "I've patched us through to

Allen. He's one of the paramedics in the ambulance on its way."

"Okay, what are your names?" came the male voice on the other end.

"I'm Sam. Christine is having the baby."

"Okay, Christine, do you feel the urge to push?"

"Yes," she said in a groan.

"That's good. That's what I want you to do. What's happening, Sam?"

"The head, it's halfway out."

"Okay, Christine, take a little breather. One, two, three. I want you to push again—hard. Sam, put your hands underneath the baby's head. You will need to catch it as it comes out. Just like you're catching a football."

Sam placed his hands in position between Christine's legs. He looked up at her. Sweat dripped from her face. "I never played sports in school."

She tried to laugh, but the overwhelming urge to push again stifled it.

"That's right, Christine. One more hard push ought to do it," Allen said from the other end.

"It's out! It's out," Sam shouted.

"Great job, both of you."

"I can hear a siren. Please tell me that's you," Sam said.

"If your truck is blue with boxes strapped to the bed along the opposite side of the road, yes, it is."

"Thank God," he said.

"Does he look healthy, Sam?" Christine asked. Her face was red and glistening with sweat.

"Yes, he looks perfect." Sam held him up.

"Yes, he does," she said with tears.

The emergency vehicle sped across the median. Two men got out, and one opened the driver's side. "Sam, I presume?"

"Yes," he said with relief.

"Okay, place the baby on the seat and exit the vehicle. Randy and I will take over from here."

Sam carefully laid the wet child back between Christine's legs. He stood outside the truck on the grassy area, watching as Allen and Randy worked. A police vehicle pulled up beside them. Two officers set out traffic cones to direct traffic around the scene. The people inside the passing cars craned their heads to the side to see what was happening. They would probably be on the evening news.

With the umbilical cord still attached, Allen picked the infant up, laid him across Christine's chest, and placed a blanket over Christine. "Okay, Christine, we are going to ease you onto the stretcher."

When both mother and child were inside the ambulance, Randy asked, "Do you want to cut the cord, Sam?"

"Should I?"

Christine, her voice audible from inside the ambulance, said, "Please, Sam, you deserve the honor."

Sam could feel the placenta still pulsing, supplying oxygen to the baby. Randy clamped the cord, and Allen handed him the scissors.

"She still has to push out the placenta. We'll take over from here, but if you want to follow us to the hospital?"

Sam could hear the baby's wail right before the double doors shut. A tear trickled down his cheek.

He felt both exhilarated and like he might pass out.

Raja and Ethel came rushing into the hospital.

"My daughter came in a little earlier. Pregnant," Raja said to the lady at the desk.

"Name?"

"Raja Sharma."

"No, your daughter's name." She laughed.

"Oh, Christine Sharma."

She looked through her files.

"She just came in," Raja said. "Can you do that a little faster?"

Ethel snickered. "Finding the right file is like spreading peanut butter on bread, isn't it, Raja?"

The woman looked at them both like they were crazy grandparents.

"They must have taken her straight back. She's not yet listed in the system. The desk on the obstetrics floor will know."

They stared blankly.

"Fourth floor," the woman said, pointing to the elevator.

Sam came running in.

"Sam?" Ethel exclaimed.

"Both Christine and the baby are fine. The ambulance just brought her in."

"The baby's already here?" Raja asked.

"It was fast."

Sam relayed the events of the birth to them in the waiting room. After forty-five minutes, Dr. Langley came out.

"Mother and son are doing well. I love mothers who make my job easy, although I hear I owe my thanks to you. I take it you are Sam?"

"Yes, I am."

Dr. Langley extended his hand.

"The baby is on its way to the nursery, and Christine is resting in her room. The three of you can go back to see her. Only a brief visit."

Christine was groggy when they walked in. She half-opened her eyes.

"Are you okay?" both her parents asked.

"Just tired and weird."

"Weird?" Ethel asked.

"Yeah, you never told me how strange your body feels after having a baby."

"Oh, yes, your body completely changes."

"I tried feeding him, but my milk hasn't come in."

"It will," Ethel said.

"Yeah, they said it could take days sometimes, but I don't think it will. I already feel my breasts swelling. He must have activated my mammary glands when he was sucking my nipple."

Christine looked over at Sam. "I'm so sorry. I'm embarrassing you."

"I think the embarrassment ship has sailed," he said, still red-faced.

"I can't keep calling him, he. They asked me what name they should write on the form, and I said I hadn't even decided on a name. I've been considering Wynn as a middle name, but he needs a first name. Do you have a middle name, Sam?"

"Noah," Sam said.

She reached for his hand.

"Noah, yes, I like that name. Noah Wynn Sharma."

A nurse came in and said, "The baby is in the nursery now if you want to see him."

Ethel and Raja kissed their daughter on the forehead and headed for the nursery. Sam stayed behind.

"He's perfect, isn't he, Sam?" Christine said.

"Yes. Thank you for letting me be a part of this, Christine."

"You said you wrote mostly from experience. I'm sure you will write about this someday."

He smiled.

CHAPTER 39

December 2018

Ethel, Luce, and Rhonda entered Filbert's Furniture.

"Would Mr. Filbert be in?" Ethel asked.

"I'm Mr. Filbert," the young man answered.

"No, the Mr. Filbert I'm looking for is an older gentleman."

"Oh, you mean my father. He's in his office. Is there anything I can help you with?"

"I need to speak to him."

The young man smirked. "Well, if you want to look around while I get him."

"Rude, don't you think?" Rhonda said.

"Afraid he would miss out on a commission," Luce said.

"I think they are just swamped in here," Ethel said while wiping her hand across a barn wood dining room table. "What do you think? Would this work in the cottage?"

"Hmm, I suppose, but there is a lot of furniture to look at. We could be here all day," Rhonda said.

"I think you may be right," Luce replied.

A man with graying hair, walking with a slight limp,

approached them. "Hello, ladies. My son said you were asking for me."

Luce whispered in Ethel's ear, "Don't you dare chicken out." She gently pushed Ethel forward.

"Mr. Filbert, I don't know if you remember me, but I purchased a chair from you several years back."

The man eyed her suspiciously and glanced at his watch.

"Do you need to be somewhere?" Ethel asked.

"My son takes care of most of the business these days. I mostly come in to putter about, help long-time customers, and do the books. I was getting ready to go home when you came in. My back's been acting up."

"Oh, I'm so sorry," Ethel said.

Luce nudged her again.

"Actually, Mr. Filbert, I'm sorry for more than your back."

"You look somewhat familiar."

"I'm the woman who practically accused you of stealing my grandmother's prayer beads." Ethel felt Luce's hand again. "Not practically, I'm afraid. I accused you outright, and I came in to apologize."

"You're the woman living in an upstairs apartment across from the park. Yes, I thought I recognized you."

"I've moved. My family and I are no longer in the apartment."

"Yes, she's in a new house, and she needs new furniture," Rhonda pronounced excitedly. Rhonda had almost dropped her pan of cookies when Ethel asked her to join her and Luce in picking out furniture.

"Yes, I do. I need almost a full house of furniture. It's my husband's and my treat to ourselves for Christmas. I would very much like for you to help with that, but you said you were leaving because your back hurt?"

"It comes and goes." He paused and looked around the

room at the sales associates, all of whom were helping customers.

"Your business looks like it's doing well," Luce said.

"Yes, I can thank my son, a brilliant manager."

He called out to his son, "Babe, I'm going to be helping these ladies. So, I'm sticking around for a while." His son gave him a thumbs-up.

"Babe? Is he named after Babe Ruth?" Luce asked.

"No, it's a nickname that just stuck. His mom and I joked we couldn't think of a name for him, so we called him Babe for several days. His proper name is Donald."

"Oh." Luce nodded.

"Well, what kind of furniture are you looking for? Did you have something specific in mind?" Mr. Filbert asked.

Rhonda had wandered off, already touching fabrics, sitting on couches, and making notes in a small pad she was carrying.

"All the furniture in the house is going, except for a massive mahogany desk and the chair I purchased from you. It still looks like new."

Ethel half expected Luce to make a snide remark about the reason it looked pristine, that it was because she never sat in it, but she kept her mouth shut.

Rhonda reappeared. "Yes, the desk is the focal point of one entire area."

"Ethel, show him the photos you took. He might have something he thinks will go with them."

Ethel pulled out her phone, pressed the picture icon, and handed her phone to him.

He looked over the top of his glasses. "Beautiful desk. Yes, I remember that chair. But I remember the two flights of stairs more."

"Again, Mr. Filbert, I'm so sorry. It's haunted me, and I feel ashamed I waited too long to apologize."

"I take it you found your grandmother's prayer beads?"

"Yes, she did," Luce offered.

"I hope you don't mind staying to help us," Ethel said.

"No, as I said before, I putter around the store now. One thing I like to do is to help long-time customers." He smiled.

Three hours later.

"Such a nice man," Rhonda said. "I think you should fit him into the book you're writing."

"You're writing a book?" Luce exclaimed. "I thought there were to be no secrets between us."

"No, no." Ethel shook her head. "I don't know if I'm writing a book. It's something I've been toying around with. Sam's the writer in the...."

"You started to say family, didn't you, Ethel?" Luce said.

"Yes, I believe she did," Rhonda agreed.

"When do you think those two will tie the knot?" Luce asked.

"Oh, you must have the wedding in my garden. I hope they can wait at least until spring."

"You two are incorrigible," Ethel exclaimed. "You sound like Raja."

"I can't wait until your new furniture arrives. Monday, he said? I have to clear my schedule. And you do, too, Luce," Rhonda said.

"Oh, most definitely, and we'll need Sam to help us move the pieces into place," Luce said and winked.

"Do you girls want to go for coffee and maybe dessert? My treat," Ethel said.

"Oh, no, Ethel, you shouldn't. You just dropped a chunk of money on new furniture. You should come to my apartment. I made lemon-drop cookies this morning. Oh, and

Ethel, you must meet the young couple who moved into your old apartment. They are so adorable," Rhonda said.

"Oh, Luce, you must see her apartment and garden," Ethel exclaimed.

"Will Raja be okay with Noah all this time?" Luce asked.

"He's a natural babysitter—a natural grandpa, that is. He spoils Noah rotten."

"This is so much fun," Rhonda exclaimed. "It's a girls' day out."

Ethel and Luce looked at each other. For a moment, they were sad, but only for a moment.

"She's smiling down on us, you know," Luce said.

After a slight look of despair, their mouths turned upward, their lips glistening like the sweet sap of a maple tree as the three hooked arms.

"Yes, it is," they all agreed.

CHAPTER 40

June 2019

The wedding was a small affair held in Rhonda's garden. Rhonda opened the French doors, allowing guests to move freely inside and outside. Compliments overflowed regarding both the culinary display and the garden.

Ethel heard Fritz say, "I could meditate here all day."

"Reminds me of a smaller version of some of Seattle's finest botanical gardens," Mr. Scranton, Sam's dad, said.

"Have you ever thought of opening a pastry shop?" Santiago asked. Leave it to Santiago to recognize it as a business opportunity.

Besides Fritz, who Ethel discovered had a minister's license and could officiate at weddings, Luce, Santiago, and the boys, Sam's parents, Mr. and Mrs. Scranton, and his younger brother, Josh, Rhonda, Ethel, Raja, and Noah Wynn were in attendance. At eight months, Noah was already babbling away and pulling himself up.

Cornelius was conspicuously absent.

Ethel looked over and saw Thaddeus watching from his yard in his wheelchair.

"How's he doing?" Ethel asked.

"Mighty good for his age," Rhonda replied. "Someone is with him around the clock now."

An array of cookies, cakes, and pastries covered Rhonda's barn wood table, the one they had eyed at Filbert's Furniture Store. She said she was ready for a change, and Mr. Filbert was such a nice man. "He gave me a deal."

Josh served as Sam's best man, and Luce was Christine's maid of honor.

When Ethel told Rhonda that the wedding would combine aspects from both America and India, she said, "I hope there won't be an elephant. An elephant would ruin my garden." Ethel had told her about her and Raja's wedding.

Ethel wore her periwinkle blue sari, and Luce wore the ivory and brown one.

"Doesn't our daughter look beautiful in the red sari?" Raja said, clasping his wife's hand.

"I've never seen her more radiant," Ethel replied. "Nor have I ever seen Sam look more handsome."

"I told you all along that boy was interested."

"Yes, Raja, you were right," she said, leaning into her husband and smiling.

CHAPTER 41

August 2019

Once again, Cornelius sat in his easy chair—a glass of whiskey, his companion. The chair was one of the few remaining pieces of furniture left in the apartment. The living room floor was knee-deep in boxes. Who would have thought a man who paid little heed to decorating could have accumulated so much over the years?

A good portion of the boxes consisted of books. Cornelius organized the boxes in piles, each marked with a black felt marker with the destination. Most of the special first editions he had acquired over the years would be donated to the bookstore, while the rest would be given to local charities. The only books not in boxes were the journals he had retrieved from Ola's cottage. He would place them in the incinerator on his way out the next day.

The only items left were the essential pieces of furniture, such as a bed, his easy chair, and a side table. He promised them to Mrs. Cline, the woman down the hall whose son was moving out and needed furniture. In return, she would see that the boxes reached their destinations.

"We will hate to see you go," she said. "You've always been such a good neighbor, so quiet."

Cornelius couldn't say the same for her son, who liked to play loud music, but then he was never around much to hear it, and ironically, neither he nor the son would be there anymore.

"Where will you be moving to?" Mrs. Cline inquired.

"I'm planning an extended stay with my sister," he lied. Cornelius rarely saw Ellen. They made it a point to call each other on their birthdays, and she would robotically invite him to holiday dinners, which he usually declined. After that night, he drifted away from his family. Ola had become his focal point.

It surprised him when Ellen came to Ola's funeral. He supposed she was offering an olive branch. If she knew the truth, she would have shunned him. Being five years younger, they had never been all that close, but they grew further apart during his drinking spree and divorce. She had married an accountant. Said she wouldn't have to worry about her husband getting killed on the job, the way their mother always worried about their father and Cornelius when he was a cop.

Even though Ellen wasn't much of a reader, she agreed the bookstore was a good thing when he decided to quit the force. Nice and safe was the way she put it. Cornelius could never see what she saw in her husband, Arnie, beyond the fact that he was nice and safe.

He took a drink of whiskey while, in his mind, he went over each task he needed to do tomorrow, the way a thorough criminal might.

Everything he could think of had been diligently taken care of. He had called the cable and utility companies. He changed the beneficiary of his life insurance policy from Ola to that of his sister. The letter he would drop off at the post office would explain everything. He even left an envelope containing a more than adequate sum in Mrs. Cline's care to give to his cleaning lady, explaining that he had moved when she arrived on Tuesday.

A manila folder lay on the table beside his drink. Not having any progeny and knowing his sister wouldn't want the bookstore, he left it to Christine. Both she and Sam were doing a fine job of running it, and it's what Ola would have wanted. He was sure Ethel would continue to work part-time when she wasn't busy looking after Noah Wynn. Tomorrow, he would take care of all the lingering little tidbits.

He would sleep in and go into the bookstore late. Finding comfort in slumber and sleeping late had become a habit.

He would offer to close up for Sam and Christine. He would leave the manila folder on her desk. It contained a copy of his will, bequeathing her the bookstore. Inside, he would whiff his last smell of books, and outside, his final breaths of fresh air while gingerly walking to the police station. He would leave a sealed envelope with the desk sergeant, asking him to give it only to Jake, who was nearing retirement.

"Tell him it's from Corn. He'll know." He didn't have the heart to face him.

From there, he would return to his apartment and rest. At dusk, he would get in his car and drive down the same road Lloyd and Amelia traversed that night.

But this time, he would be stone sober.

CHAPTER 42

Early September 2019

Yesterday, Ethel went for a walk, something she promised to do every morning from now on. Raja was in his office teaching an online class. Christine and Sam took Noah into the bookstore with them. They had turned the area near the office into a nursery. They didn't take him every day. Noah got divided between her and Raja, Sam's parents, and being at the bookstore with his parents.

The day before yesterday, there had been a graveside service for Cornelius. It was brief. In keeping with his meticulous nature, he left explicit instructions for everything, including his funeral. His sister, Ellen, carried out his wishes.

Other than his sister and her family, Christine, Sam, Luce, and she were the only ones in attendance. Raja stayed home and watched Noah. Christine placed a black ribbon on the bookstore door and closed it for the day.

Cornelius had left a sealed envelope addressed to her and Luce. He thanked them for being such good friends to Ola and hoped she and Amelia were now together. As for being sorry, he said there were no words he could say or actions he had ever taken that could make up for what he had done.

Cornelius's confession had been a shock to all of them. All except for Raja. His death had been ruled an accident, thanks to Jake.

It was nine months ago, right before the new furniture arrived, that Raja, while perusing Ola's book titles, discovered the Sisko Family Photo Albums and Ola's last journal wedged between other books.

She didn't know why she had never questioned the lack of family photos. And the Eye of Horus Journal, she remembered being on the desk with the other journals, had slipped her mind. Christine said she must have picked them up while cleaning. Somehow, the one that was smaller than the rest got shoved into the bookcase.

"So much was going on in your life. You could hardly think of everything," Rhonda said.

She called Luce to come over. "Whenever you have the time. I feel this is something we should do together."

The pictures portrayed a happy family, and every holiday was represented. There were some photos of Ola and Lloyd when they were teenagers, dating, then their wedding pictures, a small affair. Lloyd wasn't that tall but seemed so next to Ola. And both of them were so skinny. She would have never recognized Ola. She and Luce looked through the first album, commenting on the fashions. "Can you believe we once wore clothes like this?" Ethel said.

"I know," Luce replied. "It's like looking at our old high school yearbooks."

It was wonderful to see their friend so happy. Then, they became somber upon seeing Amelia's baby pictures. "She looks like her father," they both commented. It wasn't until the last album that Ethel realized the man who came to Ola's memorial, the one who sat in the back and left before she had time to talk to him, was Lloyd. Luce hadn't seen him that day.

"You know, Cornelius left right after he did. Do you think

he was going out to talk to him? If he was, I wonder what he said to him?"

Luce shook her head. "We'll never know."

They opened the journal. On the opening pages, she wrote about her Egyptian trip, Peg, and the others who were a part of it. On the last pages, Ola wrote:

> To Ethel and Luce,
> You will find this and read it after I have passed. I hope you won't think badly of me for making the decision I did.
> You have been the dearest, best friends anyone could hope for.
> Ethel, I'm sure it was a shock that I left you the house and the car. I don't know if you will decide to live there, but I hope you do. It's an excellent place to write a book. Now you have time—but maybe not with a grandbaby on the way. Yes, I hope you don't mind Christine telling me. She felt she should when I asked her to work in the store. I hope it works out for her and Cornelius.
> And Luce, I know you hardly needed my house, but I would have split everything between you if you had.
> Of course, you will have read all the journals by now. I was depressed for the longest time. Cornelius gave me a new life. Then, both of you came along and enriched it more than you will ever know.
> I told you about my experience inside the Great Pyramid. It was so much more than I could ever

express in words. I was alive for the first time.
When I looked down and saw the Earth, the people were all dead, even though they thought they were alive. As I was told telepathically during the experience, the Earth is a place of learning, where our karma unfolds.

Please think of me as truly alive and happy with Amelia.

All my love,
Ola

Yesterday's walk had been a deterrent, something to get her mind off the past year's events, the bad ones, if only for a day, and to reflect upon the good ones.

While she walked, she thought about resolutions. She had made none for the longest time. While most people made their resolutions in January, as a teacher, she divided the year's resolutions into two segments: the ones she made for the beginning of the school year and those she thought more suitable for summer vacation. Even though she was no longer a teacher, she saw no reason to change this. Some habits were hard to dislodge from her programmed brain.

In early September, the air was still warm. As summer drew to a close in the Emerald City, Ethel observed locals and tourists soaking up the much-needed sunshine that was dwindling. Both millennials and yuppies jogged or paddled along Puget Sound for that extra abdominal workout. Couples walked hand-in-hand at Pike Place Market. First-time tourists stood in the never-ending line at the first Starbucks while the locals got their daily caffeine fix at a leisurely pace at the many other coffee shops throughout the town, all while rolling their eyes and grinning at the newbies to the city. On the surface, all proceeded as usual. No one could have told by merely looking at her that the previous year had unfurled its pent-up karma in her world like a tsunami in slow motion.

CHAPTER 43

December 2019

Christmas was only two days away when two familiar-looking women entered Ola's Wise Old Bookstore. They couldn't be more different. One was tall and lean, fitting somewhere between bohemian and goth, long purple tresses falling out of a man's fedora, landing on a Peruvian poncho. Everything about this woman suggested a free spirit and a world traveler. The apparel looked authentic, pieces she had picked up on her adventures. The other one, a petite woman who appeared to shop solely at L.L. Bean, was nearly frantic.

"I hope you have a copy of *Life of Pi.* The last bookstore we were in said they were out and could order it, but I must have it by Christmas," the smaller, agitated woman said.

"I'm sure we do," Ethel said as she placed her mug of tea on the counter. "Please, follow me."

"Oh, thank goodness," the woman said as Ethel handed her the book.

"It's one of my husband's favorites."

"I blame myself," the woman with her said. "I thought a puppy would be a nice gift for my brother. I thought an adorable little puppy might relieve some of the stress my brother keeps bottled up. I gave it to him early."

"It backfired," the petite woman said.

"Well, you know how puppies are. Everything is a chew toy for them," the tall woman added.

"Yes, it chewed up one of my husband's favorite books. He was so angry that he threatened to return the puppy to the shelter where Matilda got it. Matilda rescues many animals and is a big proponent of animal rights."

"I knew I had seen you somewhere," Ethel said. "I believe we were at a rally together. I, too, am active in animal rights. By the way, I love your hair."

"Yes, now that you mention it, I remember seeing you at a rally. Oh, and my hair, I have to credit Barb, my beautician."

"Baboons?"

"Why, yes. Have you been there?"

Ethel smiled. "Yes, I have. Not for a while, though." She had snipped off the remaining Matcha Tea strands and had begun pulling them back into a bun, out of the reach of Noah, who liked to tug on her hair.

"*Life of Pi* is one of my favorites, too. Is that all? Did you want to look around?" Ethel asked.

"Another time. I'm afraid we are in a hurry."

"I will ring you up then." Ethel took the woman's credit card. The name on it, Glenda Densworth, caught her eye. Ethel looked up. "You also looked familiar." The words spilled out of her mouth before she thought. What would she think? The teacher, whom her husband let walk out without so much as an argument, was reduced to working as a clerk in a bookstore.

"You're Ethel Sharma," the woman exclaimed. "I'm so sorry. I should have recognized you. I heard you retired."

Really? Retired? Surely that wasn't what Mr. Densworth told her. Maybe he didn't discuss school affairs with her.

"And working in a bookstore. Denny would love nothing better than to work in a bookstore. Books are his greatest love."

Denny? She calls him Denny. Ethel did her best not to smile too broadly.

"My daughter is the owner. I'm helping out while she, her husband, and our grandchild are in India."

"Oh," she said, seeming to be impressed. "Matilda travels a lot."

"I've never been to India, though," Matilda said.

"Is your daughter's name Ola?" Mrs. Densworth asked.

"No, Christine. Ola is the person for whom the store is named. She was my best friend. She died a little over a year ago," Ethel stuttered. There was no need to mention Cornelius. The bookstore was not even mentioned in the newspaper article, and what little of the incident that was written didn't make front-page news. Hopefully, Mrs. Densworth or her husband knew nothing about it. "Christine and her husband now own the bookstore."

"Oh, I see. I am so sorry about your friend," Mrs. Densworth said.

"Thank you," Ethel said, handing Mrs. Densworth back her card and purchase.

The woman almost turned to leave, but mid-turn looked back at Ethel. "Mrs. Sharma, I just want to say it was a shame to see you leave the school. You were such an excellent teacher. I know Denny misses you a great deal."

"He does?" Ethel blurted it out before thinking.

"Oh, he's not one to admit such things. But I know him well enough to know when something bothers him, and when you left, well, he was an absolute beast all summer."

Ethel saw the sincerity in her eyes.

"Thank you, Mrs. Densworth. I'm sorry he was a lion... I mean beast."

Mrs. Densworth smiled. "Don't worry. He's usually a beast, just maybe more of one after you left.

"He was born a beast. I ought to know; I grew up with him," Matilda, his sister, piped in.

"I believe running into each other was serendipitous. Do you believe in such things?" Mrs. Densworth asked.

"Why yes, I do."

"Well, we must be off. I'm sure Denny will want to come to the shop. I see you carry rare editions. He is particularly interested in those. He somehow never finds the time, but he will have to make the time for many things." Mrs. Densworth placed her hand on her bulging belly. It was clear she was expecting. Her winter coat had covered up the fact at first.

"When is your baby due?"

"The end of March, maybe sooner, the way I feel," she said.

"Denny is so excited. He hopes to add a nursery to the house before spring," his sister said.

"Congratulations, and I wish you well with everything."

"I will tell Denny I ran into you." The two women waved as they exited the store.

CHAPTER 44

Early March 2020

Ethel sat Noah on a blanket on the living room floor, where he was easily visible from her desk. Transfixed by the television, a cartoon in which animals spoke like adults, she might get some writing done.

It was quite strange. Ethel had grown up on the same cartoons: animals that should walk on four legs walking on two, birds using their feathers as hands, living in tiny houses, driving little automobiles, and having the same life problems as humans. Well, maybe not as dramatic.

Ethel sat at the desk, bare except for her laptop and two books, *A Proud Peacock* and *Life of Pi*. She had only read a few pages in the one Cornelius had handed her over a year ago. She looked at the cover—such a beautiful bird, but so proud.

She pulled the curtains back to display a cornucopia of nature's bounty.

Noah giggled. Watching him laugh made *her* laugh.

The writing program had been open on her laptop since the day before. She stared at the screen. Still, no words came. She envied Sam. Words flowed like a wild, untamed stream for him. He was working on a novel, one he kept secret, even from Chrissie, the nickname Sam had given Christine.

Ethel divided her attention between Noah and the window. She watched a family of deer gingerly walk past the trees where the hammock had hung. Raja had taken it down over the winter. A squirrel scurried up the oak and back down again. The deer and the squirrel appeared to be talking to each other. A wren landed on the grass near them and joined in the conversation. What could they be saying? Maybe commenting on the weather or the food supply—the deer about the grass, the squirrel complaining about the lack of nuts this time of year, or the bird bragging about the abundance of worms? It had to be something as simple as that. Animals hardly had the complexities of life that humans endured. They could be chattering away about her. She was sure they could see her through the window. Animals always scurried away when humans approached. What did they think of humans?

Suddenly, there was a whole family of wrens, two adults and a baby. The mama bird pulled a worm from the ground. They were having a mild winter. Animals could flourish upon the Earth easily without humans—such a strange ecosystem. The lowliest of creatures sustained life on the planet. Take the insects away, and both the animals and humans would perish.

From the corner of her eye, she spied a new animal. It was Ginger, the stray cat, who sometimes came around. She didn't know if Ginger was its name, but it was what she called it. Noah had wanted to pet it the day she put a bowl of milk out for it.

"No, Noah Wynn, this cat is feral, not used to humans," she told her grandson, who only understood he wasn't supposed to touch it. He was content watching the cat slurp the milk from the doorway as Ethel held him.

Noah could name all the animals in his picture books and even read some words.

Ethel watched as the cat watched the birds from a distance. She looked at Noah to see if he was still doing okay, then looked back out the window. The cat had crept up almost beside the birds. Then, without warning, the cat swooped on top of the young one. Ethel gasped and rose from her chair. Noah let out a wail, startled by her reaction.

"Come over here," she said to him, waiting to make sure the graphicness of it was over.

Noah was walking, primarily running, all over the place. She picked him up so he could see out the window. The orange tabby's back was facing in their direction. Noah couldn't tell the cat whom Ethel no longer felt affectionate enough to bestow with a name had just finished devouring its prey. The parents were flying around and squeaking in a rage. The cat, still hovering over the spot where the baby bird was, reminded her of a lion. Then she thought of Mr. Densworth.

Noah pointed and said, "Kitty! Birds!"

"That's right, Noah Wynn."

Ethel could still only think of Principal Densworth and the hierarchy of the animal world. "If only all animals could get along," she said to her grandson. Maybe at his young age, some sliver of this hope might register.

Ginger walked away, no remorse on his face, only pride. She must get cat food on her next trip to the market. Then, maybe he wouldn't eat birds. Perhaps she and Raja would take Noah to the pound to pick out a dog. Both Sam and Christine agreed he could have a puppy.

The squirrel made her think of Sam and the story he wrote about a squirrel going on an adventure. Who would have thought Sam and Christine together? But then, both Sam and Christine were easy-going sorts. "Like two peas in a pod," Raja said.

Ethel smiled.

A butterfly landed on the outside windowsill. Noah tried to say butterfly, but it came out funny.

She must put up a hummingbird feeder. The grass had grown greener overnight. Everything in the backyard paradise seemed marvelously alive. Maybe that was what the animals were discussing—so many shades and tints of green. Ethel had read once that there were more varieties of green than any other color, nature's way of protection.

Before Ginger's frightful display, Ethel had thought the creatures in her backyard to be docile. The act of eating the bird had appalled her, but she had thought nothing of the birds eating the worms.

"Let's get you fed and put down for a nap," Ethel said.

"I don't wanna take a nap. I wanna look out the window at the woods," Noah protested. Her grandson always resisted naps, but she knew he would fall asleep after lunch today. His eyes drooped, and his head bobbed all over the place.

"You know, Noah Wynn, we should call the woods Wynn's Woods," Ethel said while placing Noah in his crib.

Ethel sat at Ola's desk. She still had trouble thinking of it as her own. With her fingers resting on her laptop, the thought of lions, tigers, and bears roaming in their midst occurred to her. What if all the creatures lived in harmony with each other? Principal Densworth was still on her mind. He wasn't a bad sort. His wife and sister were pleasant enough, having the same values as he did.

Before she knew it, a whole slew of animals occupied her backyard. Was it her imagination? A tiger, hyena, lion, polar bear, and orangutan? It seemed as natural for them to be there as the deer and the squirrels. She eyed the book on the edge of the desk, the one Cornelius had handed her that day. The peacock, actually a peahen, stood proudly in the center. Was that peahen with the emerald neck winking at her?

She thought about her grandmother—such a wise

woman. If only she could have lived to see her great-great-grandson. If only her mother and father could have seen him.

Ethel laughed, thinking of the serendipity of it all, the animals ever-present on her mind, this story she was conjuring up, and Noah, the Biblical prophet who had saved them from extinction.

The thought of Sam telling her she should start a school came back to her.

She began pecking away at the laptop.

Miss Ethel Peacock strutted and proudly displayed her plumage as she paced around Mr. Densworth Lion's waiting room. She had come unannounced, but she was so excited about the idea she had received in a dream that she dared not lose any momentum. She could have called ahead, but what if he refused to see her? No, she decided not to risk it.

With the first light of morning, Ethel roused from her nest, feeling exhilarated. It was more than a dream. It was a vision. She breathed in the cool, crisp air of early spring. Everything about the morning was perfect. Her grandmother's sage words echoed in her mind. "Ethel, bold steps are needed if one is to accomplish great things." Sharing her vision with a lion and asking him to help her make it happen was definitely a bold step.

"A peacock? A peacock, you say? What is a peacock doing here?" Mr. Densworth Lion asked his secretary in disbelief.

CHAPTER 45

December 2020

Ethel was minding the cash register when a familiar face walked in. She wanted to duck and hide, but told herself to be brave.

He went straight to the display. Christine and Sam insisted that at least fifty copies of the book be exhibited on the most prominent table in the bookstore. Sam said it would appear to be in great demand. They propped her picture up beside it. Christine insisted she wear her tie-dyed dress and the feathered tiara that Ola had given her for her author photo.

He placed three copies of *A Peculiar School* on the counter. "Christmas presents, and won't you please sign them? Mrs. Sharma, I always knew you would do great things," Mr. Densworth said as she penned her signature.

Ethel smiled, not so much at Mr. Densworth's statement but at all that had happened. She remembered the day she had looked at the bookcase filled with books, teeming with heartaches. Like in fiction, mingled with real life's sorrows was a sprinkling of happy moments and sometimes even happy endings.

Author's Note

This book came about while writing *Down the Rabbit Hole*, the sequel to *A Peculiar School*. It is an anthropomorphic tale with its main character, Ethel Peacock, who is actually a peahen. Her two best friends are Luce Pigeon and Ola Owl. I thought, what if these animals were people?

With all of the main characters being birds and best friends, it seemed appropriate to call the book *Birds of a Different Feather*.

I originally wrote *A Peculiar School* for middle school. However, many ages have read it. If you decide to read both books, it's hard to say which should be read first. It's like the chicken and the egg.

Acknowledgments

Thanks to my husband, Chris, who reads and rereads my writing and encourages me to keep at it. And always to my beta readers, Barbara Daniels Dena, Monika Martyn, Diane Olsen, and Jean Kelly. A special thanks to Harvey Holbrook regarding questions about police matters. Thanks to Cathie Harris, who shared her experiences with me about her trip to Egypt. Thanks to Emerald Barnes for her editing expertise and Vickie Bolton for excellent proofreading.

J. Schlenker, a late-blooming author, lives with her husband, Chris, in the splendid center of nowhere in the foothills of Appalachia in Kentucky, where the only things to disturb her writing are croaking frogs, screaming guineas, and the occasional sounds of hay being cut in the fields.

https://jschlenker.com/

For more information:
https://www.jschlenker.com/
jschlenkerauthor@gmail.com

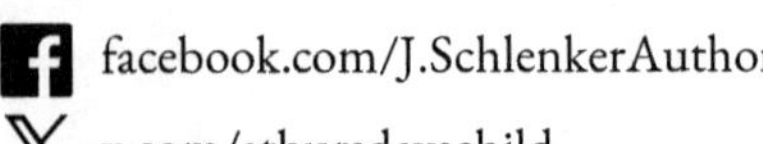

facebook.com/J.SchlenkerAuthor
x.com/athursdayschild
instagram.com/jschlenkerauthor

Also by J. Schlenker

Jessica Lost Her Wobble

The Color of Cold and Ice

Sally

A Peculiar School

Alice Black

The Innkeeper on the Edge of Paris

The Imaginary Life of Abigail Jones

Down the Rabbit Hole

The Water Spider

www.ingramcontent.com/pod-product-compliance
Lightning Source LLC
Chambersburg PA
CBHW061010120726
47910CB00006B/1864